跟她學 部落格

職場生活英語

序

　　本系列套書共分《跟**她**學部落格職場生活英語》及《跟**他**學部落格職場生活英語》兩冊，兩冊皆以辦公室所發生的事情為主題。內容寫實、饒富趣味性。

　　為了增加本系列套書的可讀性，我們在編排上做了這樣的設計：

本　　　文：也就是部落格的內容，用字簡短、洗鍊並具實用性。美籍編輯特別用了許多時下流行的俚語及慣用語，裨與現代英語接軌。

這麼說就對了！：在這個專欄中，我們將本文所涵蓋的俚語或慣用語加以精細解說，使讀者明瞭這些俚語或慣用語的意思及用法，提升讀者口語及寫作的能力。

字詞幫幫忙！：在這個專欄中，我們將本文所有的重要單詞或片語陳列出來，並附上音標及例句，方便讀者學習這些單詞或片語的正確用法。

　　讀者從以上的編排設計就可看出我們編輯本系列套書的用心。我們另外聘請 ICRT 電台的美籍專業廣播員將本系列套書的內容錄音，方便讀者跟著朗讀，提升讀者閱讀及聽力技巧。

祝大家學習成功！

目錄 TABLE OF CONTENTS

Time to Get Back into Shape

Index | *Links* | *about* | *comments* | *Photo*

May 01

A new guy started in our office today and he's totally **dreamy**! His name is Mike, and I was asked to **introduce** him to everyone and take him out for lunch. It turns out we **have a lot in common**, and I **had a crush on** him immediately. I **dare not** say anything, though. I gained so much weight last winter that I'd be too **embarrassed** to tell him I'm interested. So, I've decided to change my eating habits and **get back into shape**. Hopefully, it will help me **catch Mike's eye. Wish me luck!**

About me

Ivy

Calendar

◄ *May* ►

Sun	Mon	Tue	Wed	Thu	Fri	Sat
				1	2	3
4	5	6	7	8	9	10
11	12	13	14	15	16	17
18	19	20	21	22	23	24
25	26	27	28	29	30	31

Blog Archive

- ► May (1)
- ► April
- ► March
- ► February
- ► January
- ► December
- ► November
- ► October
- ► September
- ► August
- ► July
- ► June

Ivy at Blog 於 May 05.01. PM 02:00 發表 | 回覆 (0) | 引用 (0) | 收藏 (0) | 轉寄給朋友 | 檢舉

該減肥了！

May 01

　　今天辦公室來了個新人，他真像漫畫裡走出來的夢幻男主角！他叫麥克，我負責帶他介紹給大家認識，還有帶他去吃午餐。結果我們超合的，我馬上就煞到他。不過我什麼不敢說。之前冬天我胖太多，因此不好意思告訴他對他有好感。所以，我決定要改變吃東西的習慣，恢復我苗條的身材。希望這樣能讓麥克注意到我。祝我好運吧！

About me

Ivy

Calendar

◄			May			►
Sun	Mon	Tue	Wed	Thu	Fri	Sat
				1	2	3
4	5	6	7	8	9	10
11	12	13	14	15	16	17
18	19	20	21	22	23	24
25	26	27	28	29	30	31

Blog Archive

- ► May (1)
- ► April
- ► March
- ► February
- ► January
- ► December
- ► November
- ► October
- ► September
- ► August
- ► July
- ► June

人總有心頭小鹿亂撞、『煞到』某人的時候，這時候，你知道該怎麼用英文表達嗎？當你『煞到』某人時，你對他或她感到迷戀不已，感覺自己的理智一瞬間都被摧毀了對吧？英文裡的 crush 原來的意思就是『壓垮、摧毀』，而網誌中的 "had a crush on him" 指的就是『煞到他／迷戀他』的意思。下次你想在部落格裡抒發自己的愛意，或是想和朋友討論你的新對象，記得把這個片語拿出來用！

have a crush on sb 迷戀某人，煞到某人

crush [krʌʃ] *n.* 迷戀；壓垮

例: In high school, I had a crush on your older brother.

（高中時我曾暗戀過妳哥哥。）

 字詞幫幫忙！

1. **dreamy** [ˈdrimɪ] *a.* 夢幻般的，迷人的

   例: The broadcaster's voice is so dreamy!

   （那個廣播員的聲音超迷人的！）

2. **introduce** [ˌɪntrəˈdjus] *vt.* 介紹，引見

   introduce A to B 將某甲介紹給某乙

   例: Teresa introduced her friends to her parents.

   （泰瑞莎把她的朋友們介紹給爸媽認識。）

3. **have a lot in common** 有很多共同之處

   have nothing in common 毫無共同之處

   have something in common 有些許共同之處

   例: My sister and I have a lot in common. For example, we both love painting and watching movies.

   （我姊姊和我有很多共同點。比如說，我倆都很喜歡畫畫和看電影。）

   Maggie and her boyfriend are madly in love although they have nothing in common.

   （瑪姬和她的男友瘋狂地熱戀中，雖然他們倆無一處相同。）

4. dare not + 原形動詞　　不敢……（dare 與 not 並用或在問句中出現時均為助動詞，主詞不論第幾人稱均用 dare）

例: Sarah dare not go swimming alone.
（莎拉不敢一個人去游泳。）

Dare he do it?
（他敢做這件事嗎？）

5. embarrassed [ɪmˋbærəst] *a.* 感到尷尬的，感到難為情的
embarrassing [ɪmˋbærəsɪŋ] *a.* 令人尷尬的，令人難為情的

例: The bride was too embarrassed to kiss the groom in front of so many people.
（新娘不好意思在那麼多人面前吻新郎。）

It's embarrassing to forget to bring money on a date for men.
（男生約會時忘了帶錢時這會很令人難為情。）

6. get back into shape　　恢復身材；恢復健康
stay in shape　　身材保持很好
be in shape　　身材很好；很健康
stay out of shape　　身材走樣的；不健康的
be out of shape　　不成人樣；不健康

例: Jill stays in shape by exercising on a daily basis.
（吉兒每天運動來保持身材。）

The fashion model fell seriously ill half a year ago, and now she is out of shape.
（這位時裝模特兒半年前生了一場重病，現在的她已不成人樣。）

7. catch one's eye
吸引某人的注意（此處 eye 為不可數名詞，等於 attention）

例: Emily tried to catch Andy's eye by wearing a miniskirt.
（艾蜜莉穿迷你裙，試圖引起安迪的注意。）

8. Wish sb luck!　　祝某人好運！

例: You have a math test today, don't you? Wish you luck!
（你今天有數學考試，對吧？祝你好運！）

My First Try

Index | *Links* | *about* | *comments* | *Photo*

May 02

I decided to start off my **diet** by only drinking water today. At first I felt fine, only getting hungry at lunch. Then, by 4 p.m., I was **starving** and felt a little **light-headed**. On my way out the door to get some fresh air, I passed by Mike. He began **chatting** with me, which made me excited and the **dizziness** got worse. Suddenly, his arms were around me because I nearly **fainted**! I was so embarrassed that I **rushed to** the ladies' room without even thanking him for catching me.

About me

Ivy

Calendar

◄   *May*   ►

Sun	Mon	Tue	Wed	Thu	Fri	Sat
					1	3
4	5	6	7	8	9	10
11	12	13	14	15	16	17
18	19	20	21	22	23	24
25	26	27	28	29	30	31

Blog Archive

- ► May (2)
- ► April
- ► March
- ► February
- ► January
- ► December
- ► November
- ► October
- ► September
- ► August
- ► July
- ► June

Ivy at Blog 於 May 05.02. PM 05:16 發表 | 回覆 (0) | 引用 (0) | 收藏 (0) | 轉寄給朋友 | 檢舉

節食初體驗

May 02

　　我決定今天開始只喝水來節食。起初我覺得還好，只是在午餐時覺得有點餓。到了下午四點時，我開始感到飢腸轆轆，而且頭暈眼花。在我走出門外想呼吸點新鮮空氣時，我從麥克身邊經過。他開始跟我閒聊，這讓我很興奮，但頭也更昏了。突然間，他兩手抱住我，原來我差一點昏倒了！我覺得好窘，於是就衝到洗手間，連一句謝謝他扶住我的話也沒說。

About me

Ivy

Calendar

◄　　　　　*May*　　　　►

Sun	Mon	Tue	Wed	Thu	Fri	Sat
				1	2	3
4	5	6	7	8	9	10
11	12	13	14	15	16	17
18	19	20	21	22	23	24
25	26	27	28	29	30	31

Blog Archive

► May (2)
► April
► March
► February
► January
► December
► November
► October
► September
► August
► July
► June

英文中有許多可用來描述某人因酒醉、身體不適、興奮過度、遭受撞擊等而感到『頭暈目眩』的字詞，並可依照個人感受的程度來做區分：最輕微的應該就是 light-headed 了，顧名思義，輕飄飄的頭意指腦袋感到飄飄然，失去平衡，接著再嚴重點，可能開始覺得天旋地轉，甚至覺得噁心不舒服，也就是 dizzy，最後很有可能昏厥過去而失去知覺，那就是 faint 的程度了。以下是一些與頭暈目眩相關的字詞：

light-headed [ˌlaɪtˈhɛdɪd] *a.* 暈眩的

dizzy [ˈdɪzɪ] *a.* 頭暈目眩的

dizziness [ˈdɪzɪnɪs] *n.* 暈眩，頭昏

faint [fent] *vi.* 暈倒，昏厥

= pass out

woozy [ˈwuzɪ] *a.* 虛弱的；暈眩的（口語）

tipsy [ˈtɪpsɪ] *a.* （飲酒後）微醺的；步履不穩的

see stars　　眼冒金星，頭昏眼花

one's head is spinning　　某人頭在暈

＊spin [spɪn] *vi.* 快速旋轉（三態為：spin, spun [spʌn], spun）

例: After riding on the merry-go-round, Gary felt dizzy.

（蓋瑞坐完旋轉木馬後，覺得頭暈目眩。）

The runner was so exhausted after the race that he almost fainted.

（那位選手在跑完比賽後，累得差點昏倒。）

Jenny felt tipsy after one beer.

（阿珍喝了一罐啤酒後就覺得有點醉意了。）

Right after being punched in the face, Allen saw stars.

（艾倫被一拳揍在臉上後，當場眼冒金星。）

1. diet [ˋdaɪət] *n.* （為了治療或健康因素所做的）規定飲食

a balanced diet 均衡的飲食

be on a diet 在節食中

go on a diet 開始節食

例: Mary hasn't been eating a balanced diet recently.

（瑪麗最近的飲食一直不均衡。）

Lisa is slender because she's always on a diet.

（麗莎很苗條，因為她一直都在節食。）

＊slender [ˋslɛndɚ] *a.* 苗條的

John weighs almost 100 kilograms, so he needs to go on a diet.

（阿強重達將近 100 公斤，所以他該節食了。）

2. starve [stɑrv] *vi.* 挨餓，飢餓（starving 是 starve 的現在分詞）

be starving to death 快要餓死了（誇張用語，比喻『很餓』）

例: I'm starving to death. Do you have anything to eat?

（我餓死了。有什麼東西可以吃嗎？）

3. chat [tʃæt] *vi.* & *n.* 聊天，閒聊

chat with sb 與某人聊天 / 閒聊

= have a chat with sb

例: I chatted with Betty on the phone for two hours last night.

（我昨晚跟貝蒂講了 2 個小時的電話。）

4. rush to + 地方 衝去某地，匆促趕往某地

rush into + 地方 衝進某地

rush out of + 地方 衝出某地

例: The fire fighters rushed to the scene to put out the fire.

（消防人員趕忙到現場救火。）

The customers rushed out of the restaurant when they saw the fire in the kitchen.

（顧客看見廚房竄出火苗時，全都衝出餐廳。）

Unit 3

The Office Fool

Index | Links | about | comments | Photo

May 03

Today, I spent some time **looking up** information on the Internet about **losing weight**. I found **advice** from many different websites. Some had special diet plans to follow, while others were about the perfect exercises to do. I **printed out** the information to **go through** at home. However, I couldn't find the printouts at the printer. Then a man from the accounting department asked **in a loud voice** if anyone had printed out weight loss information. I **turned beet red** and **sheepishly** went to get my pages immediately. >_<|||

About me

Ivy

Calendar

◄   *May*   ►

Sun	Mon	Tue	Wed	Thu	Fri	Sat
				1	2	3
4	5	6	7	8	9	10
11	12	13	14	15	16	17
18	19	20	21	22	23	24
25	26	27	28	29	30	31

Blog Archive

- ► May (3)
- ► April
- ► March
- ► February
- ► January
- ► December
- ► November
- ► October
- ► September
- ► August
- ► July
- ► June

Ivy at Blog 於 May 05.03. PM 08:30 發表 | 回覆 (0) | 引用 (0) | 收藏 (0) | 轉寄給朋友 | 檢舉

10

May 03

About me

Ivy

　　今天我花了一點時間上網查詢減肥的相關資訊。我從五花八門的網站找到了一些建議。有些是介紹特別的飲食計畫，有些則是介紹超有效的油切運動。我列印出這些資料好帶回家詳讀。但我去印表機拿時卻遍尋不著列印的東西。結果會計部的一個男生大聲問誰在列印減肥資料，害我整個臉紅得像猴子屁股似的，趕緊去拿回我印的東西，真羞死人了。>_<|||

Calendar

◄　　　　*May*　　　　►

Sun	Mon	Tue	Wed	Thu	Fri	Sat
					1	2	3
4	5	6	7	8	9	10
11	12	13	14	15	16	17
18	19	20	21	22	23	24
25	26	27	28	29	30	31

Blog Archive

▸ May (3)
▸ April
▸ March
▸ February
▸ January
▸ December
▸ November
▸ October
▸ September
▸ August
▸ July
▸ June

Ivy at Blog 於 May 05.03. PM 08:30 發表｜回覆 (0)｜引用 (0)｜收藏 (0)｜轉寄給朋友｜檢舉

當你覺得很窘的時候，臉紅得像猴子屁股，英文的說法是 "turn / go red"，或者也可以說 "turn / go beet red"。beet [bit] 就是『甜菜根』，這種國外常見的植物長得就像是紅通通的菜頭，正宗的俄羅斯羅宋湯裡就有這種食材。所以下次要形容因害羞而臉紅，就可以說某人 "turn / go beet red"。以下是類似說法：

turn / go as red as a beet　　　臉紅耳赤；害羞
turn / go as red as a cherry　　　臉紅耳赤；害羞
＊cherry [ˈtʃɛrɪ] *n.* 櫻桃

flush [flʌʃ] *vi.* 臉紅
blush [blʌʃ] *vi.* 臉紅

例: David turned beet red when a little boy told him his zipper was open.
（有個小男孩告訴大衛拉鍊沒拉時，他羞得滿臉通紅。）

Sarah blushed when her prince charming passed by.
（莎拉的白馬王子經過她身旁時，她的臉紅得像猴子屁股。）

＊prince charming　　（某女孩子的）白馬王子 / 意中人

如果要說『臉色發白』，就用 " turn / go pale" 來表示。

turn / go pale　　　臉色發白，變成蒼白
＊pale [pel] *a.* （臉色）蒼白的

例: The moment she heard the bad news, Nina turned pale.
（妮娜一聽到這個壞消息馬上臉色發白。）

字 詞幫幫忙！

1. look up... / look...up　　查詢 / 查閱（資訊、字義等）

注意:
表『查字典』不可說 "look up a dictionary"，而應該說 "consult a dictionary" 或 "refer to a dictionary"。look up 接被查的單字或電話號碼；consult（請教）或 refer to（參考）之後接字典或電話簿。

例: Jim looked up the store's phone number in the phone book.
（吉姆在電話簿裡查那間商店的電話號碼。）

If I don't know the meaning of a word, I'll consult the dictionary / I'll look it up in the dictionary.
（如果我不明白一個字的意思，就會去查字典。）

2. **lose weight** 減重，變瘦

   gain weight 增重，變胖

= **put on weight**

   例: Mandy tried her best to lose weight before her wedding.

   （曼蒂為了婚禮拼命在減肥。）

   Soon after my boyfriend quit smoking, he put on a lot of weight.

   （我男友戒菸後不久就胖了許多。）

3. **advice** [əd'vaɪs] *n.* 建議，忠告（不可數）

   a piece of advice 一則建議

   不可說：an advice (×)

   例: That's a good advice. (×)

   → That's a good piece of advice. (○)

= That's a good suggestion.（suggestion 是可數名詞）

   （那是個好建議。）

4. **print out... / print...out** 列印出⋯⋯

   printout [`prɪnt͵aʊt] *n.* （電腦）列印出的資料

   例: Can you help me print out my report?

   （你可以幫我把報告列印出來嗎？）

5. **go through...** （從頭到尾）詳讀⋯⋯

   例: The boss went through all of the files that I handed in.

   （老闆詳讀了所有我呈交的文件。）

6. **in a loud voice** 以大聲說話

   in a / an...voice 用⋯⋯的聲音

   例: The boss spoke to his secretary in a loud voice.

   （老闆用大嗓門向他祕書說話。）

7. **sheepishly** [`ʃipɪʃlɪ] *adv.* 困窘地；靦腆地

   例: Vicky grinned sheepishly when she noticed the handsome man looking at her.

   （維琪發現那個帥哥在看她時，靦腆地笑了一笑。）

   *grin [grɪn] *vi.* 露齒而笑

A Fruit Failure

May 04

I tried an all-fruit diet today, and it went well at first. It wasn't hard eating bananas for breakfast and strawberries for lunch. However, just when I thought I was able to **stick to** this diet program, my best friend Monica asked me to **join** her **for** dinner. She said she needed to <u>**have a heart-to-heart with**</u> a good friend, so I couldn't **refuse**. **As a result**, my all-fruit diet **ended up** a failure the very first day. ><

About me

Ivy

Calendar

◄   *May*   ►

Sun	Mon	Tue	Wed	Thu	Fri	Sat
				1	2	3
4	5	6	7	8	9	10
11	12	13	14	15	16	17
18	19	20	21	22	23	24
25	26	27	28	29	30	31

Blog Archive

- ► May (4)
- ► April
- ► March
- ► February
- ► January
- ► December
- ► November
- ► October
- ► September
- ► August
- ► July
- ► June

Ivy at Blog 於 May 05.04. PM 09:10 發表 | 回覆 (0) | 引用 (0) | 收藏 (0) | 轉寄給朋友 | 檢舉

水果減肥餐宣告失敗

Index | *Links* | *about* | *comments* | *Photo*

May 04

　　我今天試了水果餐減肥法，一開始都很順利。早餐吃香蕉、午餐吃草莓沒什麼難的。但是就當我覺得能對水果餐堅持到底時，我的手帕交莫妮卡約我和她一起吃晚餐。她說她需要和好友談心，所以我就不能拒絕了。結果我的水果餐減肥法第一天就破功了。><

About me

Ivy

Calendar

◄　　　*May*　　　►

Sun	Mon	Tue	Wed	Thu	Fri	Sat
				1	2	3
4	5	6	7	8	9	10
11	12	13	14	15	16	17
18	19	20	21	22	23	24
25	26	27	28	29	30	31

Blog Archive

► May (4)
► April
► March
► February
► January
► December
► November
► October
► September
► August
► July
► June

Ivy at Blog 於 May 05.04. PM 09:10 發表｜回覆 (0)｜引用 (0)｜收藏 (0)｜轉寄給朋友｜檢舉

好朋友找你／妳談心，怎麼忍心拒絕呢？希望莫妮卡找作者談的事很重要，否則節食計劃泡湯還真是欲哭無淚。

說到『談心、促膝長談』，英文的表達方法十分簡單明瞭，那就是 have a heart-to-heart (talk) with sb。heart-to-heart 字面上的意思就是『心對心』，可以作名詞用，表『貼心的談話、坦率的談心』，也可以作形容詞用，表『坦率的、毫無隱瞞的』。所以你看，heart-to-heart 一聽是不是就有『誠心誠意、敞開心胸』的感覺呢？

have a heart-to-heart (talk) with sb　　與某人談心

= have a deep conversation with sb
= have an intimate conversation with sb
　＊intimate [ˈɪntəmɪt] *a.* 親密的
　例: After having a heart-to-heart talk with my good friend, I felt better about breaking up with Andrew.
　　（和好友促膝長談後，對於和安德魯分手的事我心裡便舒暢多了。）

1. **failure** [ˈfeljə] *n.* 失敗的人或事物（可數）；失敗（不可數）
　例: The party Kevin held last night was a total failure.
　　（凱文昨晚辦的派對爛透了。）

　　Failure is the mother of success.
　　（失敗為成功之母。──諺語）

2. **stick to + N/V-ing**　　堅持／不放棄……
　stick [stɪk] *vi.* 堅持，固守
　三態為：stick，stuck [stʌk]，stuck。
　例: Whatever you do, you should stick to your principles.
　　（你不論做什麼事，都要把持原則。）

3. **join sb for sth**　　和某人一起從事……
　join sb in + V-ing　　加入某人從事……

例: Would you be interested in joining me for lunch?
（你願不願意和我一塊吃午餐呢？）

Would you like to join us in going to the movies tonight?
（你今晚要不要和我們一起去看電影？）

4. **refuse** [rɪˋfjuz] *vi.* & *vt.* 拒絕

refuse to V　　拒絕（做）……

例: Kent wants to ask Lisa out, but he's afraid she might refuse.
（阿根哥想約麗莎出去，但他很怕她會拒絕。）

The actor refused to talk about his private life in the interview.
（那位演員在訪問中拒絕談論他的私生活。）

5. **As a result, S + V**　　結果 / 因此，……

例: A typhoon struck the island. As a result, all schools were closed for the day.
（颱風侵襲該島。因此，所有學校當天都停課了。）

6. **end up...**　　最後 / 到頭來……

注意:

end up 後一律接現在分詞作補語，end up 之後若是 be 動詞，一律改成現在分詞 being，而 being 可省略。

例: You can end up (being) one of the richest people in this city if you invest your money with me.
（如果你和我一起投資，你就有可能變成這座城市裡最有錢的人之一。）

The gambler ended up losing everything.
（這名賭徒到頭來失去了一切。）

＊本文最後一句 ended cop 之後省略了 being，即:

As a result, my all-fruit diet ended up (being) a failure the very first day.
（結果，我的水果裝第一天就服失敗收場。）

Unit 5

Throw off a Routine

Index | *Links* | *about* | *comments* | *Photo*

May 05

Today was **horrible**! I wanted to wear one of my favorite **outfits**, but I couldn't **squeeze into** my miniskirt! I got so **upset** I **ended up** taking longer than usual to get **dressed**. This **threw off my whole morning routine** and I got to work late. I thought my boss hadn't seen me, so I tried to **sneak** to my desk. **Unfortunately**, I found a note my boss had already written on my computer that read, "This is the third time this month!"

About me

Ivy

Calendar

◄　　*May*　　►

Sun	Mon	Tue	Wed	Thu	Fri	Sat
				1	2	3
4	5	6	7	8	9	10
11	12	13	14	15	16	17
18	19	20	21	22	23	24
25	26	27	28	29	30	31

Blog Archive

► May (5)
► April
► March
► February
► January
► December
► November
► October
► September
► August
► July
► June

Ivy at Blog 於 May 05.05. PM 02:36 發表｜回覆 (0)｜引用 (0)｜收藏 (0)｜轉寄給朋友｜檢舉

打亂例行公事

Index | *Links* | *about* | *comments* | *Photo*

May 05

今天真是糟透了！我想穿上我最愛的其中一套衣服，卻發現怎麼也塞不進去那件迷你裙裡。我好沮喪，結果花了比平常久的時間穿衣服。這打亂了我整個早上的例行公事，害我上班遲到。我以為老闆沒發現，便想偷偷溜到座位上。但衰的是，我發現電腦上有一張老闆貼的紙條，上面寫著：『這是妳這個月第三次遲到了！』

About me

Ivy

Calendar

◄ *May* ►

Sun	Mon	Tue	Wed	Thu	Fri	Sat
				1	2	3
4	5	6	7	8	9	10
11	12	13	14	15	16	17
18	19	20	21	22	23	24
25	26	27	28	29	30	31

Blog Archive

- ► May (5)
- ► April
- ► March
- ► February
- ► January
- ► December
- ► November
- ► October
- ► September
- ► August
- ► July
- ► June

Ivy at Blog 於 May 05.05. PM 02:36 發表 | 回覆 (0) | 引用 (0) | 收藏 (0) | 轉寄給朋友 | 檢舉

網誌作者因為塞不進想穿的迷你裙裡，所以搞了老半天衣服都還沒換好，打亂她每天上班前要做的例行公事，像是化妝、弄頭髮等，落得上班遲到的下場。相信許多人都有過這種經驗，像是早上醒來發現新長了顆青春痘（zit / pimple），花了 10 分鐘把它擠掉（squeeze a zit / pimple），結果卻因此來不及買早餐或沒趕上公車等等，這時 throw off one's (daily / morning...) routine 就派上用場啦。

throw off one's (daily / morning...) routine
打亂某人（每天 / 早上 / ……）的例行公事
= mess up one's (daily / morning...) routine
routine [ruˋtin] *n.* 例行公事
mess up... 　　弄亂 / 弄糟……

例: This morning, I spent 10 minutes trying to get rid of the pimples on my cheek. It totally threw off my routine.
（今天早上我花了 10 分鐘想把臉上的痘痘擠掉，結果徹底打亂我的例行公事。）
＊pimple [ˋpɪmpl̩] *n.* 青春痘（zit）

字詞幫幫忙！

1. **horrible** [ˋhɔrəbl̩] *a.*（口語）糟透的
= terrible [ˋtɛrəbl̩] *a.*
= awful [ˋɔfl̩] *a.*
例: The food at that restaurant is horrible.
（那家餐廳的食物糟透了。）

2. **outfit** [ˋautˏfɪt] *n.*（尤指整套的）服裝（可數）
例: Patrick looks stylish in that outfit.
（派屈克穿那套衣服看起來很時髦。）
＊stylish [ˋstaɪlɪʃ] *a.* 時髦的，新潮的

3. **squeeze into...** 擠進……
squeeze [skwiz] *vi.* 擠，壓 & *vt.* 擠出，榨出
例: Despite all of my efforts, I still can't squeeze into those jeans.
（儘管我再怎麼努力，還是塞不進那條牛仔褲。）

Don't squeeze your pimples unless you want scars on your face.

（除非你希望臉上有疤痕，否則就不要擠青春痘。）

4. **upset** [ʌpˋsɛt] *a.* 心煩的，苦惱的

   例: I was upset when Kathy stood me up again.

   （凱西又放我鴿子讓我很不爽。）

   ＊stand sb up　　放某人鴿子，對某人爽約

5. **end up + V-ing**　　結果／最後／到頭來……

   例: Larry ended up divorcing his wife because she was found two-timing him.

   （賴瑞最後跟他太太離婚，因為有人發現她對他劈腿。）

   ＊divorce [dəˋvɔrs] *vt.*　　與……離婚

   　two-time [ˋtuˏtaɪm] *vt.*　　（對某人）感情不忠

   The drug dealer ended up (being) in jail.

   （這個毒販最後鋃鐺入獄了。）

6. **dress** [drɛs] *vt.* 給……穿衣服，使打扮 & *vi.* 穿著，打扮

   get dressed　　　　穿好衣服

   dress up　　　　　盛裝打扮

   例: You need to get dressed right now. We're leaving in five minutes.

   （你現在趕快穿好衣服，我們 5 分鐘後就要出發了。）

   It's a formal party, so you'll have to dress up.

   （那是正式的派對，因此你必須盛裝。）

7. **sneak** [snik] *vi.* 偷偷進入／溜出

   sneak into...　　　偷偷溜進……

   sneak out of...　　偷偷溜出……

   例: The thief sneaked into the house and stole everything he saw.

   （小偷溜進屋內，把看到的一切東西都偷走了。）

8. **unfortunately** [ʌnˋfɔrtʃənɪtlɪ] *adv.* 不幸地

   fortunately [ˋfɔrtʃənɪtlɪ] *adv.* 幸運地

   例: I was late, but fortunately, the movie hadn't started yet.

   （我遲到了，所幸電影還沒開始。）

Unit 6

A Coworker's Advice

Index | Links | about | comments | Photo

May 06

I was really **frustrated** at work today, and my co-worker Janet noticed. She asked me **what was up**, and I told her about **struggling** with losing weight. She then told me about a weight-loss **clinic** her sister **had** tried and had success with. She even had the clinic's business card **on hand**. I called the clinic right away and made an **appointment** for tomorrow. I hope it **goes well**. I'm <u>keeping my fingers crossed</u>.

About me

Ivy

Calendar

◄   *May*   ►

Sun	Mon	Tue	Wed	Thu	Fri	Sat
				1	2	3
4	5	6	7	8	9	10
11	12	13	14	15	16	17
18	19	20	21	22	23	24
25	26	27	28	29	30	31

Blog Archive

- ► May (6)
- ► April
- ► March
- ► February
- ► January
- ► December
- ► November
- ► October
- ► September
- ► August
- ► July
- ► June

Ivy at Blog 於 May 05.06. PM 10:52 發表 | 回覆 (0) | 引用 (0) | 收藏 (0) | 轉寄給朋友 | 檢舉

同事的好心建議

May 06

　　今天上班真是沮喪極了，同事珍娜注意到這一點。她問我怎麼了，我就告訴她我正在跟體重奮戰。然後她告訴我她姊姊之前試過一家減肥診所超有效的。她手邊甚至有那家診所的名片。我馬上就打電話跟診所預約明天看診。希望一切順利，請保佑我能減肥成功。

About me

Ivy

Calendar

◀　　　May　　　▶

Sun	Mon	Tue	Wed	Thu	Fri	Sat
				1	2	3
4	5	6	7	8	9	10
11	12	13	14	15	16	17
18	19	20	21	22	23	24
25	26	27	28	29	30	31

Blog Archive

- ► May (6)
- ► April
- ► March
- ► February
- ► January
- ► December
- ► November
- ► October
- ► September
- ► August
- ► July
- ► June

『手指交叉』就能減肥成功？不，可沒那麼容易。keep one's fingers crossed 或 cross one's fingers 的手勢為中指與食指交叉如十字架狀，因為十字架象徵耶穌，所以有『祈求上帝保佑』的意思，藉以表達『祈求好運』。我們常在電影或影集中看到一個人若發假誓時，會把手放在背後做出中指與食指交叉的動作，就是希望自己不會因為發假誓而招來厄運。

keep one's fingers crossed (for sb)

（為某人）祈求上帝保佑，（為某人）祈求好運

= cross one's fingers (for sb)

＊cross [krɔs] *vt.* 使交叉

例: I have an interview tomorrow. Please keep your fingers crossed for me.

= I have an interview tomorrow. Please cross your fingers for me.

（我明天有個面試。請祝我好運。）

＊interview [ˈɪntə͞vju] *n.* 面試

1. **frustrated** [ˈfrʌstretɪd] *a.* 感到挫折的

   feel / be frustrated at...　因……感到挫折

   例: Michael feels frustrated at the fact that he cannot find a job.
   （麥可因為找不到工作而滿懷挫折。）

2. **What's up?**　怎麼了？

= What's (= What has) happened?

   例: Gary: Are you busy?

   Betty: Not at all. What's up?

   （蓋瑞：妳很忙嗎？）

   （貝蒂：一點也不。有什麼事嗎？）

   What's up? 亦表『有啥新鮮事？』的意思，為美國時下一般年輕人打招呼用語，對方常以 "Nothing much."（沒什麼搞頭。）回應。

3. **struggle** [ˈstrʌgḷ] *vi.* 搏鬥，掙扎

    struggle with...　　與……搏鬥

    struggle to V　　努力／掙扎（做）……

    例: Betty struggled with the zipper of her favorite jeans.

    （貝蒂拼命想拉上她最喜歡的牛仔褲拉鏈。）

    ＊zipper [ˈzɪpɚ] *n.* 拉鍊

    Mary struggled to get control of her scooter after she hit a car.

    （瑪莉撞到車子後奮力想控制住她的機車。）

4. **clinic** [ˈklɪnɪk] *n.* 診所

    a dental clinic　　牙醫診所

5. **have...on hand**　　手邊有……

    例: If you need money, I have NT$500 on hand.

    （如果你需要錢，我手頭上有 500 元。）

6. **appointment** [əˈpɔɪntmənt] *n.* 約會，約定

    make an appointment　　約時間會面

    make an appointment with sb for ＋ 時間　　和某人約在某時間會面

    例: In order to see the famous doctor, you have to make an
    appointment a week in advance.

    （為了讓那位名醫看病，你必須提早一星期預約。）

    ＊in advance　　事先，提前

    ＝ beforehand

    Marcy made an appointment with her dentist for 10:00
    tomorrow morning.

    （瑪西和她的牙醫約好明天上午 10 點看診。）

7. **go well**　　進行順利

    例: I hope your interview goes well today.

    （祝你今天的面試順利。）

    Jack: Is everything OK?

    Tom: Everything is going well.

    （傑克：一切都還好嗎？）

    （湯姆：一切都進行得很順利。）

The First Doctor's Visit

Index | Links | about | comments | Photo

May 07

I went to the clinic Janet **recommended** today. The doctor was very nice, and she said she **based** her program **on** her own weight-loss success. However, the price of the medicine was **outrageous**. I decided that I would try the program for three weeks to see if it **worked**. I figured that would be the only way to know **for sure**. Taking the **medicine** wasn't as bad as I thought. **So far so good!**

About me

Ivy

Calendar

◄   *May*   ►

Sun	Mon	Tue	Wed	Thu	Fri	Sat
				1	2	3
4	5	6	7	8	9	10
11	12	13	14	15	16	17
18	19	20	21	22	23	24
25	26	27	28	29	30	31

Blog Archive

- ► May (7)
- ► April
- ► March
- ► February
- ► January
- ► December
- ► November
- ► October
- ► September
- ► August
- ► July
- ► June

Ivy at Blog 於 May 05.07. PM 03:14 發表 | 回覆 (0) | 引用 (0) | 收藏 (0) | 轉寄給朋友 | 檢舉

May 07

　　我今天去了珍娜大推的減肥診所。醫生人超好的，而且她說她的減肥計畫可是根據她自己的成功減重經驗設計的。不過減肥藥還真是貴得離譜。我決定了，我就試這個計劃 3 個星期，看它是不是真的那麼神奇。我想這是知道真相的不二法門。吃減肥藥其實沒有我想像的那麼糟。到目前為止，一切順利！

About me

Ivy

Calendar

◄			*May*			►
Sun	Mon	Tue	Wed	Thu	Fri	Sat
				1	2	3
4	5	6	7	8	9	10
11	12	13	14	15	16	17
18	19	20	21	22	23	24
25	26	27	28	29	30	31

Blog Archive

- ► May (7)
- ► April
- ► March
- ► February
- ► January
- ► December
- ► November
- ► October
- ► September
- ► August
- ► July
- ► June

Ivy at Blog 於 May 05.07. PM 03:14 發表｜回覆 (0)｜引用 (0)｜收藏 (0)｜轉寄給朋友｜檢舉

在經濟不景氣的年代，許多商品都會讓人覺得貴得離譜，有時去買個東西荷包就輕了一半！抱怨東西太貴最常用的英文單字就是 expensive 了。不過在這個網誌中用到的 outrageous（形容詞，表『離譜的』、『過分的』）『超級貴，貴得離譜』。下次你想抱怨東西太貴時，除了用 very expensive（很貴）、too expensive（太貴），也可以用 outrageous，更能讓人感受到那種荷包大失血的切身之痛！

outrageous [aut`redʒəs] *a.* 離譜的；過分的

例: It was foolish of Alex to pay such an outrageous price for that ugly hat.
（艾力克斯花那麼多錢買那頂醜帽子還真是愚蠢。）

"So far so good!" 這句話超實用的，你可能也常聽見別人這麼說。so far 是指『到目前為止』，so good 則是指『很好』，所以 so far so good 就是表示『到目前為止都很好』。當某事仍在進行中，有人問你狀況如何，如果一切都還算順利的話，你就可以回答："So far so good!" 如果你想展露英文能力，也可以用 as of right now 或 up to the / this point 等表示『到目前為止』的片語與 so far 同義，後面再加上 it's going well 或 it's all right 等表示『事情進行順利』的短句，這樣的組合同樣有異曲同工之妙。

例: Sarah: How's your new job?
Adam: So far so good.
　　或: As of right now, it's going well.
　　或: Up to this point, it's all right.
（莎拉：你的新工作怎麼樣？）
（亞當：到目前為止，一切順利。）

字詞幫幫忙！

1. **recommend** [ˌrɛkə`mɛnd] *vt.* 推薦
strongly / highly recommend...　　強勢 / 大力推薦……
例: Rebecca highly recommended the popular book, *Twilight*, to me.
（蕾貝卡大力推薦我看《暮光之城》這本熱門書。）

2. **base A on / upon B**　　將 A 建立在 B 的基礎上

be based on / upon...　　根據……

例: The lawyer based his closing arguments on the facts of the case.

（這位律師根據案情作結辯。）

That movie is based on a famous comic book.

（那部電影是根據一本知名漫畫書改編而成的。）

3. **work** [wɜk] *vi.*（方法、計畫等）行得通；起作用

work like magic　　（方法、計畫等）非常靈驗，非常有效

例: Jill claimed that her tips on memorizing vocabulary words would work like magic.

（吉兒聲稱她的背單字撇步超有效。）

＊**tip** [tɪp] *n.* 秘訣

a tip on...　　有關……的秘訣／撇步（此處 on 等於 about，表『有關』）

memorize [ˈmɛməˌraɪz] *vt.* 記住，熟記

4. **for sure**　　肯定地，確切地

= **for certain**

例: We will have the meeting at 2:00 PM for sure.

（我們確定會在下午兩點開會。）

5. **medicine** [ˈmɛdəsn̩] *n.* 藥物

注意:

表『吃』藥的動詞用 take，表『喝』湯用 eat，而表『喝』水、『喝』飲料才用 drink。

take medicine	服藥，吃藥（非 eat medicine）
take pills	吃藥丸（非 eat pills）
eat the soup	喝湯（非 drink the soup）
drink water / tea / coffee	喝水／茶／咖啡

Clinic Diet: Day 1

Index | *Links* | *about* | *comments* | *Photo*

May 08

Today was my first **full** day to follow the diet program and take the medicine. I reread the **sheets** of information the doctor had given me. The rules were simple. I could only eat one small **bowl** of food for each meal and have two small snacks per day. Eating a small **portion** for breakfast <u>**was a breeze**</u>, but lunch proved to be more difficult. **In addition**, I discovered the convenience store by my office **lacked** any healthy snacks. I guess I'll have to prepare them myself.

About me

Ivy

Calendar

◄ *May* ►

Sun	Mon	Tue	Wed	Thu	Fri	Sat
				1	2	3
4	5	6	7	8	9	10
11	12	13	14	15	16	17
18	19	20	21	22	23	24
25	26	27	28	29	30	31

Blog Archive

► May (8)
► April
► March
► February
► January
► December
► Novombor
► October
► Ooptombor
► August
► July
► June

Ivy at Blog 於 May 05.08. PM 01:55 發表 | 回覆 (0) | 引用 (0) | 收藏 (0) | 轉寄給朋友 | 檢舉

醫療節食：第一天

May 08

　　今天是我遵照節食計劃開始吃藥的第一個整天。我再看了一次醫生給我的幾頁資料。規則很簡單。我每餐只能吃一小碗食物，一天只能吃兩次小點心。早餐吃少少的東西很容易，但午餐可就不是那麼一回事了。此外，我發現辦公室附近的便利商店沒賣什麼健康的點心。我想我得自己準備餐飲了。

About me

Ivy

Calendar

◄　　　*May*　　　►

Sun	Mon	Tue	Wed	Thu	Fri	Sat
				1	2	3
4	5	6	7	8	9	10
11	12	13	14	15	16	17
18	19	20	21	22	23	24
25	26	27	28	29	30	31

Blog Archive

▸ May (8)
▸ April
▸ March
▸ February
▸ January
▸ December
▸ November
▸ October
▸ September
▸ August
▸ July
▸ June

Ivy at Blog 於 May 05.08. PM 01:55 發表 | 回覆 (0) | 引用 (0) | 收藏 (0) | 轉寄給朋友 | 檢舉

breeze 原意表『微風、和風』，然而網誌中所用的 be a breeze 倒跟自然界的風沒啥關係，而是指『輕而易舉的事』，等同於 a piece of cake（原意為『一片蛋糕』），也就是我們日常口語中的『小 case』。同時，它們也可以在對話中表『不客氣，小事一樁』之意。以下為您介紹這類超好用的片語用法：

It's a breeze. 　　小事一樁。
= It's a piece of cake.
It's not a big deal. 　　沒什麼大不了。
It's nothing. 　　這沒什麼。
No sweat. 　　一點也不難，毫不費力。
＊sweat [swɛt] *n.* 汗水

例: Passing the exam was a piece of cake for Jeremy.
（傑瑞米輕而易舉就通過了考試。）

Paul: Thank you for going through all the trouble to get me this ticket.
Lucy: It's nothing.
（保羅：謝謝妳大費周章為我拿到這張票。）
（露西：這沒什麼啦。）

Dora: Are you sure you can lift the box yourself?
Gary: Sure, no sweat!
（朵拉：你確定你可以自己搬動那個箱子嗎？）
（蓋瑞：當然，沒問題！）

1. **full** [fʊl] *a.* （時間）整整的
a full day / week / month / year 　　一整天／一整個星期／一整個月／一整年
= a whole day / week / month / year
例: Ruth spent a full week shooting wedding photos.
（露絲花了一整個禮拜拍攝婚紗照。）

2. **sheet** [ʃit] *n.* （紙、玻璃等）一張，一片
   a sheet of paper　一張紙
   = a piece of paper
   a sheet of glass　　一片玻璃
   = a piece of glass

3. **bowl** [bol] *n.* 碗
   a bowl of rice　　一碗飯
   a bowl of noodles　一碗麵
   a bowl of soup　　一碗湯

4. **portion** [ˋpɔrʃən] *n.* 一份，一客
   a portion of...　一份 / 一客……
   例: Would you mind splitting this portion of French fries with
       me?
   （你可以跟我分這份薯條嗎？）
   ＊split [splɪt] *vt.* 分開（三態同形）

5. **In addition, S + V**　　此外 / 而且，……
   In addition to + N/V-ing, S + V　　除了……以外，……
   例: The job pays well. In addition, I get a one-week vacation
       yearly.
   （這份工作待遇不錯，此外，我每年有一星期的假期。）

   In addition to an extra battery, what else comes with this
   cell phone?
   （除了另送一顆電池，買這隻手機還送什麼其他的？）

6. **lack** [læk] *vt.* & *n.* 沒有；缺乏
   例: The school lacks money to build a swimming pool.
   （該校缺乏建游泳池的經費。）

   A lack of vitamin D has a negative effect on one's health.
   （缺乏維生素 D 對我們的健康有負面影響。）

My Beating Heart

Index | Links | about | comments | Photo

May 09

I'm **getting used to** my new eating habits. I've also been good about **selecting** healthy **snack options**. But the exciting news for today is about Mike. He **stopped by** my desk today to let me know he would be out of the office **on a business trip** for a few days. He was wearing his blue shirt, which really **looked good on** him. He looked so handsome and **my heart started beating out of control**. It seemed so loud I was sure he could hear it.

About me

Ivy

Calendar

◄   *May*   ►

Sun	Mon	Tue	Wed	Thu	Fri	Sat
				1	2	3
4	5	6	7	8	9	10
11	12	13	14	15	16	17
18	19	20	21	22	23	24
25	26	27	28	29	30	31

Blog Archive

- ► May (9)
- ► April
- ► March
- ► February
- ► January
- ► December
- ► November
- ► October
- ► September
- ► August
- ► July
- ► June

Ivy at Blog 於 May 05.09. PM 02:03 發表 | 回覆 (0) | 引用 (0) | 收藏 (0) | 轉寄給朋友 | 檢舉

小鹿亂撞

May 09

　　我慢慢習慣新的飲食習慣了，對於挑選健康的零嘴也變得很在行。但今天令人興奮的消息是跟麥克有關。他今天走到我辦公桌旁，告訴我他要出差幾天。他穿著藍色襯衫，那件襯衫穿在他身上真是好看極了。這傢伙實在太帥了，害我心頭小鹿亂撞！我覺得心跳那麼大聲，他一定可以聽得到！

About me

Ivy

Calendar

◄ May ►

Sun	Mon	Tue	Wed	Thu	Fri	Sat
					1	2	3
4	5	6	7	8	9	10
11	12	13	14	15	16	17
18	19	20	21	22	23	24
25	26	27	28	29	30	31

Blog Archive

- ► May (9)
- ► April
- ► March
- ► February
- ► January
- ► December
- ► November
- ► October
- ► September
- ► August
- ► July
- ► June

Ivy at Blog 於 May 05.09. PM 02:03 發表｜回覆 (0)｜引用 (0)｜收藏 (0)｜轉寄給朋友｜檢舉

35

就算你沒談過戀愛，一定也有心頭『小鹿亂撞』的經驗吧！英文裡描述這種心情的句子不少，像網誌裡的 one's heart beats out of control，這字面上的意思就是『心跳到失去控制』，一聽就知道是看到喜歡的人才會有的反應。

另外，中文裡有『小鹿』，英文裡則是用『蝴蝶』來表示，像是 have butterflies in one's stomach，一群蝴蝶在胃裡飛來飛去？那豈不是令人坐立難安，怎麼樣都不對勁？沒錯！這個說法原先是用來形容人因為緊張而心裡七上八下。遇到心儀對象時，不是同樣也會有這種反應嗎？你看，這是不是栩栩如生地把忐忑不安的心情全都描述出來了！

one's heart beats out of control　　某人小鹿亂撞，心跳加速

have butterflies in one's stomach　　某人心裡七上八下，忐忑不安

＊butterfly [ˈbʌtɚˌflaɪ] *n.* 蝴蝶

　　stomach [ˈstʌmək] *n.* 胃

例: Every time Lucy came close to me, my heart began beating out of control.

（每次露西靠近我時，我的心就會開始狂跳不止。）

I had butterflies in my stomach as I asked my girlfriend to marry me.

（當我向女友求婚時，心裡感到忐忑不安。）

字詞幫幫忙！

1. get used to + N/V-ing　　習慣於……

＝　get accustomed to + N/V-ing

　　used to V　過去曾經……

例: It isn't easy getting used to waking up early after summer vacation.

（暑假過後，要習慣早起可不是件容易的事。）

Alex used to be an actor and was featured in many plays.

（艾力克斯曾經是演員，還主演過很多舞台劇。）

2. select [səˈlɛkt] *vt.* 挑選，選擇

例: Sarah selected a pink dress to wear to her friend's wedding.

（莎拉挑了一件粉紅色的洋裝穿去參加朋友的婚禮。）

3. snack [snæk] *n.* 點心 & *vi.* 吃點心

snack on...　　吃……（當點心）

例: Do you have anything in your house to snack on? I'm starving.

（你家裡有什麼可以吃的嗎？我餓死了。）

4. option [ˈɑpʃən] *n.* 選擇

have no option but to V　　別無選擇只好……

= have no choice but to V

例: Because the airport was closed, we had no option but to drive home.

（因為機場關閉，我們別無選擇只好開車回家。）

5. stop by...　　到……短暫停留；順道拜訪……

例: I stopped by the convenience store on my way home.

（我在回家途中順道去了便利商店。）

Do you mind if I stop by your house this evening?

（你介不介意我今晚順路到你家坐一坐？）

6. on a business trip　　出差

例: Mr. Wang is on a business trip. Do you need me to give him a message?

（王先生出差去了。需要我幫您留言給他嗎？）

7. sth looks + adj. + on sb　　……穿／戴在某人身上看起來……

sb looks + adj. + in sth　　某人穿／戴……時看起來很……

例: The red dress looks great on you. You should wear it more often.

（這件紅色洋裝穿在妳身上很好看。妳應該常穿。）

Jason looks very handsome in his soldier uniform.

（傑森穿軍服時看起來很帥。）

Unit 10

Success

Index | *Links* | *about* | *comments* | *Photo*

May 10

Today was my **weigh-in** day. I only weigh myself once a week because I don't want to **get obsessed with** numbers. When I got on the **scale**, I found that I had already lost two kilograms, so <u>**I was totally pumped!**</u> This success is really the **encouragement** I need to keep working hard towards **achieving** my goal. To **reward** myself, I decided that if I lost another two kilograms next week, I would buy myself a new miniskirt. **Yippee!**

About me

Ivy

Calendar

◄ *May* ►

Sun	Mon	Tue	Wed	Thu	Fri	Sat
				1	2	3
4	5	6	7	8	9	10
11	12	13	14	15	16	17
18	19	20	21	22	23	24
25	26	27	28	29	30	31

Blog Archive

- ▸ May (10)
- ▸ April
- ▸ March
- ▸ February
- ▸ January
- ▸ December
- ▸ November
- ▸ October
- ▸ September
- ▸ August
- ▸ July
- ▸ June

Ivy at Blog 於 May 05.10. PM 08:36 發表 | 回覆 (0) | 引用 (0) | 收藏 (0) | 轉寄給朋友 | 檢舉

May 10

　　今天是量體重的日子。我每個星期只量一次體重，因為我不想太過執著於體重計上的數字。站上體重計後，發現我已經減了兩公斤，因此讓我士氣大振！這個成就實在是我需要的鼓勵，好讓我繼續努力，朝目標的體重邁進。我決定如果下星期再瘦兩公斤的話，我就要買條迷你裙犒賞自己。好耶！

Ivy at Blog 於 May 05.10. PM 08:36 發表｜回覆 (0)｜引用 (0)｜收藏 (0)｜轉寄給朋友｜檢舉

不管是達到主管的要求、成功完成一件專案，或是只是單純達到自己所定的目標，這時內心一定覺得自己的努力沒有白費、士氣大振，有動力繼續努力向前。

pump [pʌmp] 當名詞作『幫浦』解，當動詞時原表『給……打氣』，像是 pump air into a flat tire（為沒氣的輪胎打氣），而網誌裡所用的 "I was totally pumped." 照字面翻譯就是『我徹底地被打氣。』，衍生出來的意思就是『士氣大振』。也可以在 be pumped 之後加上 up 來加強語氣，因為 up 有『完全地』的意思。另外，be pumped (up) 還可用來表『興奮』，等同於 be excited，當你士氣大振時，通常心情也是很興奮的囉。

be pumped (up)　　士氣大振；感到興奮

例: Our team was pumped (up) by the news of winning the championship.
（我們這隊奪得冠軍的消息讓大家士氣大振。）

Tommy was so pumped (up) that he couldn't sleep.

= Tommy was so excited that he couldn't sleep.
（湯米興奮到睡不著覺。）

字 詞幫幫忙！

1. **weigh-in** [ˋweˌɪn] *n.* 稱體重
   weigh [we] *vt.* 量（體重），稱（重量）
   weight [wet] *n.* 體重
   例: Since Rita went on a diet, she has been weighing herself every morning.
   （麗塔自從開始節食後，每天早上都會量體重。）

   How much do you weigh?
   = What's your weight?
   （你的體重是多少？）

   My little brother weighs 80 kilograms.
   （我家小弟體重 80 公斤。）

2. **get / be obsessed with...**　　滿腦子想的都是……；著迷於……
   obsess [əbˋsɛs] *vt.* 使縈繞；使著迷（常用被動）

例: The poor man was obsessed with how to make money.
（這個窮光蛋滿腦子想的都是如何賺錢。）

Gary is obsessed with Diane. He thinks of nothing but her.
（蓋瑞迷戀黛安，成天想的都是她。）

3. **scale** [skel] *n.* 體重計；磅秤

例: Lisa thought she gained some weight and was scared to get on the scale.
（麗莎覺得她胖了，不敢站在磅秤上量體重。）

4. **encouragement** [ɪnˋkɝdʒmənt] *n.* 鼓勵
encourage [ɪnˋkɝdʒ] *vt.* 鼓勵
encourage sb to V　　鼓勵某人從事……

例: I owe my success to my girlfriend's encouragement.
（我的成功要歸功於女友的鼓勵。）

Judy's parents encouraged her to pursue her dream.
（茱蒂的父母鼓勵她追求自己的夢想。）

＊pursue [pɚˋsu] *vt.* 追求

5. **achieve** [əˋtʃiv] *vt.* 完成，實現
achieve one's goal(s)　　實現某人的目標
= attain one's goal(s)
= accomplish one's goal(s)

例: If you work hard, you will eventually achieve your goals.
（如果你努力，最後一定會達成目標。）

＊eventually [ɪˋvɛntʃʊəlɪ] *adv.* 最後

6. **reward** [rɪˋwɔrd] *vt.* 獎賞，獎勵 & *n.* 報酬
reward sb with...　　以……獎賞某人
as a reward for...　　作為……的回報

例: The mother rewards her children with cookies when they do well in school.
（孩子在學校表現良好時，這位媽媽就會給他們餅乾作為獎賞。）

I gave John a watch as a reward for his help.
（我送約翰一只手錶來回報他的協助。）

7. **yippee** [ˋjɪpi] *int.* 好耶（用來表達興奮、開心的歡呼聲）

例: Edward jumped up and down and yelled "Yippee!" when he won the game.
（艾德華贏得比賽時，邊跳邊大喊『好耶！』。）

Sweet Temptations

Index | *Links* | *about* | *comments* | *Photo*

May 11

At work today, Karen brought in a cheesecake she made **from scratch**. I **turned down** her **offer** to cut me a slice, but she **insisted** that I try it. It was so **tasty** that I ended up having another slice **later on**! I feel so **guilty** right now. I'm never going to **get rid of** my double **chin** if I can't **resist** being tempted by **sweets**.

About me

Ivy

Calendar

◄   *May*   ►

Sun	Mon	Tue	Wed	Thu	Fri	Sat
				1	2	3
4	5	6	7	8	9	10
11	12	13	14	15	16	17
18	19	20	21	22	23	24
25	26	27	28	29	30	31

Blog Archive

▸ May (11)
▸ April
▸ March
▸ February
▸ January
▸ December
▸ November
▸ October
▸ September
▸ August
▸ July
▸ June

天啊，誘惑出現了

May 11

　　凱倫今天帶了自己做的起司蛋糕來公司。她本來要切一塊給我，可是我跟她說不用了，但她很堅持我一定要嚐嚐看。蛋糕真是超好吃，所以我接著又吃了第二塊！我現在好有罪惡感。如果我沒辦法抗拒甜食的誘惑，就別想消掉我的雙下巴了。

About me

Ivy

Calendar

◄　　　*May*　　　►

Sun	Mon	Tue	Wed	Thu	Fri	Sat
				1	2	3
4	5	6	7	8	9	10
11	12	13	14	15	16	17
18	19	20	21	22	23	24
25	26	27	28	29	30	31

Blog Archive

- ► May (11)
- ► April
- ► March
- ► February
- ► January
- ► December
- ► November
- ► October
- ► September
- ► August
- ► July
- ► June

Ivy at Blog 於 May 05.11. PM 04:45 發表｜回覆 (0)｜引用 (0)｜收藏 (0)｜轉寄給朋友｜檢舉

scratch 當名詞時，原意為『刮痕，抓痕』，像是 a scratch on the car（車上的刮痕）或是 the scratches on my back（我背上的抓痕）；此外，scratch 還有『起跑線』的意思（想像一下用石頭在地上劃出一道刮痕，不就可以當起跑線了嗎？），所以網誌中所用的 from scratch 就是『從頭開始、從零開始』之意，用在這裡指的是作者的同事 Karen 帶來的起司蛋糕是她自己親自動手，從頭到尾完成的點心。類似的用法還有：from the very beginning、from the ground up。

from scratch　　從頭開始，從零開始

scratch [skrætʃ] *n.* 刮痕，抓痕；起跑線 & *vt.* 抓，搔

例: The old man built his business from scratch.

= The old man built his business from the ground up.

（這個老先生白手起家，創立了他的事業。）

If you scratch my back, I'll scratch yours.

（如果你抓我的背，我也會抓你的。／如果你幫助我，我也會幫助你。）

1. **temptation** [tɛmpˋteʃən] *n.* 誘惑，引誘

   tempt [tɛmp] *vt.* 引誘，誘惑

   tempt sb to V　　引誘／誘惑某人從事⋯⋯

   例: It is hard to resist temptation.

   （抗拒誘惑很難。）

   John's older brother tempted him to steal their parents' money.

   （阿強他老哥誘使他偷爸媽的錢。）

2. **turn down...**　　拒絕⋯⋯

   例: David turned down the job because the salary was too low.

   （大衛因薪資太低而拒絕了那份工作。）

3. **offer** [ˋɔfɚ] *n.* & *vt.* 提供；給予

4. **insist** [ɪnˋsɪst] *vt.* 堅持
   insist that + S + (should) + V　　堅持……
   例: Mary insisted that Sam (should) apologize to her.
   （瑪莉堅持山姆應該向她道歉。）

5. **tasty** [ˋtestɪ] *a.* 美味的，可口的
   = delicious [dɪˋlɪʃəs] *a.*

6. **later on**　　之後，稍後

7. **guilty** [ˋgɪltɪ] *a.* 內疚的；有罪的

8. **get rid of...**　　擺脫 / 除去……
   例: Let's get rid of all this trash in the room.
   （咱們把房間裡的垃圾都清掉吧。）

9. **chin** [tʃɪn] *n.* 下巴
   double chin　　雙下巴
   keep one's chin up　　振作起來；不沮喪
   例: After losing three matches in a row, it's difficult for the
   tennis player to keep his chin up.
   （連輸 3 場比賽後，想要那名網球選手不沮喪也難啊。）

10. **resist** [rɪˋzɪst] *vt.* 抗拒
    例: The official couldn't resist the temptation and took the
    bribe.
    （那個政府官員禁不住誘惑而接受了賄賂。）
    ＊bribe [braɪb] *n.* 賄賂

11. **sweets** [swits] *n.* 甜點，糖果（恆用複數）
    例: My little brother enjoys sweets.
    = My little brother has a sweet tooth.（此處片語恆用單數
    tooth）
    （我小弟喜歡吃甜食。）

Measuring Success

May 12

I **went shopping** with Monica today to a new **boutique downtown**. She had heard about their many **gorgeous** dresses and needed one for her sister's wedding. On the sale **rack** I found a **lovely knee-length** dress. Although it is too small for me right now, I decided to buy it and use it to **measure** my success. When I can **fit into** it, <u>**I'll have reached my target weight.**</u>

About me

Ivy

Calendar

◄   *May*   ►

Sun	Mon	Tue	Wed	Thu	Fri	Sat
				1	2	3
4	5	6	7	8	9	10
11	12	13	14	15	16	17
18	19	20	21	22	23	24
25	26	27	28	29	30	31

Blog Archive

- ► May (12)
- ► April
- ► March
- ► February
- ► January
- ► December
- ► November
- ► October
- ► September
- ► August
- ► July
- ► June

Ivy at Blog 於 May 05.12. PM 09:53 發表 | 回覆 (0) | 引用 (0) | 收藏 (0) | 轉寄給朋友 | 檢舉

測量是否減肥成功

May 12

　　我今天和莫妮卡到市中心新開的一家精品店血拼。她聽說那家店有許多漂亮的洋裝，她要買一件穿去參加她姊姊的婚禮。我在打折區的架子上看到一件漂亮的及膝洋裝。雖然它現在對我來說太小件，我還是決定買下它，用來測量我減肥是否成功。當我穿得下的時候，我就已經達到目標體重了。

Calendar

◄　　　May　　　►

Sun	Mon	Tue	Wed	Thu	Fri	Sat
				1	2	3
4	5	6	7	8	9	10
11	12	13	14	15	16	17
18	19	20	21	22	23	24
25	26	27	28	29	30	31

Blog Archive

► May (12)
► April
► March
► February
► January
► December
► November
► October
► September
► August
► July
► June

Ivy at Blog 於 May 05.12. PM 09:53 發表 | 回覆 (0) | 引用 (0) | 收藏 (0) | 轉寄給朋友 | 檢舉

還記得電影《穿著 Prada 的惡魔》裡，第一助理艾蜜莉對第二助理安卓雅說：『再來一個腸胃炎我就能達到理想體重』嗎？這句話的英文是 "I'm just one stomach flu away from my goal weight."。在本網誌中，target weight 表示『目標體重』之意，和 goal weight 有相同的意思。goal [gol] 和 target ['tɑrgɪt] 均表『目標』，所以『達到某人的目標體重』除了可用網誌中所說的 reach one's target weight，還可以說 reach one's goal weight。以下再介紹幾種不同的表達方式：

reach one's objective weight　　達到某人的目標體重

＊objective [əb'dʒɛktɪv] *a.* 目標的

cross the finish line　　達成目標（字面上原為『衝過終點線』之意）

＊the finish line　　終點線

one's mission will be complete　　某人將達成任務

＊mission ['mɪʃən] *n.* 任務

complete [kəm'plit] *a.* 完成的

例: Only by eating less and exercising more can you reach your objective weight.

（只有少吃多運動你才能達到目標體重。）

Jackie crossed the finish line by losing 20 kilograms.

（潔姬達成目標瘦了 20 公斤。）

My mission will be complete if I lose five more kilograms.

（要是我再減個 5 公斤，就達成任務了。）

字詞幫幫忙！

1. **measure** ['mɛʒɚ] *vt.* 測量 & *n.* 措施

    take measures to V　　採取措施做……

    例: The carpenter measured the length of the floor.

    （木匠測量那面地板的長度。）

    We must take measures to control the spread of this disease.

    （我們必須採取措施來防止這種疾病的蔓延。）

2. **go shopping**　血拼，購物

   例: I like to go shopping on weekends with Jane.
   （我喜歡在週末和阿珍一起去血拼。）

3. **boutique** [bu'tik] *n.* 精品店

4. **downtown** [ˌdaun'taun] *adv.* 在市中心

   例: I ran into my boss downtown today.
   （今天我在市中心碰見老闆。）
   ＊run into sb　和某人不期而遇
   ＝ bump into sb

5. **gorgeous** ['gɔrdʒəs] *a.* 漂亮的（＝ beautiful）

   例: Wow! Your sister is gorgeous.
   （哇！你妹妹好漂亮。）

6. **rack** [ræk] *n.* 架子，掛物架

   a sale rack　　擺有特價服飾的架子

   a magazine rack　雜誌架

   例: There are several interesting magazines on the rack.
   （架上有許多有趣的雜誌。）

7. **lovely** ['lʌvlɪ] *a.* 漂亮的

   例: My sister has a lovely daughter.
   （我姊姊有個漂亮的女兒。）

8. **knee-length** ['niˌlɛŋθ] *a.* 長度及膝的

   ankle-length ['æŋklˌlɛŋθ] *a.* 長及腳踝的

   floor-length ['flɔrˌlɛŋθ] *a.* 長度垂至地板的

   例: The movie star tripped over her floor-length gown on the
   red carpet.
   （那位影星走星光大道時被自己拖地的禮服裙襬給絆倒了。）
   ＊trip [trɪp] *vi.* 絆倒
   trip over sth　被某物給絆到
   gown [gaun] *n.*（女生的）長禮服

9. **fit into...**　穿得下……（尤指衣物）

   例: Henry is too fat to fit into that shirt.
   （亨利太胖了，穿不下那件襯衫。）

Surprising Compliments

Index | *Links* | *about* | *comments* | *Photo*

May 13

Jamie's wedding was today, and I **attended** it with Karen. **To my surprise**, we were **seated** at a table with Jack, someone I had taken an English class with three years ago. We hadn't seen each other since, and I was **flattered** when he **complimented** me on how I looked. However, Jamie was the real **knock-out** in her wedding dress. Every woman **stared at** her with **envy**, including me!

About me

Ivy

Calendar

◄　　*May*　　►

Sun	Mon	Tue	Wed	Thu	Fri	Sat
				1	2	3
4	5	6	7	8	9	10
11	12	13	14	15	16	17
18	19	20	21	22	23	24
25	26	27	28	29	30	31

Blog Archive

▸ May (13)
▸ April
▸ March
▸ February
▸ January
▸ December
▸ Novombor
▸ October
▸ Soptombor
▸ August
▸ July
▸ June

Ivy at Blog 於 May 05.13. PM 11:20 發表｜回覆 (0)｜引用 (0)｜收藏 (0)｜轉寄給朋友｜檢舉

May 13

　　今天我和凱倫一起去參加潔咪的婚禮。怎麼都想不到，我們居然和傑克坐在同一桌，我在 3 年前和他一起上過英文課，後來就沒再見過面，所以當他稱讚我變漂亮時，我感到受寵若驚。不過，穿著結婚禮服的潔咪才是真正的大美女。每個女人都用羨慕的眼光看著她，當然也包括我啦！

About me

Ivy

Calendar

◀　　　May　　　▶

Sun	Mon	Tue	Wed	Thu	Fri	Sat
				1	2	3
4	5	6	7	8	9	10
11	12	13	14	15	16	17
18	19	20	21	22	23	24
25	26	27	28	29	30	31

Blog Archive

▸ May (13)
▸ April
▸ March
▸ February
▸ January
▸ December
▸ November
▸ October
▸ September
▸ August
▸ July
▸ June

想要討女生歡心，稱讚她變美絕對是上上之策！看來這個傑克還真懂女人心！ flatter 這個字原為『奉承、諂媚』之意，乍聽之下好像不是什麼正面的字眼，不過如果是用被動式 be flattered 的話，就另當別論了。"I am / was flattered." 通常是因為出乎意外被讚美或是受邀做某件事而感到『受寵若驚』，此時 flattered 是用來表示說話者驚喜的心情，相當於 pleasantly surprised（又驚又喜）。

flatter [ˋflætɚ] *vt.* 奉承，諂媚；使受寵若驚

例: I was flattered when Mr. Chang invited me to attend the grand opening of his shop.

（當張先生邀請我參加他的店隆重的開幕典禮時，我感到受寵若驚。）

＊grand [grænd] *a.* 隆重的

Don't trust people who flatter you.

（別相信那些拍你馬屁的人。）

Brian is popular among girls in the office because he is good at flattering them.

（布萊恩很受公司女同事歡迎，因為他很會獻殷勤。）

看到『正妹』卻不知如何用英文告訴外國朋友嗎？最道地的說法就是 knock-out。knock out 原為動詞片語，表示『擊敗、使失去知覺』，想像一下，當一個女孩子美到讓你失去知覺，那不是『正』到翻了？愛看美女是人的天性，所以英文裡形容美女的字詞還不少，以下列舉數個常見的名詞，下次要和人分享看到美女時，就不怕詞窮了。

knock-out [ˋnɑkˏaut] *n.*（美到讓人失去知覺的）美女
stunner [ˋstʌnɚ] *n.*（美到讓人驚艷的）尤物
head-turner [ˋhɛd ˏtɝnɚ] *n.*（讓人轉過頭去看的）美女

例: George told everyone he was dating a knock-out, but no one believed him.

（喬治告訴大家他和一個正妹在交往，但沒人相信他。）

Carrie is such a stunner that she has many admirers.

（凱莉是個超級尤物，所以她有許多愛慕者。）

＊admirer [ədˋmairɚ] *n.* 愛慕者，崇拜者

We saw a head-turner in the pub, and she turned out to be our friend's new girlfriend.

（我們在酒吧看到一個大美女，結果她居然是我們朋友的新女友。）

1. **compliment** [ˈkɑmpləmənt] *n.* & [ˈkɑmpləˌmɛnt] *vt.* 讚美，
   恭維

   compliment sb on sth　　就某事稱讚某人

   例: The compliment I gave Tracy made her smile.
   （我讚美崔西的話讓她展開笑顏。）

   The boss complimented Jeff on his excellent performance.
   （老闆稱讚傑夫工作表現優異。）

2. **attend** [əˈtɛnd] *vt.* 出席，參加

3. **To one's surprise, S + V**　　令某人驚訝的是，……

4. **seat** [sit] *vt.* 使就座 & *n.* 座位

   be seated　　坐下
   =   seat oneself

   例: The waitress seated me by the window.
   （服務生把我安排坐在窗邊。）

   Everyone must be seated before the plane takes off.
   （飛機起飛前每個人都要坐在自己的位子上。）

5. **stare at...**　　盯著……看

   例: Why are you staring at me like that? Is there something
   on my face?
   （你為什麼那樣盯著我？我臉上有什麼東西嗎？）

6. **envy** [ˈɛnvɪ] *n.* & *vt.* 羨慕

   envious [ˈɛnvɪəs] *a.* 羨慕的
   be envious of...　　羨慕……

   例: Everyone envies Debby because she has a rich
   boyfriend.
   =   Everyone is envious of Debby because she has a rich
   boyfriend.
   （每個人都羨慕黛比，因為她有個多金的男友。）

Back at the Doctor's Office

May 14

At my doctor's appointment today, I found out that I had lost 5 kilograms **in total**. The doctor said I was **making** good **progress** and that I should **keep up** the good work. She also **suggested** I start exercising **regularly** to **tone** my body. We also talked about ways to avoid **pigging out** when I'm feeling **stressed** or **depressed**. Her advice will be very helpful when I**'m faced with** those situations in the future.

About me

Ivy

Calendar

◄   *May*   ►

Sun	Mon	Tue	Wed	Thu	Fri	Sat
				1	2	3
4	5	6	7	8	9	10
11	12	13	14	15	16	17
18	19	20	21	22	23	24
25	26	27	28	29	30	31

Blog Archive

▸ May (14)
▸ April
▸ March
▸ February
▸ January
▸ December
▸ November
▸ October
▸ September
▸ August
▸ July
▸ June

Ivy at Blog 於 May 05.14. PM 08:30 發表 | 回覆 (0) | 引用 (0) | 收藏 (0) | 轉寄給朋友 | 檢舉

回診所複診

Index | *Links* | *about* | *comments* | *Photo*

May 14

今天看診時我發現自己總共瘦了 **5** 公斤。醫生說我進展不錯,應該要繼續保持。她還建議我開始規律運動來讓身體更結實。我們還談到當我覺得壓力大或沮喪時,要如何避免暴飲暴食。她的建議讓我以後若碰到這種情況時將無比受用。

About me

Ivy

Calendar

◄   *May*   ►

Sun	Mon	Tue	Wed	Thu	Fri	Sat
				1	2	3
4	5	6	7	8	9	10
11	12	13	14	15	16	17
18	19	20	21	22	23	24
25	26	27	28	29	30	31

Blog Archive

- ► May (14)
- ► April
- ► March
- ► February
- ► January
- ► December
- ► November
- ► October
- ► September
- ► August
- ► July
- ► June

Ivy at Blog 於 May 05.14. PM 08:30 發表 | 回覆 (0) | 引用 (0) | 收藏 (0) | 轉寄給朋友 | 檢舉

現代人面對壓力和情緒失調時，往往會藉由吃東西來達到安慰自己的作用。這就是所謂的 comfort eating（安慰進食）或 emotional eating（情緒進食）。

在情緒影響下進食容易造成 overeating（吃過多），over- 即有『超過』之意。甚或像網誌所說失去淑女矜持、喪失理智地 pig out（大吃特吃、暴飲暴食），不需多作解釋，大家都看過豬怎麼吃東西吧！除了豬之外，馬也是英文界中的大胃王，若說某人 eat like a horse，就是用來描述人食量驚人，相當於中文說的『食大如牛』。相反地，要形容一個人『食量很小』，就用 eat like a bird。

諸位，若要減肥成功，千萬要先做好情緒管理，戒掉安慰食品（comfort food）才行！

overeat [ˌovəˈit] *vi.* & *vt.* 吃得過飽，暴食
三態為：overeat, overate [ˌovəˈet], overeaten [ˌovəˈitn̩]。

pig out　　　　　　大吃特吃
eat like a horse　　食量很大，吃得很多
eat like a bird　　　食量很小，吃得很少

例: Jodie felt sick after overeating at the all-you-can-eat restaurant.

（裘蒂在吃到飽餐廳吃太多而感到不舒服。）

People tend to pig out during the Chinese New Year holidays.

（大家在農曆新年期間往往會大吃大喝。）

Although Lily is skinny, she eats like a horse.

（莉莉瘦歸瘦，她可是個大胃王。）

My sister always eats like a bird.

（我妹妹總是吃很少。）

1. in total　　總共，共計（與數字並用）

2. make progress 有進步，有進展

progress [ˋprɑɡrɛs] *n.* 進步，進展

例: Nick made some progress in his Japanese class over the summer vacation.

（尼克暑假期間在日文課上有些許進步。）

3. keep up... （繼續）保持⋯⋯

例: Rita's boss told her to keep up the good work.

（莉塔的老闆要她繼續好好幹。）

4. suggest [səgˋdʒɛst] *vt.* 建議

5. regularly [ˋrɛɡjələlɪ] *adv.* 規律地，定期地

= **on a regular basis**

例: I have my hair trimmed regularly.

（我都會定期去剪頭髮。）

＊trim [trɪm] *vt.* 修剪

6. tone [ton] *vt.* 使結實，使強健（常與 up 並用）

tone up one's muscles 鍛鍊肌肉

例: Kevin does push-ups to tone up his muscles every day.

（凱文每天做伏地挺身來鍛鍊他的肌肉。）

＊push-up [ˋpuʃˏʌp] *n.* 伏地挺身

7. stressed [strɛst] *a.* 焦慮的，緊張的（不用於名詞前）

be / feel stressed out 飽受壓力的，非常緊張的

例: David often feels stressed from work.

（大衛經常為工作感到焦慮。）

Jack is stressed out because he has too much work.

（傑克因為工作太多而飽受壓力。）

8. depressed [dɪˋprɛst] *a.* 感到沮喪的，消沈的

9. be faced with... 面臨 / 面對⋯⋯

例: Recently, a lot of companies are faced with bankruptcy.

（近來有許多公司都面臨倒閉。）

＊bankruptcy [ˋbæŋkrʌptsɪ] *n.* 破產，倒閉

Where to Exercise

Index | Links | about | comments | Photo

May 15

I **stopped by** a **gym** today to ask about becoming a member. I **was shocked at** how expensive it was. However, when I got home, I realized my tiny apartment was not a **suitable** place to exercise. I called the gym to ask about getting a **discount**. They said we could **negotiate** the fee if I was willing to prepay for six months. I told them I would have to **sleep on it**.

About me

Ivy

Calendar

◄　　　May　　　►

Sun	Mon	Tue	Wed	Thu	Fri	Sat
				1	2	3
4	5	6	7	8	9	10
11	12	13	14	15	16	17
18	19	20	21	22	23	24
25	26	27	28	29	30	31

Blog Archive

- ► May (15)
- ► April
- ► March
- ► February
- ► January
- ► December
- ► November
- ► October
- ► September
- ► August
- ► July
- ► June

Ivy at Blog 於 May 05.15. PM 10:05 發表 | 回覆 (0) | 引用 (0) | 收藏 (0) | 轉寄給朋友 | 檢舉

上哪運動好呢？

May 15

　　今天我順便去了健身房，詢問加入會員的事。我被那麼高的費用給嚇壞了。不過回到家後，我發現我的小公寓不適合運動。我便打了通電話去健身房問能不能打折。他們說要是我願意先預付 6 個月會費，價錢是可以談的。我告訴他們我得好好想一下才行。

About me

Ivy

Calendar

◄　　　　*May*　　　　►

Sun	Mon	Tue	Wed	Thu	Fri	Sat
				1	2	3
4	5	6	7	8	9	10
11	12	13	14	15	16	17
18	19	20	21	22	23	24
25	26	27	28	29	30	31

Blog Archive

► May (15)
► April
► March
► February
► January
► December
► November
► October
► September
► August
► July
► June

Ivy at Blog 於 May 05.15. PM 10:05 發表 | 回覆 (0) | 引用 (0) | 收藏 (0) | 轉寄給朋友 | 檢舉

這麼說就對了！

要花大錢之前的確是得好好考慮才行。不過關『睡覺』（sleep）什麼事？sleep on it 在英文中是很常用到的俚語，指的就是『好好考慮』的意思。

面對重大事情或決定時，我們往往都需要時間思考斟酌，從字面上就可以知道，這句話表示等到回家睡覺時再好好想個清楚，等到第二天再做出決定。

另外，語意相似且同樣很有意思的就是 chew on / over it，chew [tʃu] 原為『咀嚼、嚼碎』，chew on / over... 便引申為『仔細考慮……』的意思。

sleep on...　　仔細考慮……

= chew on / over...

例: Take your time and sleep on my offer. You can tell me your decision tomorrow.

（不用急，好好考慮一下我的提議。你可以明天再告訴我你的決定。）

About your proposal, the board needs more time to chew on it.

（關於你的提案，董事會需要多點時間考慮。）

＊proposal [prəˈpozl̩] *n.* 提案

1. **stop by...**　　在……稍作停留

   例: Stop by my office someday and we can go out for lunch together.

   （哪天到我公司來吧，我們可以一道吃午餐。）

2. **gym** [dʒɪm] *n.* 健身房；體育館

= gymnasium [dʒɪmˈneziəm] *n.*

3. **be shocked at...**　　對……感到震驚

   shocked [ʃɑkt] *a.* 震驚的

例: We were shocked at the news of Larry's sudden death.
（聽到賴瑞突然去世的消息令我們很震驚。）

4. **suitable** [ˋsutəb!̩] *a.* 合適的

be suitable for...　　適合……

例: Bright clothes are not suitable for funerals.
（參加喪禮時不適合穿鮮豔的衣服。）

＊funeral [ˋfjunərəl] *n.* 喪禮

5. **discount** [ˋdɪskaʊnt] *n.* 折扣

at a discount of + 10 / 20 / 30... + percent

以 9 折 / 8 折 / 7 折 /……的價錢

get a discount of + 10 / 20 / 30... + percent on sth

用 9 折 / 8 折 / 7 折 /……買到某物

give sb a + 10 / 20 / 30... + percent discount on sth

就某物給予某人 9 折 / 8 折 / 7 折 /……的優惠

例: I bought these shoes at a discount of 15%.
（我以 85 折的價錢買下這雙鞋子。）

＊15% = 15 percent

Students can get a discount of 20 percent on movie tickets.
（學生買電影票有 8 折優惠。）

The vendor gave me a 40 percent discount on the shirt.
（那件襯衫小販給我打 6 折。）

＊vendor [ˋvɛndɚ] *n.* 攤販

6. **negotiate** [nɪˋgoʃɪˏet] *vt.* 通過談判達成 & *vi.* 談判，協商

negotiate a price　　議價

negotiate with...　　和……協商 / 交涉

例: Henry decided to negotiate the rent with his landlord.
（亨利決定與他的房東協商房租。）

Mary is negotiating with her boss for a raise.
（瑪麗正和她老闆協商要求加薪。）

Unit 16

The Needed Push

Index | *Links* | *about* | *comments* | *Photo*

May 16

I went back to the gym to **take a tour of** their **facilities**. In the **weightlifting** room, I saw many **muscular men**, and one of them **happened to** be Mike! **What a coincidence!** He came over to say hello right away and told me he **worked out** there at least four times a week. This news was the **push** I needed to become a member.

成為會員所需的動力

Index | Links | about | comments | Photo

May 16

　　我回到健身房四處參觀了一下他們的設備。在舉重室裡，我看見許多肌肉男，其中一個嘟嘟好是麥克，真是太巧了！他馬上過來跟我打招呼，還說他一星期至少來這裡運動 4 次。這個消息正是我成為會員所需要的動力。

About me

Ivy

Calendar

◄ *May* ►

Sun	Mon	Tue	Wed	Thu	Fri	Sat
					1	2	3
4	5	6	7	8	9	10
11	12	13	14	15	16	17
18	19	20	21	22	23	24
25	26	27	28	29	30	31

Blog Archive

▸ May (16)
▸ April
▸ March
▸ February
▸ January
▸ December
▸ November
▸ October
▸ September
▸ August
▸ July
▸ June

Ivy at Blog 於 May 05.16. PM 07:52 發表 | 回覆 (0) | 引用 (0) | 收藏 (0) | 轉寄給朋友 | 檢舉

63

健身房內常會有許多 muscular men 在練肌肉，muscular [ˈmʌskjələ˙] 的意思就是『肌肉發達的』，a muscular man 就是我們常聽到的『肌肉男』。在英文中，還可以用以下幾種說法來形容肌肉發達的男性：

hunk [hʌŋk] n. 肌肉男；英俊且性感的男人
macho man [ˌmatʃo ˈmæn] n. 強壯的男子，勇猛的男子漢
stud [stʌd] n. 性感的壯男

例: Tom's wife is more muscular than he is.
（湯姆的老婆比他還肌肉發達。）

Sandy has a crush on Jim because she thinks he is a hunk.
＊have a crush on sb　　迷戀某人
（珊蒂很迷戀吉姆，因為她認為他是個性感的肌肉男。）

　　Lucy: Look at the stud over there. I'd like to talk to him.
Mandy: That's my gay co-worker, Patrick. He wouldn't be
　　　　interested in you.
（露西：瞧那邊那個猛男。我想過去跟他聊個天。）
（曼蒂：那是我同事派屈克，他是同志。他對妳沒『性』趣的啦。）
＊gay [ge] a. 男同性戀的（要說："He is gay." 而不要說："He is a gay."）

coincidence [koˈɪnsədəns] 就是『巧合』的意思。在本網誌中，由於女主角心儀的對象麥可剛好在同一家健身房健身，所以她忍不住在心中吶喊："What a coincidence!"（真是太巧了！）。在這種情況，還有其他說法可以當作你心中的旁白：

It must be fate.　　這一定是命中注定。
＊fate [fet] n. 命運
What dumb luck.　　真是太走運了。
＊dumb [dʌm] a. 愚蠢的
Lucky for me.　　我出運了。

例: Jack and I share many interests. It must have been fate when we met.
（我和傑克有許多共同的興趣。我們當初相遇是命中注定的。）

I had a blind date last night, and the guy was really my type. Lucky for me.
（我昨晚去相親，而對方正是我的菜。我想我出運了。）
＊be one's type　　是某人喜歡的那一型

1. **push** [pʊʃ] *n.* 動力 & *vt.* 促使，逼迫
   push sb to V　　促使 / 逼某人從事……
   例: Hannah pushed her husband to take the high-paying job.
   （漢娜逼她先生接下這份高薪的工作。）

2. **take a tour of...**　　到處參觀 / 四處逛逛……
   tour [tʊr] *n.* 參觀，遊覽；巡迴表演
   be on tour　　巡迴表演
   例: I took a tour of the office on my first day at work.
   （我上班的第一天四處參觀了一下辦公室。）
   My band will be on tour for the next few months.
   （我的樂團在接下來幾個月要巡迴表演。）

3. **facilities** [fəˈsɪlətɪz] *n.* 設施，設備（恆用複數）
   例: The college I went to has great athletic facilities.
   （我唸的那所大學有很棒的運動設施。）
   ＊athletic [æθˈlɛtɪk] *a.* 運動的

4. **weightlifting** [ˈwetˌlɪftɪŋ] *n.* 舉重
   lift weights　　舉重
   例: Tommy took up weightlifting after he joined the football team.
   （湯米加入橄欖球隊後開始練舉重。）
   Mark is muscular because he lifts weights at a gym every day.
   （馬克肌肉很發達，因為他每天在一家健身房舉重。）

5. **happen to V**　　碰巧 / 剛好……
   例: I happened to sit by my boss at the concert.
   （在音樂會上我碰巧坐在老闆旁邊。）

6. **work out**　　運動，健身
   例: Peter works out on a daily basis.
   （彼得每天運動。）

An Official Member

Index \ *Links* \ *about* \ *comments* \ *Photo*

May 17

I signed the **contract** at the gym today and **paid up front** for a one-year **membership**. I also **signed up for** a couple of classes they offer in the evening-yoga and **aerobics**. The personal trainer **suggested** them **to** me because yoga will increase my strength and **flexibility** and aerobics will make me **sweat like a pig**. I'm **on my way to** becoming a **hot and sexy** woman!

About me

Ivy

Calendar

◄   *May*   ►

Sun	Mon	Tue	Wed	Thu	Fri	Sat
				1	2	3
4	5	6	7	8	9	10
11	12	13	14	15	16	**17**
18	19	20	21	22	23	24
25	26	27	28	29	30	31

Blog Archive

► May (17)
► April
► March
► February
► January
► December
► November
► October
► September
► August
► July
► June

正式會員

May 17

　　我今天跟健身房簽了合約，並預付一年的會費。我還報名幾堂他們晚上的課程，包括瑜珈和有氧舞蹈。私人教練向我推薦這些課程，因為瑜珈能夠增強體力和柔軟度，有氧舞蹈則可以讓我盡情飆汗。我已經一步步朝著火辣性感女神的路邁進囉！

About me

Ivy

Calendar

◄　　*May*　　►

Sun	Mon	Tue	Wed	Thu	Fri	Sat
				1	2	3
4	5	6	7	8	9	10
11	12	13	14	15	16	**17**
18	19	20	21	22	23	24
25	26	27	28	29	30	31

Blog Archive

▸ May (17)
▸ April
▸ March
▸ February
▸ January
▸ December
▸ November
▸ October
▸ September
▸ August
▸ July
▸ June

Ivy at Blog 於 May 05.17. PM 01:43 發表 | 回覆 (0) | 引用 (0) | 收藏 (0) | 轉寄給朋友 | 檢舉

台灣叫『辣妹』，港仔稱『靚女』，英文中也有不少形容身材火辣美女的形容詞，如網誌中所提的 hot and sexy（火辣性感），hot 通常用來指天氣『炎熱』或食物『辛辣』，用在女人身上便引伸為『身材火辣的』。因此男生若看到某個辣妹從眼前經過，便常會說 "She's hot!" 或 "What a hot babe!"。

要特別注意的是，雖然英國的 Spice Girl 樂團中文譯為『辣妹合唱團』，但 spice [spaɪs] 指的是『香料』，而非形容女人的身材，因此盡量避免使用 a spice girl 或 a spicy girl 來形容女生，這在國外並非慣用語。

hot [hɑt] *a.* 熾熱的；辛辣的；（人）性感火辣的
sexy [ˈsɛksɪ] *a.* 性感的
babe [beb] *n.*（尤指年輕貌美的）小妞
例: Last night, I met some hot babes at the bar.
　（昨晚我在酒吧認識了幾個辣妹。）

1. contract [ˈkɑntrækt] *n.* 合約
　　sign a contract with sb　與某人簽約
　　例: The singer has signed a three-year contract with the record company.
　　　（這位歌手和唱片公司簽了 3 年的合約。）

2. pay up front　預先／事先付款
= 　pay in advance
　　例: We need to pay NT$5,000 up front to rent the hotel room.
　　　（我們訂旅館房間前要先預付 5,000 元。）

3. membership [ˈmɛmbɚˌʃɪp] *n.* 會員資格，會員身分
　　a membership card　會員卡
　　apply for membership　申請會員資格
　　例: Show your membership card when you enter.
　　　（進入時請出示會員卡。）

To apply for membership of this golf club, you are supposed to pay an annual fee of $20,000..

（你若要申請該高爾夫球俱樂部就須年繳會費 2 萬美元。）

4. sign up for... 報名上……的課

例: Betty signed up for an intensive English course.

（貝蒂報名參加了一個英語密集班。）

＊intensive [ɪn'tɛnsɪv] *a.* 密集的

5. aerobics [ɛ'robɪks] *n.* 有氧舞蹈

aerobic [ɛ'robɪk] *a.* 有氧的

aerobic exercise 有氧運動

6. suggest sth to sb 向某人推薦某事物

= recommend sth to sb

例: Mike suggested that restaurant to me.

（麥克向我推薦那間餐廳。）

7. flexibility [ˌflɛksə'bɪlətɪ] *n.* 柔軟度；彈性

flexible ['flɛksəbḷ] *a.* 具柔軟度的；有彈性的

例: There is not much flexibility in our schedule.

（我們的行程表彈性空間不大。）

After taking ballet for a long time, Emma's legs are very flexible.

（艾瑪長期學習芭蕾舞，因此她的腿柔軟度非常好。）

＊ballet [bæ'le / 'bæle] *n.* 芭蕾舞

8. sweat like a pig 汗流浹背，揮汗如雨

sweat [swɛt] *vi.* 流汗

例: Could you turn on the fan? I'm sweating like a pig.

（可以麻煩你開電風扇嗎？我滿身大汗。）

9. be on one's way to + N/V-ing 某人正邁向……的途中

on one's way to + 地方 某人往某地的途中

例: Jenny is on her way to becoming a partner in the law firm.

（珍妮即將成為那家律師事務所的合夥人。）

If you keep working hard, you will be on your way to success.

（如果你繼續努力，便會邁向成功之路。）

Dan got robbed on his way to the office.

（阿丹去上班的途中被搶劫。）

What Am I Doing Wrong

Index | *Links* | *about* | *comments* | *Photo*

May 18

I have been **making every effort to get Mike's attention**, but nothing seems to be working. I wonder what I am doing wrong. Is it possible I **am** just **not his type**? I think I'll **pay close attention from now on** to whom he looks at. Maybe it will give me some **clues** as to which type of person he**'s attracted to**.

About me

Ivy

Calendar

◄   *May*   ►

Sun	Mon	Tue	Wed	Thu	Fri	Sat
				1	2	3
4	5	6	7	8	9	10
11	12	13	14	15	16	17
18	19	20	21	22	23	24
25	26	27	28	29	30	31

Blog Archive

- ► May (18)
- ► April
- ► March
- ► February
- ► January
- ► December
- ► November
- ► October
- ► September
- ► August
- ► July
- ► June

Ivy at Blog 於 May 05.18. PM 12:56 發表 | 回覆 (0) | 引用 (0) | 收藏 (0) | 轉寄給朋友 | 檢舉

May 18

　　我費盡心機要讓麥克注意我，但似乎都不管用。我在想自己到底是哪裡做錯了。因為我不是他的菜嗎？我想從現在起，我要密切注意他都在看誰。也許這會給我一些線索，看看『蝦咪款』的人會吸引他。

About me

Ivy

Calendar

◀　　　*May*　　　▶

Sun	Mon	Tue	Wed	Thu	Fri	Sat
					1	2	3
4	5	6	7	8	9	10
11	12	13	14	15	16	17
18	19	20	21	22	23	24
25	26	27	28	29	30	31

Blog Archive

▸ May (18)
▸ April
▸ March
▸ February
▸ January
▸ December
▸ November
▸ October
▸ September
▸ August
▸ July
▸ June

Ivy at Blog 於 May 05.18. PM 12:56 發表｜回覆 (0)｜引用 (0)｜收藏 (0)｜轉寄給朋友｜檢舉

get one's attention 就是『吸引某人的注意』，也可以說成 catch / attract one's attention。另外，catch one's eye 也有同樣的意思，表『吸引某人的目光』，此時 eye 等同於 attention [əˋtɛnʃən]，表『注意（力）』之意，為不可數名詞，因此，無論前面是表單數或複數的所有格，eye 及 attention 都不可以在字尾加上 -s。

例: Zoe's style always attracts my attention.

（柔依的舉止行為總是吸引我的注意。）

Grace dressed up to catch Vincent's eye at the party.

（葛莉絲盛裝打扮，希望在派對上吸引文森的目光。）

＊dress up　　盛裝打扮

be not one's type 為『不是某人喜歡的那一型』之意。在英文口語中，也可以說 be not one's cup of tea，這跟我們口語中『不是某人的菜』，是不是有異曲同工之妙呢？以下再介紹幾個類似的說法：

be not what sb is looking for　　不是某人所尋找的
be the complete opposite　　根本是完全相反（的類型）
＊opposite [ˋɑpəzɪt] n. 相反的人或事物

例: Susan said I am a nice guy, but not really her cup of tea.

（蘇珊說我是個好人，只不過我不是她的菜。）

Iris adores good-looking guys, but her boyfriend is the complete opposite.

（艾麗絲喜歡帥哥，但她的男朋友卻完全不符合這個條件。）

＊adore [əˋdɔr] vt. 崇拜；喜歡

至於『是某人喜歡的那一型、是某人的菜』，除了 be one's type 的說法外，還可用下列方式來表達：

be the perfect one for sb　　對某人來說是理想的對象
be one's soul mate　　是某人的心靈伴侶

例: Out of all the people in the world, David is the perfect one for me.

（全世界就只有大衛和我最速配。）

I could tell Tommy was my soul mate the first time we met.

（我們第一次見面時，我就知道湯米是我的心靈伴侶。）

1. make every effort to V 盡全力（做）……

= spare no effort to V

effort [ˋɛfət] *n.* 努力

例: John makes every effort to please his girlfriend on each Valentine's Day.

（約翰每年情人節都費盡心思來取悅女友。）

＊Valentine's Day [ˋvæləntaɪnz ˏde] *n.* 情人節

2. pay (close) attention to... （密切）注意……

例: Nina always pays close attention to fashion trends.

（妮娜隨時密切注意服裝的流行趨勢。）

＊trend [trɛnd] *n.* 趨勢

Pay attention to the signs while driving.

（開車時要注意交通號誌。）

3. from now on 從今以後

4. clue [klu] *n.* 線索，頭緒（其後常與介詞 to、about 或 as to 並用）

do not have a clue (as to) + 疑問詞引導的名詞子句

對……一無所知／毫無頭緒

例: Miss Lin gave me a clue to solving the difficult math problem.

（林老師給我一個解開這道數學難題的線索。）

I don't have a clue (as to) what's going on here.

（我對這裡發生的事一無所知。）

5. be attracted to sb 被某人所吸引

attract [əˋtrækt] *vt.* 吸引

attractive [əˋtræktɪv] *a.* 有吸引力的

例: Billy acts indifferent, but I know he's attracted to you.

（比利表現得毫不在乎，但我知道他拜倒在妳的石榴裙下。）

＊indifferent [ɪnˋdɪfərənt] *a.* 不關心的，不在乎的

All the men couldn't help looking at that attractive woman.

（所有的男人都忍不住盯著那個迷人的女人瞧。）

Not His Type

Index | Links | about | comments | Photo

May 19

I went to the gym again today and **worked up a good sweat** on the **treadmill**. I also saw Mike, and you'll never **guess** what happened! He started <u>**hitting on**</u> the guy **lifting** weights next to me! <u>**I couldn't believe my eyes**</u>. But then again, that would **make sense** since I've never seen him **check out** any girls. I finally understand what has been going on!

About me

Ivy

Calendar

◄ *May* ►

Sun	Mon	Tue	Wed	Thu	Fri	Sat
				1	2	3
4	5	6	7	8	9	10
11	12	13	14	15	16	17
18	**19**	20	21	22	23	24
25	26	27	28	29	30	31

Blog Archive

► May (19)
► April
► March
► February
► January
► December
► November
► October
► September
► August
► July
► June

原來我不是他的菜

Index | Links | about | comments | Photo

May 19

我今天又去了一趟健身房，在跑步機上跑得香汗淋漓。我還見到麥克，但你一定猜不到發生什麼事！他竟然向我旁邊一個舉重男搭訕了起來！我看了真是傻眼。話說回來，這也說明了一切，因為我從不曾看他打量過任何女孩子。我終於明白這一切是怎麼回事了！

About me

Ivy

Calendar

◀ *May* ▶

Sun	Mon	Tue	Wed	Thu	Fri	Sat
				1	2	3
4	5	6	7	8	9	10
11	12	13	14	15	16	17
18	19	20	21	22	23	24
25	26	27	28	29	30	31

Blog Archive

- ► May (19)
- ► April
- ► March
- ► February
- ► January
- ► December
- ► November
- ► October
- ► September
- ► August
- ► July
- ► June

Ivy at Blog 於 May 05.19. PM 03:36 發表 | 回覆 (0) | 引用 (0) | 收藏 (0) | 轉寄給朋友 | 檢舉

從字面上看來，hit on sb 感覺像是『打了某人』，但實際上是『向某人搭訕』的意思，這種說法是不是還蠻生動的？以下再介紹幾個和搭訕或打情罵俏有關的用法：

flirt with sb　　和某人調情，與某人打情罵俏

＊flirt [flɜt] *vi.* 調情

make eyes at sb　　　　向某人拋媚眼，向某人送秋波
make a move on sb　　向某人大獻殷勤；追求某人
= put the moves on sb

例: I hate to say this, but I saw your boyfriend hit on a girl in the bar last night.
（我很不想說，但我昨晚看到妳男友在夜店跟一個美眉搭訕。）

I'll never forgive you for flirting with my boyfriend.
（我永遠不會原諒妳和我男朋友調情的事。）

Tammy made eyes at me at the party. I think she's interested in me.
（黛咪在派對上向我拋媚眼。我想她對我有意思。）

I can't believe my eyes. The groom just made a move on the maid of honor.
（我簡直是看傻了眼。那個新郎剛剛竟然向伴娘大獻殷勤。）

＊groom [grum] *n.* 新郎
bride [braɪd] *n.* 新娘
maid of honor　　　伴娘
best man　　　　　伴郎

"I couldn't believe my eyes." 直譯為『我不敢相信我的眼睛。』，也就是我們所說的『我真是傻眼。』

例: I couldn't believe my eyes when I saw a man running naked down the street.
（我簡直不敢相信我竟然看到一個男的在街上裸奔。）

＊naked [ˋnekɪd] *a.* 裸體的

類似用法:
can't believe one's ears　　　無法相信某人親耳所聞

例: Emma couldn't believe her ears when her parents told her that they were getting a divorce.
（當艾瑪的父母告訴她他們要離婚時，她不敢相信自己聽到的是真的。）

1. **work up a (good) sweat** 因鍛鍊身體或辛苦工作而汗流浹背

   例: Frank enjoys working up a sweat after work.

   （法蘭克喜歡下班後去運動，享受汗流浹背的感覺。）

2. **treadmill** [ˈtrɛdˌmɪl] *n.* 跑步機

3. **guess** [gɛs] *vt.* 猜測

   Guess what?　猜猜看是什麼事？

   = Can you guess what happened?

   例: Tom: Guess what? A man called and said I won the lottery!

   Jerry: That must be a scam.

   （湯姆：猜猜看發生什麼事？有個男的打電話來說我中樂透了！）

   （傑瑞：那一定是個騙局。）

   ＊scam [skæm] *n.* 騙局

4. **lift** [lɪft] *vt.* 舉起，抬起

   lift weights　練舉重

   例: Diana lifted the big rock with ease.

   （黛安娜輕而易舉就舉起那塊大石頭。）

5. **make sense**　有道理；有意義

   例: It doesn't make sense to go to the beach in such bad weather.

   （天氣這麼糟去海邊實在沒道理。）

   When David drinks beer, nothing he says makes sense.

   （大衛一喝啤酒就胡說八道。）

6. **check out... / check...out**　看一看……，瞧一瞧……

   check out　（旅館客人）結帳退房 / 離開

   check in　（旅館客人）登記住宿

   例: You should check out Brad Pitt's new movie.

   （你該去看看布萊德·彼特的新片。）

   We checked in at the hotel at 2:00 this afternoon.

   （我們今天下午兩點住進這家飯店。）

Feeling Down

May 20

I got really upset when I realized that my **dreamboat** was actually **gay**. I really have no luck in the love **department**. **Nonetheless**, I still feel I should **stick to** my goal of losing weight. **After all**, the goal is really about me, not about some guy. Also, Mandy **promised** to take me out to help **cheer** me **up**. I hope it works!

About me

 Ivy

Calendar

◄   *May*   ►

Sun	Mon	Tue	Wed	Thu	Fri	Sat
					1	2	3
4	5	6	7	8	9	10
11	12	13	14	15	16	17
18	19	20	21	22	23	24
25	26	27	28	29	30	31

Blog Archive

► May (20)
► April
► March
► February
► January
► December
► November
► October
► September
► August
► July
► June

Ivy at Blog 於 May 05.20. PM 02:45 發表 | 回覆 (0) | 引用 (0) | 收藏 (0) | 轉寄給朋友 | 檢舉

心情盪到谷底

May 20

　　發現我的夢中情人竟然是個同性戀的時候，我的心情沮喪到不行。我跟愛情實在無緣了。儘管如此，我覺得我還是應該要堅持減肥的目標。畢竟這目標是為了我自己，而不是某個男人。而且曼蒂答應要帶我出去替我打打氣。希望那有用囉！

About me

Ivy

Calendar

◀　　　*May*　　　▶

Sun	Mon	Tue	Wed	Thu	Fri	Sat
					1	2	3
4	5	6	7	8	9	10
11	12	13	14	15	16	17
18	19	20	21	22	23	24
25	26	27	28	29	30	31

Blog Archive

▸ May (20)
▸ April
▸ March
▸ February
▸ January
▸ December
▸ November
▸ October
▸ September
▸ August
▸ July
▸ June

Ivy at Blog 於 May 05.20. PM 02:45 發表 | 回覆 (0) | 引用 (0) | 收藏 (0) | 轉寄給朋友 | 檢舉

作者發現苦苦暗戀的對象竟是同性戀，這打擊肯定不小。在英文中，泛指男同性戀最常用的就是 gay [ge] 這個字。gay 為形容詞，原表『快樂的』，但此種說法已作古，所以開心的時候還是不要使用 "I'm very gay!"（我好快樂喔！／我是不折不扣的同性戀！）的說法為妙。

此外，gay 表同性戀時多作形容詞用，因此常聽到外國人說 "He's gay." 而非 "He's a gay."。反之，straight [stret] 則是用來表『異性戀的』。前一陣子紅遍全美的情境秀《酷男的異想世界》其英文原名為 Queer Eye for the Straight Guy，其中 queer [kwɪr] 原表『奇怪的』之意，但現在亦用來表『同性戀的』，雖較為戲謔，但普遍為現代人所接受。以下就為您介紹其他表同性戀的說法：

lesbian [ˈlɛzbɪən] *n.* 女同性戀者 & *a.* 女同性戀的
＊不同於 gay 的用法，lesbian 常作名詞用。
homosexual [ˌhomoˈsɛkʃuəl] *n.*（泛指男女）同性戀者 & *a.* 同性戀的
例: Paul: Do you think that Diana has a boyfriend?
Tina: Don't be silly. She's a lesbian.
（保羅：妳覺得黛安娜有男朋友嗎？）
（蒂娜：別傻了。她是女同志。）
＊silly [ˈsɪlɪ] *a.* 愚蠢的
That famous singer is said to be a homosexual.
（據說那位名歌手是同性戀者。）

字詞幫幫忙！

1. **feel down**　　感到沮喪，感到消沉
= feel depressed
　　＊depressed [dɪˈprɛst] *a.* 感到沮喪的，消沉的
　　注意:
　　此處的 down [daʊn] 為形容詞，表『沮喪的、消沉的』之意。
例: George felt down when his girlfriend dumped him.
　　（喬治被女友甩掉時心情盪到了谷底。）
　　＊dump [dʌmp] *vt.* 拋棄（某人）

2. **dreamboat** [`drim,bot] *n.* 夢中情人；好看而有吸引力的人

    例: Greg is such a dreamboat that almost every girl in the office adores him.
    （葛瑞是個萬人迷，辦公室裡幾乎每個女生都愛慕他。）

3. **department** [dɪ`partmənt] *n.* 部門

    in the love department   在愛情這部分

4. **nonetheless** [,nʌnðəˋlɛs] *adv.* 儘管如此，但是（= however）

    例: The apartment is small. Nonetheless, it is all Daisy can afford.
    （雖然這間公寓很小，但這是黛西唯一能負擔得起的。）
    *afford [əˋfɔrd] *vt.* 負擔得起（與 can 或 cannot 並用）

5. **stick to ...**   堅持……

    例: Although under a lot of pressure, Bill still sticks to his belief.
    （雖然承受巨大壓力，比爾仍堅守自己的信念。）
    *pressure [ˋprɛʃə] *n.* 壓力
    belief [bɪˋlif] *n.* 信念

6. **after all**   畢竟；終究

    例: You should forgive Laura. She is your sister after all.
    （你應該原諒蘿拉，畢竟她是你妹妹啊。）

7. **promise** [ˋpramɪs] *vt. & n.* 承諾

    promise to V   承諾會……
    keep one's promise   信守承諾
    break one's promise   違背承諾，失信

    例: Shelly promised to keep the secret for me.
    （雪莉承諾會幫我保守這個秘密。）

    I have to leave now and pick up my girlfriend, or I'll break my promise to her.
    （我現在得離開去接我女友，不然就會對她失信。）
    *pick up sb / pick sb up   接送某人

8. **cheer sb up / cheer up sb**   使某人振作起來，鼓舞某人
    cheer up   振作起來

    例: I tried to cheer Beth up after she broke up with her boyfriend.
    （貝絲和男友分手後，我設法讓她振作起來。）

    Cheer up, Matt! Losing a job is not the end of the world.
    （麥特，振作點！丟掉工作又不是世界末日。）

Unit 21

Can You Believe It

Index | *Links* | *about* | *comments* | *Photo*

May 21

Mandy took me out to a bar tonight just like she had promised. After a few drinks, she **convinced** me to **spill the beans**. I told her all about my **heartache**, and she said the same thing once happened to her. Then, the **unthinkable** happened. Mike walked into the bar with a guy. To **add insult to injury**, that was the guy I'd seen Mike talking to at the gym!

About me

Ivy

Calendar

◄   *May*   ►

Sun	Mon	Tue	Wed	Thu	Fri	Sat
				1	2	3
4	5	6	7	8	9	10
11	12	13	14	15	16	17
18	19	20	21	22	23	24
25	26	27	28	29	30	31

Blog Archive

► May (21)
► April
► March
► February
► January
► December
► Novombor
► October
► September
► August
► July
► June

Ivy at Blog 於 May 05.21. PM 11:05 發表 | 回覆 (0) | 引用 (0) | 收藏 (0) | 轉寄給朋友 | 檢舉

居然有這種事？

May 21

　　曼蒂之前說要帶我去酒吧，所以今晚她帶我去了。幾杯黃湯下肚後，她說服我說出心裡的秘密。我告訴她我的情傷，她說她也曾經發生過同樣的事。接著令人難以置信的事發生了。麥克和一個男的走進酒吧。那個男的竟然就是麥克在健身房搭訕的傢伙，這真的是在傷口上灑鹽！

About me

Ivy

Calendar

◀　　　　　May　　　　▶

Sun	Mon	Tue	Wed	Thu	Fri	Sat
					1	2	3
4	5	6	7	8	9	10
11	12	13	14	15	16	17
18	19	20	21	22	23	24
25	26	27	28	29	30	31

Blog Archive

▸ May (21)
▸ April
▸ March
▸ February
▸ January
▸ December
▸ November
▸ October
▸ September
▸ August
▸ July
▸ June

Ivy at Blog 於 May 05.21. PM 11:05 發表｜回覆 (0)｜引用 (0)｜收藏 (0)｜轉寄給朋友｜檢舉

spill the beans 的原意為『灑出豆子』，但是豆子和秘密為什麼會有關聯呢？據說是因為古希臘一些秘密社團收社員時，會讓舊社員把豆子放進瓶子進行投票，白豆表示贊成，紅豆表示反對。由於這是秘密投票，開票前是不會知道結果的，可是如果瓶子無意中被打翻而讓豆子倒了出來，那可就『洩漏了秘密』。

這個片語現在一般是用在某人『大嘴巴』而不小心說出秘密，但在作者的日誌裡，指的是說出自己心裡的秘密。而如果你想和曼蒂一樣，鼓勵朋友說出你想聽的事，你還可以說 fill me in on sth，fill in 原為『填寫、填滿』之意，『填滿我』指的當然就是『快告訴我發生什麼事吧』！

spill the beans　　洩漏秘密
＊spill [spɪl] *vt.* 使溢出
fill sb in on sth　　將某事詳細告訴某人，向某人提供某事的最新消息
例: Angela knew she shouldn't have spilled the beans, but she just couldn't help it.
　　（安琪拉知道她不該洩露秘密，但她就是忍不住。）
　　Patty asked me to fill her in on how my date with her brother went.
　　（派蒂要我告訴她我和她哥哥約會的情況如何。）

和朋友大吐苦水聊情傷時，居然遇到讓你心碎的人？這時候還真的只能用『在傷口上灑鹽』來形容自己的感覺吧？日誌中用到的 add insult to injury，字面上的意思是『在傷口上又加以侮辱』，引申為『雪上加霜』、『在傷口上灑鹽』之意。其實英文裡的確是有完全對照中文的說法，那就是 rub salt in a wound（在傷口上抹鹽巴）。

另外，add insult to injury 其實還有『落井下石』之意，意同於另外一個片語 kick sb when he / she is down（在某人消沉時踢他／她一腳），人家已經情緒低落了，你還補上一腳，這豈不就是落井下石嗎？

add insult to injury　　雪上加霜；在傷口上灑鹽；落井下石
＊insult [ˈɪnsʌlt] *n.* 侮辱
＊injury [ˈɪndʒərɪ] *n.* 傷害
rub salt in a / the / one's wound　　在（某人的）傷口上灑鹽
＊rub [rʌb] *vt.* 擦上
＊wound [wund] *n.* 傷口
kick sb when he / she is down　　落井下石

例: Gina was badly hurt in the car accident. To add insult to injury, her boyfriend left her.

（吉娜在那場車禍中受重傷。雪上加霜的是，她的男友棄她而去。）

Jack rubbed salt in Ed's wound by telling everyone he was dumped yesterday.

（傑克告訴大家艾德昨天被甩了，簡直是在他傷口上灑鹽。）

Watch out for Steven! I heard he likes to kick others when they're down.

（你要提防史蒂芬。我聽說他喜歡落井下石。）

＊watch out for...　　注意／防備……

1. **convince** [kənˈvɪns] vt. 說服；使相信

　convince sb to V　　說服某人（做）……

= persuade sb to V

　＊persuade [pɚˈswed] vt. 說服

　convince sb of sth　　使某人相信某事

　例: You will never convince me to cheat on the test.

　（你是絕不可能說服我考試作弊的。）

　　What Kevin said convinced me of his innocence.

　（凱文的話讓我相信他是清白的。）

　　＊innocence [ˈɪnəsəns] n. 無罪；清白

2. **heartache** [ˈhɑrtˌek] n. 痛心，悲痛

　例: You should try to get over your heartache and keep going no matter how hard it is.

　（不管有多困難，你都應該克服這段悲痛，繼續過生活。）

　　＊get over...　　克服／熬過……

3. **unthinkable** [ʌnˈθɪŋkəbḷ] a. 難以想像的，難以置信的

= unbelievable [ˌʌnbɪˈlivəbḷ] a.

= incredible [ɪnˈkrɛdəbḷ] a.

　例: Jeff just worked here for two days. It's unthinkable that he got fired already.

　（傑夫才來這裡上班兩天，真不敢相信他已經被開除了。）

Distractions

Index | *Links* | *about* | *comments* | *Photo*

May 22

Work has been terrible because **every time** I see Mike, I feel sad and embarrassed. Therefore, I've been trying to **distract** myself by shopping online more often and **allowing** myself **snacks** that had been **forbidden**. I'm sure I'll feel better **eventually**. Till then, I am just trying to **pull myself together** and **keep my mind on** work.

About me

Ivy

Calendar

◄   *May*   ►

Sun	Mon	Tue	Wed	Thu	Fri	Sat
				1	2	3
4	5	6	7	8	9	10
11	12	13	14	15	16	17
18	19	20	21	22	23	24
25	26	27	28	29	30	31

Blog Archive

- ► May (22)
- ► April
- ► March
- ► February
- ► January
- ► December
- ► November
- ► October
- ► September
- ► August
- ► July
- ► June

Ivy at Blog 於 May 05.22. PM 02:15 發表 | 回覆 (0) | 引用 (0) | 收藏 (0) | 轉寄給朋友 | 檢舉

分散注意力

May 22

　　我的工作狀況愈來愈糟，因為每當我看到麥克就覺得既難過又尷尬。所以我一直試圖藉由更常在網路上購物，還有吃之前被禁吃的零食來分散注意力。我確信自己最後一定會好起來。但在那之前，我只能設法打起精神，把心思放在工作上。

日誌中所用的 pull myself together（把我自己拉在一起），照字面上看來似乎毫無道理可言，但其實 pull oneself together 是表『打起精神』或『振作起來、冷靜下來』之意。可以想像當我們因為某件事而沮喪不已、頹廢喪志，或是驚慌失措、抓狂時，是不是有種身心快爆炸裂開的感覺呢？所以 pull oneself together 照字面解釋是整頓好自己，把快要裂開的自己拉在一起，也就是『打起精神』或『振作起來、冷靜下來』之意啦。網誌作者因為感情問題，無法專心於工作上，於是便激勵自己打起精神，好好工作。除了 pull oneself together，以下再介紹另一個類似的用法：

regain one's composure　　（心情）恢復平靜

＊regain [rɪˋgen] *vt.* 恢復

＊composure [kəmˋpoʒɚ] *n.* 鎮靜，沈著

例: You're acting hysterically. Pull yourself together.

（你太歇斯底里了。冷靜一點好不好。）

＊hysterically [hɪsˋtɛrɪkəlɪ] *adv.* 歇斯底里地

Sally found it difficult to regain her composure after having a big fight with Albert.

（和艾伯特大吵一架後，莎莉發現自己很難恢復平靜。）

字詞幫幫忙！

1. **distraction** [dɪˋstrækʃən] *n.* 使人分心的事物

   例: I need to focus on my homework, but the music you're playing is a distraction.

   （我必須專心寫功課，但你現在放的音樂讓我分心。）

2. **Every time + S + V, S + V**　　句首/每次……，……

   = Each time + S + V, S + V

   = Whenever + S + V, S + V

   例: Every time my grandfather watches TV, he falls asleep.

   （每次我爺爺看電視就會睡著。）

3. **distract** [dɪˋstrækt] *vt.* 使分心
   distract sb from... 　　使某人分心而無法專心於……
   例: The baby's cries distracted the mother from cooking dinner.
   （寶寶的哭聲使媽媽分心而無法專心煮晚餐。）

4. **allow** [əˋlaʊ] *vt.* 允許，容許

5. **snack** [snæk] *n.* 零食，點心 & *vi.* 吃點心
   a midnight snack 　　宵夜
   snack on... 　　吃……（當點心）
   例: I decided to have a midnight snack when I couldn't fall asleep last night.
   （昨晚我睡不著覺，便決定吃個宵夜。）
   　　Do you have anything in your house to snack on?
   （你家裡有什麼可以吃的嗎？）

6. **forbid** [fɚˋbɪd] *vt.* 禁止
   三態為：forbid, forbade [fɚˋbæd / fɚˋbed], forbidden [fɚˋbɪdn̩]。
   forbid sb to V 　　禁止某人從事……
   = prohibit sb from + V-ing
   ＊prohibit [prəˋhɪbɪt] *vt.* 禁止
   例: Fishing is forbidden here.
   （此處禁止釣魚。）
   　　My father forbids us to smoke in the house.
   = 　My father prohibits us from smoking in the house.
   （父親不准我們在屋內抽煙。）

7. **eventually** [ɪˋvɛntʃʊəlɪ] *adv.* 最後，最終
   例: Thanks to your advice, we eventually worked out the problem.
   （多虧你的建議，我們終於解決了那個問題。）

8. **keep one's mind on...** 　　專注於……
   = concentrate on...
   = focus on...
   ＊concentrate [ˋkɑnsən͵tret] *vi.* 專心，專注（與介詞 on 並用）
   例: I can't keep my mind on my work because it's too noisy here.
   （我無法專心工作，因為這裡太吵了。）

Getting Better

May 23

Things aren't as **awkward** between Mike and me as they were a while ago. In fact, I have learned he makes a great **workout buddy**. It's easier to stay **motivated** to go to the gym when you have someone to work out with. I have also **kept my mouth shut about** Mike's **personal** life. I hate to **gossip**, and I don't want to **rule out** any chances of us at least becoming friends.

About me

Ivy

Calendar

◄   *May*   ►

Sun	Mon	Tue	Wed	Thu	Fri	Sat
					1	2	3
4	5	6	7	8	9	10
11	12	13	14	15	16	17
18	19	20	21	22	23	24
25	26	27	28	29	30	31

Blog Archive

- ► May (23)
- ► April
- ► March
- ► February
- ► January
- ► December
- ► November
- ► October
- ► September
- ► August
- ► July
- ► June

Ivy at Blog 於 May 05.23. PM 03:09 發表 | 回覆 (0) | 引用 (0) | 收藏 (0) | 轉寄給朋友 | 檢舉

重新出發

May 23

我和麥克之間已經沒有之前那麼尷尬了。事實上，我還覺得他是一起健身的好夥伴。當有人和妳一起健身時，比較容易保持動力上健身房。對於麥克的私生活，我嘴巴緊得很。我最恨跟人說長道短了，而且我不會排除至少還能和他當朋友的機會。

About me

Ivy

Calendar

◄ *May* ►

Sun	Mon	Tue	Wed	Thu	Fri	Sat
					1	2	3
4	5	6	7	8	9	10
11	12	13	14	15	16	17
18	19	20	21	22	23	24
25	26	27	28	29	30	31

Blog Archive

- ► May (23)
- ► April
- ► March
- ► February
- ► January
- ► December
- ► November
- ► October
- ► September
- ► August
- ► July
- ► June

飯可以亂吃，但話不可亂講，尤其是他人的私生活或秘密，保持沉默可說是一種美德。表『對某事三緘其口』的英文很簡單，就是 keep one's mouth shut about sth。shut [ʃʌt] 為及物動詞，表『關上、關閉』之意，三態均為 shut，此處的 shut 是過去分詞，表『被關閉的』，因此 keep one's mouth shut 便是指『把嘴巴緊緊關牢』。

還有，你是不是常在外國電影中，看到老外會用手作勢將嘴唇像用拉鍊拉起來，英文就是用 zip（把拉鍊拉上）這個字，因此你也可以說 "I'll keep my lips zipped." 來表示口風很緊，不會亂放話。

此外，one's lips are sealed（某人的雙唇密封起來）也很常見，seal [sil] 是『密封、封住』的意思，所以 one's lips are sealed 就是中文的『封口、守口如瓶』啦。

keep one's mouth shut (about sth)　　（對某事）保持緘默
keep one's lips zipped　　某人把嘴巴閉上
= keep one's lips buttoned
　＊zip [zɪp] vt. 把拉鍊拉上 & n. 拉鍊
　＊button [ˈbʌtn̩] vt. 把釦子扣上 & n. 鈕釦
　　one's lips are sealed　　某人守口如瓶／嚴守秘密
　＊lip [lɪp] n. 嘴唇（因有上下兩片嘴唇，故常用複數）
　例: You can tell me what happened, and I promise to keep my
　　　lips zipped.
　　　（你可以跟我說發生了什麼事，我保證我會閉嘴，不會跟別人說。）
　　　You can tell me your secret. My lips are sealed.
　　　（你可以把秘密告訴我。我口風很緊。）

1. awkward [ˈɔkwəd] a. 尷尬的
　　例. Anita felt a bit awkward when she was alone with her
　　　boss in the elevator.
　　　（安妮塔和她老闆單獨坐電梯時，她覺得有點尷尬。）
　　　＊elevator [ˈɛləˌvetə] n. 電梯

2. workout [ˈwɜkˌaut] n.（由指運動的）鍛鍊，訓練
　　work out　　鍛鍊，健身

例: You need some serious workouts to get rid of your beer belly.
（你需要好好鍛鍊一下來消除你的啤酒肚。）
* beer belly [`bɪr ,bɛlɪ] n. 啤酒肚
Randy makes it a rule to work out in the gym every day.
（蘭帝習慣每天上健身房鍛鍊身體。）
* make it a rule to V　　養成做……的習慣

3. **buddy** [`bʌdɪ] n. 死黨，哥兒們（口語，= good friend）
例: Daniel and I have been good buddies since college.
（丹尼爾和我自大學時期就是哥兒們了。）

4. **motivated** [`motə,vetɪd] a. 積極的；受到激勵的
motivate [`motə,vet] vt. 激發，激勵
stay motivated　　保持積極的態度
motivate sb to V　　激發 / 激勵某人從事……
例: It's important to stay motivated when it comes to learning
a new language.
（說到學習新語言，保持積極主動是很重要的。）
* when it comes to + N/V-ing　　說到……
Sarah's heart attack finally motivated her to lose weight.
（莎拉心臟病發作，終於激發她減肥。）

5. **personal** [`pɝsənḷ] a. 個人的，私人的
one's personal life　　某人的私生活
= one's private life
例: The actor never talks about his personal life.
（那名男演員從不談論自己的私生活。）

6. **gossip** [`gɑsəp] vi. 說閒話，說長道短（與 about 並用）& n. 閒話
（不可數）
例: Nora loves to gossip about her co-workers.
（諾拉喜歡聊同事的八卦。）
Gina filled me in on the latest gossip this morning.
（吉娜今早跟我說了最新的八卦。）

7. **rule out... / rule...out**　　排除……
例: We didn't rule out the possibility that it was Jack who
stole the money.
（我們不排除偷錢的人是傑克的可能性。）

A Promising Future

Index | *Links* | *about* | *comments* | *Photo*

May 24

The **theme** for today is "**What doesn't kill you makes you stronger**." This is how I feel about my **experience** with Mike. I'm happy to report that he and I are pretty good friends now. Today, he said a friend of his would be **perfect** for me. He even **offered to <u>fix us up</u>. What's more**, he said he knew a few other guys he could **introduce me to**. Maybe Mike really is my **key** to love after all!

About me

Ivy

Calendar

◄   May   ►

Sun	Mon	Tue	Wed	Thu	Fri	Sat
				1	2	3
4	5	6	7	8	9	10
11	12	13	14	15	16	17
18	19	20	21	22	23	**24**
25	26	27	28	29	30	31

Blog Archive

- ► May (24)
- ► April
- ► March
- ► February
- ► January
- ► December
- ► November
- ► October
- ► September
- ► August
- ► July
- ► June

Ivy at Blog 於 May 05.24. PM 03:39 發表 | 回覆 (0) | 引用 (0) | 收藏 (0) | 轉寄給朋友 | 檢舉

戀愛路放光明

Index | *Links* | *about* | *comments* | *Photo*

May 24

　　今天的主題是『打斷筋骨顛倒勇！』這就是我現在對麥克這段經驗的感想。我很高興跟大家說我和他現在是好麻吉。今天他說他有個朋友很適合我，甚至還要撮合我們。而且還說他認識幾個可以介紹給我的人。麥克最後說不定還是我尋找真愛的橋樑呢！

About me

Ivy

Calendar

◀　　　　*May*　　　　▶

Sun	Mon	Tue	Wed	Thu	Fri	Sat
				1	2	3
4	5	6	7	8	9	10
11	12	13	14	15	16	17
18	19	20	21	22	23	24
25	26	27	28	29	30	31

Blog Archive

▸ May (24)
▸ April
▸ March
▸ February
▸ January
▸ December
▸ November
▸ October
▸ September
▸ August
▸ July
▸ June

Ivy at Blog 於 May 05.24. PM 03:39 發表｜回覆 (0)｜引用 (0)｜收藏 (0)｜轉寄給朋友｜檢舉

自己戀愛順利時，有時候就會忍不住想把朋友『送作堆』，讓大家都能一起幸福。這時候要怎麼用英文表達呢？除了日誌中的 fix us up 和 introduce A to B 之外，常見的還有 set us / them up 和 hook us / them up。不過要特別注意的是，set sb up 還有『設計 / 陷害某人』之意，所以要小心使用。

fix us / them up　　撮合我們倆 / 他們倆
= set us / them up
= hook us / them up
　fix A up with B　　撮合某甲和某乙
= set A up with B
= hook A up with B
　＊hook [hʊk] *vt.* （用鉤）固定住
introduce A to B　　把某甲介紹給某乙
introduce [ˌɪntrəˋdjus] *vt.* 介紹，引見
set sb up　　設計陷害某人

例: My friends Eric and Judy have a lot in common. I really want to fix them up.
（我的朋友艾瑞克和茱蒂有很多共同點。我很想撮合他們。）

Karen has tried to set me up with a good friend of hers, but I'm not interested.
（凱倫一直想撮合我和她的一名好友，但我沒興趣。）

Laura introduced me to her brother after I broke up with John.
（我和約翰分手後，蘿拉把我介紹給她的哥哥。）

I was mad upon learning that my best friend had set me up.
（一獲知我最好的朋友陷害我時，我氣壞了。）

字 詞 幫幫忙！

1. **promising** [ˋprɑmɪsɪŋ] *a.* 有希望的，有前途的
　例: Luke is a promising young businessman.
　　（路克是位年輕有為的生意人。）

2. **future** [ˋfjutʃɚ] *n.* 未來
　carve out a bright future　　開創光明的前途
　＊carve [kɑrv] *vt.* 開創；雕刻

例: If you want to carve out a bright future, you should work harder than anyone else.
（如果你想開創光明的前途，就應該比任何人都更努力。）

3. **What doesn't kill you makes you stronger.**
你會愈挫愈勇。（出自尼采語錄）

4. **theme** [θim] *n.* 主題，題材
a theme park　　主題樂園

5. **experience** [ɪkˋspɪrɪəns] *n.* 經驗 & *vt.* 體驗；經歷
experienced [ɪkˋspɪrɪənst] *a.* 有經驗的
have a lot of experience in...　　在……方面經驗豐富
例: Mary has a lot of experience in babysitting.
= 　Mary is (well) experienced in babysitting.
（瑪麗當保母的經驗豐富。）
＊babysit [ˋbebɪˌsɪt] *vi.* 當臨時保姆
Kent experienced a period of hardship after he was laid off.
（肯特被裁員之後經歷了一段苦日子。）
＊hardship [ˋhɑrdʃɪp] *n.* 困苦

6. **perfect** [ˋpɝfɪkt] *a.* 完美的，理想的
例: Andy looks like a perfect husband, but actually, he is unfaithful to his wife.
（安迪看似完美的丈夫，但他其實對老婆不忠。）
＊unfaithful [ʌnˋfeθfəl] *a.* 不忠實的

7. **offer to V**　　主動提議／願意……
例: I offered to drive Amy home.
（我主動提議開車送艾咪回家。）

8. **What's more, S + V**　　而且／此外，……
例 Elle is getting married. What's more, she's doing it in a castle.
（愛莉要結婚了。不僅如此，她的婚禮將會在一間城堡舉行。）
＊castle [ˋkæsl̩] *n.* 城堡

9. **key** [ki] *n.* 關鍵（人物）；祕訣
the key to + N/V-ing　　……的關鍵／祕訣
＊此處的 to 為介詞，表『針對……』之意。
例 The key to winning Emily's heart is being nice to her friends.
（要贏得艾蜜莉的芳心，祕訣就是討好她的朋友。）

Getting A Date

Index | *Links* | *about* | *comments* | *Photo*

May 25

Mike told me today that he would **for sure** find a date for me this weekend. I feel **skeptical** about **being set up on a blind date**, but I'm **putting my trust in** Mike. I made him **swear** that he wouldn't tell anyone about the blind date **just in case** it went poorly. **That way**, I could **save myself some embarrassment**.

About me

Ivy

Calendar

◄   *May*   ►

Sun	Mon	Tue	Wed	Thu	Fri	Sat
				1	2	3
4	5	6	7	8	9	10
11	12	13	14	15	16	17
18	19	20	21	22	23	24
25	26	27	28	29	30	31

Blog Archive

- ► May (25)
- ► April
- ► March
- ► February
- ► January
- ► December
- ► November
- ► October
- ► September
- ► August
- ► July
- ► June

有了約會對象

May 25

　　麥克今天告訴我，他這個週末一定會幫我找到約會的對象。我對於被安排相親這檔事持懷疑的態度，但我信任麥克。我要他發誓不會告訴任何人關於相親的事，以防萬一進行得不順利。這麼一來，我就能讓自己免去一些尷尬。

Ivy at Blog 於 May 05.25. PM 02:52 發表｜回覆 (0)｜引用 (0)｜收藏 (0)｜轉寄給朋友｜檢舉

a blind date（盲目的約會）就是兩個素未謀面的人，經由親友介紹的第一次約會，類似我們所說的『相親』。網誌中的 be set up on a blind date 就是『被安排相親』的意思。此外，a blind date 除了指『相親』，也可用來指『相親的對象』。

be set up on a blind date　　被安排相親
set sb up on a blind date　　　　幫某人安排相親
= set up a blind date for sb
= arrange a blind date for sb

例: Tony's sister was set up on a blind date after her divorce.
（東尼的姊姊離婚後被安排去相親。）

Rose's parents set up a blind date for her, but she didn't like the man.
（蘿絲的父母幫她安排一場相親，但她卻不喜歡那個男的。）

Joyce made a good impression on her blind date.
（喬伊絲給她的相親對象留下一個好印象。）

＊impression [ɪmˋprɛʃən] n. 印象

1. for sure　　肯定地，確定地（常修飾句中動詞如 tell、know 等）
= for certain
　　例: I can tell you for sure that I'm not going to attend Mary's party.
　　　　（我可以很肯定地告訴你，我不會去參加瑪莉的派對。）

2. skeptical [ˋskɛptɪkl̩] a. 懷疑的
feel / be skeptical about / of...　　對……表示懷疑
= feel / be suspicious about / of...
　　＊suspicious [səˋspɪʃəs] a. 懷疑的
　　例: Jane is always skeptical about everyone she meets.
　　　　（阿珍對見到的每個人都疑神疑鬼。）

3. put one's trust in sb　　相信某人
= trust sb
　　例: You should never put your trust in a man like Jerry.
　　　　（你絕對不能相信像傑瑞那樣的人。）

4. **swear** [swɛr] *vt.* 發誓

三態為：swear, swore [swɔr], sworn [sworn]。

swear + that 子句　　發誓……

swear to V　　發誓要（做）……

例: Peter swore that he would never tell anyone about my secret.
（彼得發誓他絕不會把我的秘密告訴任何人。）

John swore to help me if I should ever need him.
（約翰發誓只要我需要他，他就會幫助我。）

5. **(just) in case + S + V**　　以防／倘若……

＊just in case 也可單獨使用，此時表『以防萬一』之意。

in case of...　　以防／倘若……

例: My father brought a flashlight in case we needed it for camping.
（我爸爸買了支手電筒以防露營時會用到它。）

＊flashlight [ˈflæʃˌlaɪt] *n.* 手電筒

Sally keeps a spare key on hand just in case.
（莎莉總是會帶著備用鑰匙以防萬一。）

＊spare [spɛr] *a.* 備用的

In case of an emergency, you can call me at this number.
（萬一有緊急狀況，你可以打這支號碼給我。）

6. **(In) that way, S + V**　　那樣一來，……

(In) this way, S +V　　如此一來，……

例: Jack saved NT$50 a day. This way, he was soon able to buy himself a bicycle.
（傑克每天存 50 元。如此一來，他很快就可以給自己買一輛自行車了。）

7. **save oneself some embarrassment**　　讓自己不會感到尷尬

embarrassment [ɪmˈbærəsmənt] *n.* 尷尬，困窘

embarrassed [ɪmˈbærəst] *a.* 感到尷尬／困窘的

embarrassing [ɪmˈbærəsɪŋ] *a.* 令人尷尬／困窘的

例: I saved myself some embarrassment when I saw that my zipper was down before I went out.
（我出門前發現石門水庫沒關，讓自己免去了尷尬的時刻。）

＊zipper [ˈzɪpɚ] *n.* 拉鍊

The singer felt very embarrassed when he forgot the lyrics to his hit song.
（那名歌手在演唱會當中忘記自己暢銷金曲的歌詞時，感到很尷尬。）

＊lyrics [ˈlɪrɪks] *n.* 歌詞（恆用複數）

It's embarrassing to forget to bring money on a date.
（約會時忘了帶錢是件很令人難為情的事。）

Unit 26

The Phone Call

Index   Links   about   comments   Photo

May 26

Mike said his friend Luke would **give me a ring** today, and he just did. Luke sounded very **friendly** and had a deep voice, which I like. We decided to meet on Saturday afternoon to have lunch and see a movie **afterwards**. He said he'd be the guy in the restaurant with a **bouquet** of red roses. Now, I **can't stop imagining** what he looks like.

About me

Ivy

Calendar

◄　　*May*　　►

Sun	Mon	Tue	Wed	Thu	Fri	Sat
				1	2	3
4	5	6	7	8	9	10
11	12	13	14	15	16	17
18	19	20	21	22	23	24
25	**26**	27	28	29	30	31

Blog Archive

▸ May (26)
▸ April
▸ March
▸ February
▸ January
▸ December
▸ November
▸ October
▸ September
▸ August
▸ July
▸ June

Ivy at Blog 於 May 05.26. PM 04:22 發表 | 回覆 (0) | 引用 (0) | 收藏 (0) | 轉寄給朋友 | 檢舉

來電相約

May 26

　　麥克說他的朋友路克今天會打電話給我，他也真的打了。路克聽起來挺友善的，而且嗓音低沈，是我喜歡的那種。我們決定要在星期六下午碰面，一起吃個中飯，之後再去看電影。他說他會在餐廳裡拿著一束紅玫瑰。我現在忍不住一直想像他到底長什麼模樣。

About me

Ivy

Calendar

◄　　*May*　　►

Sun	Mon	Tue	Wed	Thu	Fri	Sat
				1	2	3
4	5	6	7	8	9	10
11	12	13	14	15	16	17
18	19	20	21	22	23	24
25	**26**	27	28	29	30	31

Blog Archive

▸ May (26)
▸ April
▸ March
▸ February
▸ January
▸ December
▸ November
▸ October
▸ September
▸ August
▸ July
▸ June

根據網誌中的上下文，give sb a ring 在這裡指的可不是給某人一只戒指，畢竟沒有人會在還沒見面前，就要送對方這麼貴重的禮物吧！ring 除了指『戒指』外，還可表『電話鈴聲』，因此 give sb a ring，其字面直譯為『給某人電話鈴聲』，進而引申為『打電話給某人』。以下就為您介紹其他打電話給某人的常用說法：

give sb a ring　　打電話給某人

= give sb a call

= give sb a buzz

= ring sb

= call sb (up)

= phone sb

ring [rɪŋ] *n.* 鈴聲；戒指 & *vt.* 給……打電話

三態為：ring, rang [ræŋ], rung [rʌŋ]。

buzz [bʌz] *n.* 嗡嗡聲；電話聲

phone [fon] *n.* 電話 & *vt.* 給……打電話

例: Lyla asked her daughter to give her a buzz when she got home.

（萊拉要她女兒到家時打電話給她。）

David called me up to see if I wanted to go to the movies with him.

（大衛打電話問我要不要和他去看電影。）

Nick stopped phoning his girlfriend after they had a big fight.

（尼克和他女友大吵一架後就不再打電話給她了。）

字 詞 **幫幫忙**！

1. friendly [ˈfrɛndlɪ] *a.* 友好的，友善的

be friendly with sb　　對某人友善

例: The waitress wore a friendly smile while serving us.

（那名女服務生面帶友善的笑容服務我們。）

Richard is friendly with his new neighbor.

（李察對他的新鄰居很友善。）

2. **afterwards** [`ˈæftɚwɚdz`] *adv.* 隨後，後來
=   afterward [`ˈæftɚwɚd`] *adv.*
    例: The car crashed into a gas station, and afterwards there
    was a huge explosion.
    （車子撞上加油站，隨即便發生了大爆炸。）
    ＊crash into...　　撞上……
    explosion [ɪkˈsploʒən] *n.* 爆炸

3. **bouquet** [buˈke] *n.* 花束
    a bouquet of flowers　　一束花
=   a bunch of flowers
    ＊bunch [bʌntʃ] *n.* 一束
    例: Eddie sent his wife a huge bouquet of lilies on their
    wedding anniversary.
    （艾迪在結婚週年紀念那天送了他老婆一大束百合花。）
    ＊lily [ˈlɪlɪ] *n.* 百合（花）
    anniversary [ˌænəˈvɝsrɪ] *n.* 週年紀念（日）

4. **can't stop + V-ing**　　忍不住（做）……
=   can't help + V-ing（此處 help 表『抗拒』，而非『幫助』）
=   can't resist + V-ing
    ＊resist [rɪˈzɪst] *vt.* 抗拒
    例: Emily is so cute that I can't stop staring at her.
    （愛蜜莉長得太可愛了，我忍不住一直盯著她看。）

5. **imagine** [ɪˈmædʒɪn] *vt.* 想像
    imagine what / how / why...　　想像什麼／如何／為什麼……
    imagine + V-ing　　想像（做）……
    imagine A as B　　把 A 想像成 B
    例: Toby couldn't imagine why his friend got fired.
    （托比想不出為何他的朋友會被開除。）
    Doris can't imagine working in the office without air-
    conditioning in the summer.
    （桃樂絲無法想像夏天待在沒有冷氣的辦公室裡工作是什麼滋味。）
    ＊air-conditioning [ˈɛrkən ˌdɪʃnɪŋ] *n.* 空調，冷氣（不可數）
    air-conditioner [ˈɛrkən ˌdɪʃənɚ] *n.* 冷氣機（可數）
    Billy imagined his blind date as a quiet and gentle woman.
    （比利想像他的相親對象是個安靜、溫柔婉約的女人。）

What a Disaster

Index | *Links* | *about* | *comments* | *Photo*

May 27

I **took** a couple of hours **off work** yesterday to get a **manicure**, pedicure, and facial treatment so that I would look great for my date. I even had my hair **styled** on Saturday morning, but it **was** all **a waste of time**. Luke **turned out to be** a real jackass. He kept **teasing** me the whole time and making **rude comments**. After our lunch, I **faked** feeling sick and just went home.

About me

Ivy

Calendar

◄　　May　　►

Sun	Mon	Tue	Wed	Thu	Fri	Sat
				1	2	3
4	5	6	7	8	9	10
11	12	13	14	15	16	17
18	19	20	21	22	23	24
25	26	**27**	28	29	30	31

Blog Archive

▸ May (27)
▸ April
▸ March
▸ February
▸ January
▸ December
▸ November
▸ October
▸ September
▸ August
▸ July
▸ June

Ivy at Blog 於 May 05.27. PM 06:18 發表 | 回覆 (0) | 引用 (0) | 收藏 (0) | 轉寄給朋友 | 檢舉

史上最糟約會

May 27

　　為了讓自己約會時看起來很美，我昨天向公司請了幾個小時的假，去修手指甲和腳指甲，還做了臉。我甚至還在星期六早上去做頭髮，但這一切全都是浪費時間。路克竟然是個大混蛋。他不停地嘲弄我，而且言談粗俗。吃完午餐後，我就假裝不舒服，然後回家去了。

About me

Ivy

Calendar

◄　　　*May*　　　►

Sun	Mon	Tue	Wed	Thu	Fri	Sat
				1	2	3
4	5	6	7	8	9	10
11	12	13	14	15	16	17
18	19	20	21	22	23	24
25	26	**27**	28	29	30	31

Blog Archive

► May (27)
► April
► March
► February
► January
► December
► November
► October
► September
► August
► July
► June

這麼說就對了！

jackass [ˋdʒækˌæs] 原意為『公驢』，但在口語中通常是指愚蠢的人，也就是『傻瓜』或『混蛋』。這個字曾經被作為美國某個電視節目名稱，中文翻為『蠢蛋搞怪秀』。顧名思義，這個節目內容就是以一群人表現出稀奇古怪、荒誕不經的惡搞行徑為特色。像是試圖搶走警察的步槍，遭警察追打，或是跳進滿是毒蛇的水池中、坐滑板滑下樓梯等等。此節目備受爭議，因為很多青少年會模仿當中的危險動作而受傷。但也因為這個節目，讓大家以後在使用 jackass 這個字時，腦海中就會自動出現愚蠢行為的寫實畫面。但是請讀者特別注意，這個字是較粗俗的用法，不建議在正式的場合中使用。以下介紹其他可用來形容人愚蠢的字：

blockhead [ˋblɑkˌhɛd] *n.* 傻瓜；混蛋
= bonehead [ˋbonˌhɛd] *n.*
= dolt [dolt] *n.*
= idiot [ˋɪdɪət] *n.*

例: A jackass cut in line in front of me at the post office.

（在郵局的時候，有個混蛋在我的前面插隊。）

Tina felt like an idiot when she couldn't answer the simple question.

（當蒂娜回答不出那個簡單的問題時，她覺得自己像個白痴。）

1. **disaster** [dɪˋzæstɚ] *n.* 災難，大失敗；災害

   a natural disaster　　天災

   例: The party Jack held yesterday was a total disaster.

   （傑克昨晚辦的派對真是糟透了。）

2. **take + 一段時間 + off work / school**

   請……（一段時間）的假不上班 / 不上課

   take + 一段時間 + off　　請……（一段時間）的假

   例: Jenny took two days off work last week.

   （珍妮上星期請了兩天假沒上班。）

   Harry took a week off to spend time with his family.

   （哈利請了一星期的假陪家人。）

3. **manicure** [ˈmænɪ͵kjʊr] *n.* 修指甲
   pedicure [ˈpɛdɪk͵jʊr] *n.* 修腳指甲
   facial treatment [͵feʃəl ˈtritmənt] *n.* 臉部護理 / 保養

4. **style** [staɪl] *vt.* 設計，將……做造型
   例: Mandy is used to having her hair styled in that beauty salon.
   （曼蒂習慣在那家美容院做頭髮。）
   ＊salon [səˈlɑn] *n.* 美容院（= beauty salon）

5. **be a waste of time** 浪費時間（的事）
   waste [west] *n.* 浪費
   例: Playing video games all day is a waste of time.
   （整天打電玩很浪費時間。）

6. **turn out (to be) + N/adj.** （結果）竟然是……
   例: I used to hate Barney, but he has turned out to be one of
   my best friends.
   （我以前很討厭巴尼，但他後來竟成為我最要好的朋友之一。）

7. **tease** [tiz] *vt.* 嘲笑，揶揄

8. **rude** [rud] *a.* 粗魯的，無禮的

9. **comment** [ˈkɑmɛnt] *n.* 評論
   make a comment on... 對……發表評論
   例: The lawyer would not make a comment on the case he
   was working on.
   （那位律師不願對他正在處理的案子發表評論。）

10. **fake** [fek] *vt.* 假裝 & *a.* 假的 & *n.* 假貨，冒牌貨
    a fake painting 假畫（an authentic painting 真畫）
    fake illness 裝病

Unit 28

Dare I Date Again

Index | Links | about | comments | Photo

May 28

When I told Mike about my date with Luke, he felt **awful** and **apologized repeatedly**. He also promised that the next guy would be better. I **couldn't help but frown at the thought of** going on another date, so I said no. However, he still seemed **determined** to **convince** me to **give it another shot**.

About me

ivy

Calendar

◄   *May*   ►

Sun	Mon	Tue	Wed	Thu	Fri	Sat
					1	2	3
4	5	6	7	8	9	10
11	12	13	14	15	16	17
18	19	20	21	22	23	24
25	26	27	**28**	29	30	31

Blog Archive

▸ May (28)
▸ April
▸ March
▸ February
▸ January
▸ December
▸ November
▸ October
▸ September
▸ August
▸ July
▸ June

Ivy at Blog 於 May 05.28. PM 02:32 發表 | 回覆 (0) | 引用 (0) | 收藏 (0) | 轉寄給朋友 | 檢舉

約會怕怕

May 28

　　當我告訴麥克我跟路克約會的情形後，他覺得糟透了，並且不停跟我道歉。他也承諾下一個男人一定會更好。一想到還要去約會，我忍不住皺了皺眉頭，所以我就拒絕他了。但是他看起來仍是一付打定主意要說服我再試一次的樣子。

About me

Ivy

Calendar

◄　　*May*　　►

Sun	Mon	Tue	Wed	Thu	Fri	Sat
				1	2	3
4	5	6	7	8	9	10
11	12	13	14	15	16	17
18	19	20	21	22	23	24
25	26	27	**28**	29	30	31

Blog Archive

▸ May (28)
▸ April
▸ March
▸ February
▸ January
▸ December
▸ November
▸ October
▸ September
▸ August
▸ July
▸ June

Ivy at Blog 於 May 05.28. PM 02:32 發表│回覆 (0)│引用 (0)│收藏 (0)│轉寄給朋友│檢舉

shot 原本表『射擊；注射』，例如：

The policeman fired a shot at the criminal.

（那名警察朝罪犯開了一槍。）

The nurse gave me a shot.

（護士幫我打針。）

但網誌裡的 give it another shot 可不能翻成『再給它一槍／一針』。
give sth a shot 表示『試試看……』，此處的 shot 是『嘗試』的意思。

give...a shot 試試看……

= give...a try

= take a crack at...

＊crack [kræk] *n.* 嘗試（口語用法）

例: Do you want to give the new restaurant a shot? I heard the food is delicious.

（你想不想試試那家新開的餐廳啊？我聽說食物變好吃的。）

I failed the test, but the teacher will let me take another crack at it.

（我這次的考試不及格，但是老師答應讓我再考一次看看。）

1. **awful** [ˋɔfḷ] *a.* 糟糕的；差勁的

=   terrible [ˋtɛrəbl] *a.*

例: James drank too much last night, and he feels awful today.

（昨晚詹姆士酒喝多了，他今天感覺難受極了。）

2. **apologize** [əˋpɑləˏdʒaɪz] *vi.* 道歉

apology [əˋpɑlədʒɪ] *n.* 道歉

apologize to sb for sth　因某事向某人道歉

例: Ryan apologized to Rachel for shouting at her, but she didn't forgive him.

（萊恩因為對瑞秋大吼而向她道歉，但她沒原諒他。）

Jake offered no apology for his rude behavior.

（傑克並沒有為他粗魯的行為表示歉意。）

Now that you've admitted making the mistake, I'll accept your apology / apologies.

（你既然已經坦承認錯，我會接受你的道歉。）

3. **repeatedly** [rɪˋpitɪdlɪ] *adv.* 一再地

4. **can't help but +** 原形動詞　　忍不住……，不禁……

= can't help + V-ing（此處 help 表『抗拒』，而非『幫助』）

例: I can't help but wonder if Lisa is keeping something from me.

= I can't help wondering if Lisa is keeping something from me.

（我不禁要懷疑莉莎是不是有事情瞞著我。）

5. **frown** [fraʊn] *vi.* 皺眉，表示不滿（與介詞 at 或 upon 並用）& *n.* 皺眉

frown at sb　　對某人皺眉頭，表示不悅

frown upon sth　　對某事表不贊同，反對某事

例: Linda frowned at me for turning down her request.

（琳達因為我拒絕她的請求而對我表示不悅。）

My father frowned upon my late return home.

（我爸爸對我晚回家不以為然。）

6. **at the thought of...**　　一想到……

例: I cried at the thought of my dog that died two days ago.

（我一想到兩天前死翹翹的狗狗就會哭泣。）

7. **determined** [dɪˋtɝmɪnd] *a.* 下定決心的

be determined to V　　下定決心要……

例: I'm determined to finish the project on time no matter what.

（不管怎麼樣，我決定要準時完成這項專案。）

8. **convince** [kənˋvɪns] *vt.* 說服；使確信，使信服

convince sb to V　　說服某人（做）……

A Surprise Visitor

Index | Links | about | comments | Photo

May 29

I went to lunch with Mike and his friend, Eric. Afterwards, Mike **confessed** that he had Eric meet me **so that** I could see how nice he was. He even told me that he **used to** have a crush on Eric until he found out he was **straight. Eventually**, he **persuaded** me **to** see Eric again. **After all**, I don't want to be a member of <u>the lonely hearts club forever</u>.

About me

Ivy

Calendar

◄ May ►

Sun	Mon	Tue	Wed	Thu	Fri	Sat
					1	2	3
4	5	6	7	8	9	10
11	12	13	14	15	16	17
18	19	20	21	22	23	24
25	26	27	28	**29**	30	31

Blog Archive

- ► May (29)
- ► April
- ► March
- ► February
- ► January
- ► December
- ► November
- ► October
- ► September
- ► August
- ► July
- ► June

Ivy at Blog 於 May 05.29. PM 02:47 發表 | 回覆 (0) | 引用 (0) | 收藏 (0) | 轉寄給朋友 | 檢舉

意外的訪客

May 29

我、麥克和他的朋友艾瑞克一起去吃午飯。之後，麥克坦承他要艾瑞克來見見我，好讓我知道他有多好。他甚至還告訴我說他曾經暗戀過艾瑞克，直到發現他是異性戀才作罷。最後，他說服我和艾瑞克再見一次面。畢竟，我也不想成為『寂寞芳心俱樂部』的終生會員啊。

About me

Ivy

Calendar

◄　　　*May*　　　►

Sun	Mon	Tue	Wed	Thu	Fri	Sat
				1	2	3
4	5	6	7	8	9	10
11	12	13	14	15	16	17
18	19	20	21	22	23	24
25	26	27	28	29	30	31

Blog Archive

▸ May (29)
▸ April
▸ March
▸ February
▸ January
▸ December
▸ November
▸ October
▸ September
▸ August
▸ July
▸ June

lonely [ˈlonlɪ] *a.* 寂寞的

例: I feel so lonely without you here.

（你不在這裡我好寂寞。）

網誌中的 the lonely hearts club 就是我們中文所說的『寂寞芳心俱樂部』，想當然爾，會員一定都是單身（single [ˈsɪŋɡl̩]），不免希望自己能找到一個好對象，好擺脫『老處女』（old maid）的行列。以下是『寂寞芳心俱樂部』的幾個分會，希望眾姐妹及早擺脫它們的行列：

the singles club 　　單身俱樂部

the old maids' club 　　老處女俱樂部

（切勿說成 "the old virgins' club)

＊maid [med] *n.* （未婚的）年輕女子

＊virgin [ˈvɝdʒɪn] *n.* 處女

例: Tina got married last week. Now she is no longer a member of the singles club.

（蒂娜上星期結婚了。現在她再也不是單身俱樂部的一員了。）

1. **confess** [kənˈfɛs] *vt.* & *vi.* 坦承

   confess (to sb) + that 子句　　（向某人）坦承……

   confess to + V-ing　　承認（做）……

= admit (tʊ) + V-ing

= own up to + V-ing

   例: The man confessed to the police that he was the murderer.

   （這名男子向警方坦承他就是兇手。）

   ＊murderer [ˈmɝdərɚ] *n.* 兇手

   My little brother finally confessed to stealing my mother's money.

   （我的小弟終於承認偷了我媽的錢。）

2. **so that + S + V**　　如此／以便……

= in order that + S + V

例: Joseph took the day off so that he could pick up his parents at the airport.
（約瑟夫那天請假以便去機場接他父母。）
＊pick up sb　　接送某人

3. used to V　　以前曾經 / 常常……
例: Monica used to live in LA, but now she lives in New York.
（莫妮卡以前住在洛杉磯，但她現在住在紐約。）

4. straight [stret] *a.* 異性戀的
例: Alex is a straight guy with many gay friends.
（艾力克斯是異性戀，卻擁有許多同志友人。）

5. eventually [ɪˋvɛntʃʊəlɪ] *adv.* 最後；終於
例: Nate persisted in his studies and eventually became a lawyer.
（奈特苦讀不懈，最後終於成為一名律師。）
＊persist [pəˋsɪst] *vi.* 堅持（與介詞 in 並用）

6. persuade sb to V　　說服某人去做……
persuade [pəˋswed] *vt.* 說服
反義字:
dissuade [dɪˋswed] *vt.* 勸阻
dissuade sb from V-ing　　勸阻某人做……
例: Deborah tried to persuade David to quit smoking.
（黛伯拉設法說服大衛戒菸。）
Mr. and Mrs. Lee dissuaded their son from dropping out of college.
（李先生和李太太勸他們的兒子不要從大學退學。）

7. after all　　畢竟，終究
例: Tom shouldn't be blamed. After all, it was your fault.
（湯姆不該受到指責。畢竟，那是你的錯。）
＊blame [blem] *vt.* 責備，指責

8. forever [fəˋɛvɚ] *adv.* 永遠
= for good
例: My boyfriend promised that his love for me would last forever.
（我男友承諾他對我的愛會持續到永遠。）

A Real Date

Index | Links | about | comments | Photo

May 30

Eric and I met for coffee yesterday. He's not a **total hunk**, but he's very **sweet** and **charming**. We chatted about books we had recently read and found out we liked many of the same authors. We had so much **fun** that **before we knew it**, it was almost **midnight** ! **All in all**, we really **hit it off** and made plans to see each other again soon.

About me

Ivy

Calendar

◄   *May*   ►

Sun	Mon	Tue	Wed	Thu	Fri	Sat
				1	2	3
4	5	6	7	8	9	10
11	12	13	14	15	16	17
18	19	20	21	22	23	24
25	26	27	28	29	**30**	31

Blog Archive

▸ May (30)
▸ April
▸ March
▸ February
▸ January
▸ December
▸ November
▸ October
▸ September
▸ August
▸ July
▸ June

Ivy at Blog 於 May 05.30. PM 08:00 發表 | 回覆 (0) | 引用 (0) | 收藏 (0) | 轉寄給朋友 | 檢舉

真正的約會

May 30

　　我昨天和艾瑞克碰面喝杯咖啡。他並不是個猛男，但他很貼心，也很迷人。我們聊最近看過的書，發現我們有很多共同喜歡的作者。我們聊得很愉快，不知不覺中居然已經半夜。總之，我們倆一拍即合，也約好很快下次再見面。

About me

Ivy

Calendar

◄　　　May　　　►

Sun	Mon	Tue	Wed	Thu	Fri	Sat
					1	2	3
4	5	6	7	8	9	10
11	12	13	14	15	16	17
18	19	20	21	22	23	24
25	26	27	28	29	**30**	31

Blog Archive

► May (30)
► April
► March
► February
► January
► December
► November
► October
► September
► August
► July
► June

hit 當動詞時，有『打、擊』之意，例如：

Philip hit me in the face for no reason.

（菲利普沒來由的朝我臉上打了一拳。）

但網誌中的 hit it off 可不是把某件東西打下來的意思。hit it off 是用來形容兩人初次見面，即因共同興趣或話題而相談甚歡，也就是『合得來』之意，這跟中文所說的『一拍即合』有異曲同工之妙，而且這個用法異性與同性之間均適用。

hit it off (with sb)　　（與某人）合得來／一拍即合

= be on the same wavelength (with sb)

＊wavelength [ˈwevˌlɛŋθ] *n.* 波長

例: Gary and Amy hit it off the moment they met.

（蓋瑞和艾咪第一次見面就情投意合。）

還有另一個常用片語 get along 也表『合得來』或『相處融洽』。

例: Jill doesn't really get along with her new co-worker.

（吉兒跟她的新同事處不來。）

若是專指男女之間很來電，則可用以下說法：

A and B have a spark　　A 和 B 之間很來電

＊spark [spɑrk] *n.* 火花

例: I can feel that you and Brett have a spark. He can't take his eyes off you.

（我覺得妳跟布萊特之間很來電，他沒辦法把視線從妳身上移開。）

 字 詞 幫幫忙！

1. **total** [ˈtotl̩] *a.* 完全的；全部的

totally [ˈtotl̩ɪ] *adv.* 完全地；全部地

例: The man was a total stranger to me. I don't know why he yelled at me.

（我完全不認識那位先生。我不知道他為什麼要對我大吼大叫。）

Are you totally sure you want to do this? A tattoo is forever, you know.

（你確定真的要這麼做嗎？你要知道刺青可是會留一輩子的。）

＊tattoo [tæˈtu] *n.* 刺青

2. **hunk** [hʌŋk] *n.* 肌肉男，猛男

3. **sweet** [swit] *a.* 貼心的；芳香的
   例: It was very sweet of you to send me a gift on my birthday.
   （你在我生日當天送我禮物真是貼心。）

4. **charming** [ˈtʃɑrmɪŋ] *a.* 迷人的，有魅力的
   charm [tʃɑrm] *vt.* 使著迷
   be charmed with / by... 為……著迷
   例: Though Julie is not beautiful, Sam still finds her very charming.
   （雖然茱莉不漂亮，但山姆還是覺得她很迷人。）
   We were charmed by the stories that Jack told us.
   （我們都被傑克所說的故事迷住了。）

5. **fun** [fʌn] *n.* 樂趣（不可數）& *a.* 有趣的
   比較:
   funny [ˈfʌnɪ] *a.* 好笑的，滑稽的
   a fun person　　有趣的人
   a funny person　　滑稽的人
   例: It was a great party, and everyone had a lot of fun.
   （這個派對很棒，大家都玩得很開心。）
   Living in the dormitory is fun, but there isn't much privacy.
   （住在宿舍很有趣，但沒什麼隱私可言。）
   ＊dormitory [ˈdɔrməˌtɔrɪ] *n.* 宿舍
   privacy [ˈpraɪvəsɪ] *n.* 隱私
   Jimmy told a funny story.
   （吉米說了個好笑的故事。）

6. **before sb knows it**　　在某人不知不覺中
   例: If you don't think about going home, before you know it,
   class will be over.
   （如果你不要想著回家的事，課堂會在你不知不覺中就結束了。）

7. **midnight** [ˈmɪdˌnaɪt] *n.* 午夜，半夜 12 點

8. **All in all, S + V**　　總之，……
   ＝ To sum up, S + V
   例: All in all, I'd say the meeting was a success.
   （總而言之，我想這次會議很成功。）

Unit 31

Anticipation

Index | Links | about | comments | Photo

May 31

I get to see Eric tomorrow, and **I can hardly wait** ! After our coffee date, I couldn't sleep all night because **I was so giddy**. It was so much fun being with him. I don't want to **push my luck**, but I think I'll send him a **text message** later saying I'm **looking forward to** tomorrow.

About me

Ivy

Calendar

◄   *May*   ►

Sun	Mon	Tue	Wed	Thu	Fri	Sat
					1	2	3
4	5	6	7	8	9	10
11	12	13	14	15	16	17
18	19	20	21	22	23	24
25	26	27	28	29	30	**31**

Blog Archive

▸ May (31)
▸ April
▸ March
▸ February
▸ January
▸ December
▸ November
▸ October
▸ September
▸ August
▸ July
▸ June

Ivy at Blog 於 May 05.31. PM 02:16 發表 | 回覆 (0) | 引用 (0) | 收藏 (0) | 轉寄給朋友 | 檢舉

又期待又怕受傷害

May 31

我快等不及明天要和艾瑞克見面了！我們喝咖啡約會之後，我整夜無法入眠，因為我整個人感覺飄飄然的。和他在一起真是開心。我不想得寸進尺，但我想我等一下會傳簡訊給他，告訴他我很期待明天的見面。

About me

Ivy

Calendar

◀　　　May　　　▶

Sun	Mon	Tue	Wed	Thu	Fri	Sat
				1	2	3
4	5	6	7	8	9	10
11	12	13	14	15	16	17
18	19	20	21	22	23	24
25	26	27	28	29	30	**31**

Blog Archive

► May (31)
► April
► March
► February
► January
► December
► November
► October
► September
► August
► July
► June

Ivy at Blog 於 May 05.31. PM 02:16 發表｜回覆 (0)｜引用 (0)｜收藏 (0)｜轉寄給朋友｜檢舉

giddy 是『頭暈目眩的』之意，而網誌中的 "I was so giddy." 不是用來形容『我頭很暈。』而是『我整個人感覺飄飄然的。』這是用來形容很開心的狀態。

giddy [ˋɡɪdɪ] *a.* 頭暈目眩的

例: Jane felt giddy when Alan proposed to her.

（當亞倫向阿珍求婚時，她整個人感覺飄飄然的。）

＊propose [prəˋpoz] *vi.* 求婚（與介詞 to 並用）

另外，我們也可以用 as happy as a clam 來形容一個人開心得不得了。clam [klæm] 是指『蛤蠣』，as happy as a clam 字面上的意思是『跟蛤蠣一樣開心』。蛤蠣跟開心有什麼關係呢？其實這個用法完整的說法是 as happy as a clam at high tide（像漲潮時的蛤蠣一樣快樂），high tide 就是『漲潮』。人們通常在退潮時才會去海灘撿蛤蠣，所以漲潮時的蛤蠣既不用擔心有生命危險，又可以飽食海中的浮游生物，當然很開心。沿用到後來 at high tide 被省略了，所以就用 as happy as a clam 來形容一個人開心得不得了。

例: Patty was as happy as a clam when she got a promotion.

（當佩蒂獲得升遷時，她開心得不得了。）

＊promotion [prəˋmoʃən] *n.* 升遷

字 詞幫幫忙！

1. **anticipation** [æn͵tɪsəˋpeʃən] *n.* 期待，期望

   anticipate [ænˋtɪsə͵pet] *vt.* 期待，期望

   in anticipation of...　　　期待／期望……

   anticipate + V-ing　　　期待／期望……

   ＝ expect to V

   例: Lucy sat beside the phone in anticipation of Nick's call.

   （露西坐在電話旁，期待接到尼克的電話。）

   Mary anticipates getting married this June.

   ＝ Mary expects to get married this June.

   （瑪麗期盼著在今年當六月新娘。）

2. I can hardly wait. 我幾乎等不及了。

can hardly wait to V 幾乎等不及要（做）……

can't wait to V 等不及／迫不及待要（做）……

例: Sam can hardly wait to visit his friend in Tokyo.

（山姆幾乎等不及要去探視他住在東京的朋友。）

Bill can't wait to go on the company trip.

（比爾等不及要去員工旅遊了。）

3. push one's luck 期望好運持續下去；得寸進尺

例: Lenny pushed his luck when he asked his sister for a second loan.

（藍尼得寸進尺再度向他姊姊借錢。）

＊loan [lon] n. 借貸；貸款

4. text message [ˋtɛkst ͵mɛsɪdʒ] n. 簡訊

message [ˋmɛsɪdʒ] n. 訊息

send sb a text message 傳簡訊給某人

leave a message 留言，留話

take a message 記下留話／留言

例: Beth said she sent me a text message, but I didn't get it.

（貝絲說她有傳簡訊給我，但我卻沒收到。）

Secretary: I'm sorry, but Mr. Lin is not in. How may I help you?

William: May I leave a message with you?

（祕書：抱歉，林先生目前不在。我可以幫什麼忙嗎？）

（威廉：可以請妳替我留個話嗎？）

David: May I speak to Michelle, please?

Helen: I'm sorry, but she's not in right now. May I take a message?

（大衛：可以請蜜雪兒聽電話嗎？）

（海倫：抱歉，她現在不在。要我為您留話嗎？）

5. look forward to + N/V-ing 期待……

= anticipate + N/V-ing

例: Anita looks forward to graduating from college.

（艾妮塔期待趕快大學畢業。）

Unit 32

Fall Head over Heels

June 01

I **had a great time** seeing Eric again. We went to dinner and then saw a movie. **The more** time we spend together, **the more** I **adore** him. **Truth be told**, I'm already <u>**head over heels for**</u> him. I **wonder** if he **feels the same way** about me. I'm really **anxious** to find out.

About me

Ivy

Calendar

◄   *June*   ►

Sun	Mon	Tue	Wed	Thu	Fri	Sat
1	2	3	4	5	6	7
8	9	10	11	12	13	14
15	16	17	18	19	20	21
22	23	24	25	26	27	28
29	30					

Blog Archive

▸ June (1)
▸ May
▸ April
▸ March
▸ February
▸ January
▸ December
▸ November
▸ October
▸ September
▸ August
▸ July

為愛神魂顛倒

June 01

再見到艾瑞克真的很開心。我們一起吃了晚餐，然後去看電影。我們相處的時間愈多，我就愈喜歡他。說真的，我已經為他神魂顛倒了。不知道他對我是否有一樣的感覺。我真是超想知道的。

About me

Ivy

Calendar

◀   *June*   ▶

Sun	Mon	Tue	Wed	Thu	Fri	Sat
1	2	3	4	5	6	7
8	9	10	11	12	13	14
15	16	17	18	19	20	21
22	23	24	25	26	27	28
29	30					

Blog Archive

- ► June (1)
- ► May
- ► April
- ► March
- ► February
- ► January
- ► December
- ► November
- ► October
- ► September
- ► August
- ► July

Ivy at Blog 於 June 06.01. PM 11:05 發表 | 回覆 (0) | 引用 (0) | 收藏 (0) | 轉寄給朋友 | 檢舉

127

戀愛初期，總是讓人失去理智、愛到不知東南西北。在英文中，表示某人愛到沖昏了頭會用 be head over heels in love 來形容，直譯為『愛到頭和腳跟顛倒了過來』，表示愛情使一切變得不合邏輯，讓原本是頭的位置變成腳跟，而腳跟變成頭，就類似中文裡所說的『愛到神魂顛倒』。其實 head over heels 在英文古文獻中表『翻跟斗』之意，因此讓看的人有頭腳錯置的感覺。如今 head over heels 常與 in love 並用，來表示深墜愛河。

be / fall head over heels for sb 為某人神魂顛倒，深深愛著某人

= be / fall head over heels in love with sb

= be / fall crazily / madly / deeply in love with sb

= be crazy about sb

 ＊heel [hil] *n.* 腳後跟

例: Stanly fell head over heels in love with Lisa after they dated for a month.

（和莉莎交往了一個月後，史丹利已經深深愛上了她。）

It is obvious that Helen is madly in love with Mark.

（海倫顯然瘋狂地愛上馬克。）

My brother is crazy about a girl he just met on the Internet, which worries me.

（我弟弟對一個他剛在網路上認識的女孩深深著迷，這讓我很擔心。）

字 詞幫幫忙！

1. **have a great / good time + V-ing** 做……很開心 / 很愉快

 have a hard time + V-ing 做……有困難

 例: Jimmy is having a good time playing online games.

 （吉米打線上遊戲玩得正開心。）

 When Toby first got here, he had a hard time adapting to his new job.

 （托比剛來本公司時，挺難適應他的新工作。）

 ＊adapt [ə'dæpt] *vi.* 適應（與介詞 to 並用）

2. The more..., the more....　愈……，就愈……

例: The more you worry, the more you can't fall asleep.
（你愈煩惱就愈睡不著。）

3. adore [ə`dɔr] *vt.* 愛慕；喜歡

例: Jerry is adored by his friends because of his generosity.
（傑瑞的個性慷慨大方，因此深受朋友喜愛。）
＊generosity [ˌdʒɛnə`rɑsətɪ] *n.* 慷慨

4. truth be told　老實說

= to tell the truth

例: Truth be told, Betty doesn't like you at all.
（老實說吧，貝蒂根本就不喜歡你。）

5. wonder [`wʌndə] *vt.* 納悶，想知道

wonder + if / whether + S + V　　納悶 / 想知道是否……
wonder + 疑問詞（what, when, where, why, how 等）
引導的名詞子句納悶 / 想知道……

例: I wonder whether my friend will lend me money.
（我不知道我朋友會不會借錢給我。）

James kept wondering why Cathy changed her mind.
（詹姆士一直很納悶為什麼凱西會改變她的心意。）

6. feel the same way　感覺一樣

= the feeling is mutual

＊mutual [`mjutʃʊəl] *a.* 相互的，彼此的

例: Roger: After swimming for two hours, I'm really tired.
Helen: I feel the same way.
（羅傑：游泳兩個小時後，我累死了。）
（海倫：我也有同感。）

I enjoyed talking with Jamie, and she said the feeling was mutual.
（我喜歡和潔米聊天，而她說她也有同感。）

7. anxious [`æŋkʃəs] *a.* 渴望的，急切的

Somebody's Girl

Index | Links | about | comments | Photo

June 02

Today Eric called me and said he had an **odd** question he wanted to ask me. He said he was going to see his parents and wanted to know if he could tell them I was his girlfriend. I **giggled** happily and said nothing would make me happier. Afterwards, I couldn't stop smiling. I was **officially** someone's "girl." **What a dream come true!** I **immediately** told Mandy, and she **congratulated** me.

About me

Ivy

Calendar

◀ June ▶

Sun	Mon	Tue	Wed	Thu	Fri	Sat
1	2	3	4	5	6	7
8	9	10	11	12	13	14
15	16	17	18	19	20	21
22	23	24	25	26	27	28
29	30					

Blog Archive

▸ June (2)
▸ May
▸ April
▸ March
▸ February
▸ January
▸ December
▸ November
▸ October
▸ September
▸ August
▸ July

Ivy at Blog 於 June 06.02. PM 06:30 發表 | 回覆 (0) | 引用 (0) | 收藏 (0) | 轉寄給朋友 | 檢舉

June 02

　　艾瑞克今天打電話給我，說他有個怪問題想問我。他說他要去看他爸媽，想知道他可不可以告訴他們我是他的女朋友。我開心地咯咯笑，告訴他沒有什麼能比這件事更讓我開心了。之後，我忍不住地一直微笑。我終於正式成為某人的『女友』了。這真是美夢成真！我立刻打電話告訴曼蒂，而她也向我道賀。

Ivy at Blog 於 June 06.02. PM 06:30 發表 | 回覆 (0) | 引用 (0) | 收藏 (0) | 轉寄給朋友 | 檢舉

131

經過這麼多波折，女主角終於找到她的真命天子（**Mr. Right** 或 **Prince Charming**）了！說是『美夢成真』一點也不為過。網誌裡所使用的 **"What a dream come true!"** 也可以說成 **"It's totally a dream come true!"**（這簡直就是美夢成真！）在這兩種說法裡，都是把 **a dream come true** 當作名詞使用，其實這是從 **a dream which has / had come true** 省略 **which has / had** 簡化而來的，**come true** 為動詞片語，表『實現』之意。

例: It was totally a dream come true when I knew that I was accepted into Harvard Law School.

（當我知道自己被錄取要進入哈佛法學院時，簡直就是美夢成真。）

表『使某人的夢想成真、實現某人的夢想』則有下列幾種說法：

make one's dream(s) come true

carry out one's dream(s)

realize one's dream(s)

fulfil one's dream(s)

＊fulfil / fulfill [fulˋfɪl] *vt.* 完成，實現（夢想）

例: My mom made my dream come true by taking me on a trip to Canada last summer.

（去年暑假媽媽帶我去加拿大旅遊，一圓我的美夢。）

John finally fulfilled his dream of becoming a lawyer.

（約翰終於實現當律師的夢想了。）

不過，人生有美夢成真的時候，當然也會有夢想破滅之時，這時候又該怎麼用英文表達呢？以下為你列舉幾種常見的說法：

It's the end of one's dream. 某人的夢想破滅。

= One's dream has fallen apart.

= One's dream is dashed.

＊fall apart （結果）失敗，崩散

＊dash [dæʃ] *vt.* 使破滅（尤指希望、夢想等）

例: It was the end of Paul's dream when he was eliminated from the singing contest.

（保羅在歌唱比賽中被淘汰時，他的夢想便破滅了。）

＊eliminate [ɪˋlɪməˏnet] *vt.* 淘汰，剔除

1. **odd** [ɑd] *a.* 奇怪的，怪異的

   oddly [`ɑdlɪ] *adv.* 奇怪地，怪異地

   oddly enough　　說來奇怪

   例: A number of odd happenings took place in that old house.

   （那棟老房子裡曾發生過一些怪事。）

   ＊happening [`hæpənɪŋ] *n.* 事情，事件

   Oddly enough, Kent's dog only barks at girls wearing skirts.

   （說來奇怪，肯特的狗只對穿裙子的女生吠叫。）

   ＊bark [bɑrk] *vi.* 吠叫

2. **giggle** [`gɪg!̩] *vi.* 咯咯地笑

3. **officially** [ə`fɪʃəlɪ] *adv.* 正式地

   例: Tim and Judy have officially announced their engagement.

   （提姆和茱蒂正式宣佈他們訂婚的消息。）

   ＊engagement [ɪn`gedʒmənt] *n.* 訂婚

4. **immediately** [ɪ`midɪɪtɪlɪ] *adv.* 立刻，馬上

   ＝　at once

5. **congratulate** [kən`grætʃə͵let] *vt.* 恭喜，祝賀

   congratulations [kən͵grætʃə`leʃənz] *n.* 祝賀（恆用複數）

   congratulate sb on sth　　向某人道賀某事

   例: Andy called last night to congratulate me on getting promoted.

   （安迪昨晚打電話來恭喜我升遷。）

   ＊promote [prə`mot] *vt.* 使晉升

   Congratulations on successfully passing the test!

   （恭喜你通過考試！）

Walking on Air

Index | Links | about | comments | Photo

June 03

My co-workers have noticed a change in me since Eric and I became **official**. I have a **permanent** smile on my face, and I'm **light-hearted** and **easygoing** about everything at work. It seems nothing can **get me down**. For example, my boss got upset about a file that was not **filled out correctly** and **lectured** me on being careful. Something like that would usually **ruin** my day, but not today. I'm still **walking on air**!

About me

Ivy

Calendar

◄   *June*   ►

Sun	Mon	Tue	Wed	Thu	Fri	Sat
1	2	**3**	4	5	6	7
8	9	10	11	12	13	14
15	16	17	18	19	20	21
22	23	24	25	26	27	28
29	30					

Blog Archive

► June (3)
► May
► April
► March
► February
► January
► December
► November
► October
► September
► August
► July

Ivy at Blog 於 June 06.03. PM 02:26 發表 | 回覆 (0) | 引用 (0) | 收藏 (0) | 轉寄給朋友 | 檢舉

漫步在雲端

June 03

　　自從和艾瑞克正式交往後，我的同事都注意到我的改變。我的臉上總是帶著笑容，心情輕鬆自在，對工作上的事也都很隨和，好像沒有任何事會打亂我的好心情。舉例來說，老闆對於我沒有把一張表格填好很不高興，還把我訓了一頓，說要細心。通常這樣的事會毀了我一整天的心情，但今天則不然。我現在的心情仍然好到像漫步在雲端！

About me

Ivy

Calendar

◄			June			►
Sun	Mon	Tue	Wed	Thu	Fri	Sat
1	2	3	4	5	6	7
8	9	10	11	12	13	14
15	16	17	18	19	20	21
22	23	24	25	26	27	28
29	30					

Blog Archive

- ► June (3)
- ► May
- ► April
- ► March
- ► February
- ► January
- ► December
- ► November
- ► October
- ► September
- ► August
- ► July

135

中文裡的『高興地飛上天、快樂的好似漫步在雲端』，若是換成英文該怎麼說呢？英文可是有個非常相似而且生動的說法，那就是 **walk on air**。walk on air 就是 feel extremely joyful（感到極度愉快）的意思。從字面上看來，walk on air 是『在空中漫步』，當一個人『樂不可支』時，不就是會有飄飄然彷彿可以飛起來的感覺嗎？網誌作者因為和男友正式公開交往，所以心情當然會好到 walk on air。

例: That actor felt he was walking on air after he won the Academy Award.

（那名男演員贏得奧斯卡金像獎後，高興得像飛上天去了。）

此外，中文裡也有『整個人高興到飛到九霄雲外』的說法，其對照的英文用法為 be on cloud nine。be on cloud nine 字面意思是『在九重雲霄上』，美國氣象局用數字把雲系加以分類，因為第 9 號雲的位置最高，也最接近天堂，於是大家就用 be on cloud nine 來形容一個人『開心無比』。

例: Ever since Jane received his marriage proposal, Alan has been on cloud nine.

（自從阿珍接受他的求婚後，亞倫就一直開心得不得了。）

字 詞幫幫忙！

1. **official** [əˋfɪʃəl] a. 正式的 & n. 官員（尤指文官）
   officer [ˋɔfəsɚ] n. 官員（尤指武官，如警察、軍人等）

2. **permanent** [ˋpɝmənənt] a. 永久的
   temporary [ˋtɛmpəˏrɛrɪ] a. 短暫的

3. **light-hearted** [ˏlaɪtˋhɑrtɪd] a. 輕鬆愉快的

4. **easygoing** [ˋizɪˏgoɪŋ] a. 隨和的

5. **get sb down**　　使某人心情沮喪
   注意:
   down [daʊn] 在此作形容詞，表『消沉的、沮喪的』，等於 depressed [dɪˋprɛst]。
   例: Nothing can get Susan down because her favorite band

例: Nothing can get Susan down because her favorite band is coming to town.
（任何事都不會打壞蘇珊的心情，因為她最愛的樂團就要進城了。）

6. **fill out...** 填寫……（表格等）

= fill in...

例: Fill out this form, and we will call you when we are ready to set up an interview.
（填妥這份表格，屆時我們會電話通知面試事宜。）

*interview [`ɪntə͵vju] *n.* 面試

7. **correctly** [kə`rɛktlɪ] *adv.* 正確地

例: Carrie was the first person to answer the question correctly.
（凱莉是第一個答對問題的人。）

8. **lecture** [`lɛktʃə] *vt.* 告誡，訓斥 & *n.* 講課，講授

lecture sb on sth   針對某事訓斥某人

give a lecture to sb   對某人講課

例: My mother lectured me on being lazy.
（我媽媽訓斥我懶惰。）

The teacher gave a lecture to his class on the human body.
（這名老師對他的班級講授關於人體的課程。）

9. **ruin** [`rʊɪn] *vt.* 毀掉，破壞

ruin one's day   毀了某人的一整天

例: A phone call from an annoying client totally ruined Jack's day.
（一名討厭顧客的來電讓傑克的一整天全毀了。）

The scandal ruined Martha's reputation.
（這個醜聞毀了瑪莎的名譽。）

*scandal [`skænd!] *n.* 醜聞

reputation [͵rɛpjə`teʃən] *n.* 名聲

A Romantic Night

Index | Links | about | comments | Photo

June 04

Tonight Eric took me up to Yangmingshan so we could enjoy the night view from up there. I was **shocked** when I saw his car. It was the **latest** BMW **on the market**. It was **luxurious** to ride in. We parked in a **deserted lot** that **overlooked** part of Taipei. Eric kept saying how happy he was to be there with me. It all seemed **like a scene out of a romantic movie**.

About me

Ivy

Calendar

◄ **June** ►

Sun	Mon	Tue	Wed	Thu	Fri	Sat
1	2	3	**4**	5	6	7
8	9	10	11	12	13	14
15	16	17	18	19	20	21
22	23	24	25	26	27	28
29	30					

Blog Archive

- June (4)
- May
- April
- March
- February
- January
- December
- November
- October
- September
- August
- July

Ivy at Blog 於 June 06.04. PM 11:58 發表 | 回覆 (0) | 引用 (0) | 收藏 (0) | 轉寄給朋友 | 檢舉

浪漫的夜晚

Index | *Links* | *about* | *comments* | *Photo*

June 04

今晚艾瑞克帶我上陽明山，從那裡欣賞美麗的夜景。我看見他的轎車時很震驚。那是市面上最新款的 BMW。坐在裡頭的感覺實在有夠奢華。我們把車停在一處廢棄的空地，在那裡能將一部分的台北盡收眼底。艾瑞克一直說他很開心和我一起到那裡。這一切簡直就像愛情片裡的故事情節一樣。

About me

Ivy

Calendar

◄   *June*   ►

Sun	Mon	Tue	Wed	Thu	Fri	Sat
1	2	3	**4**	5	6	7
8	9	10	11	12	13	14
15	16	17	18	19	20	21
22	23	24	25	26	27	28
29	30					

Blog Archive

- ► June (4)
- ► May
- ► April
- ► March
- ► February
- ► January
- ► December
- ► November
- ► October
- ► September
- ► August
- ► July

romantic [roˈmæntɪk] *a.* 關於愛情的；浪漫的

romance [roˈmæns] *n.* 戀情；浪漫（氣氛）

an office romance　　辦公室戀情

例: Sam prepared a romantic dinner for Tracy on Valentine's Day.

（山姆在情人節那天為崔西準備了一頓浪漫的晚餐。）

Jack and Rose wanted to keep their romance a secret from their parents.

（傑克和蘿絲想把他們倆的戀情瞞著雙親。）

The romance has gone out of their marriage.

（他們的婚姻生活已不再浪漫。）

scene [sin] 是指電影或書中的『場景』，a romantic movie 就是指『愛情片』。在網誌中，**like a scene out of a romantic movie** 就是我們常說的『就像愛情片裡的故事情節一樣』，用來形容他們的約會實在『浪漫到不行』。此時，也可以用 "It's like a dream." （這簡直像做夢一樣。）來形容。

例: Greg proposed to Maggie in front of a fountain. It was really like a scene out of a romantic movie.

（葛雷在一座噴水池前向瑪姬求婚，簡直就像愛情片裡的情節一般。）

　＊fountain [ˈfauntn̩] *n.* 噴泉，噴水池

 字詞幫幫忙！

1. **shocked** [ʃɑkt] *a.* 感到震驚的

   shocking [ˈʃɑkɪŋ] *a.* 令人震驚的

2. **latest** [ˈletɪst] *a.* 最新的；最近的

   例: The salesman showed us the latest flat-screen TV.

   （推銷員把最新的平面電視展示給我們看。）

   ＊flat-screen [ˌflætˈskrin] *a.* 平面的

3. **on the market** 上市（in the market 則表『在市場裡』）

例: The new computer my company is designing is not on the market yet.

（我們公司尚在設計中的新款電腦還沒正式上市。）

I ran into an old friend of mine in the market this morning.

（今天早上我在市場裡巧遇我的一位老友。）

4. **luxurious** [lʌgˋʒʊrɪəs] *a.* 奢侈的；豪華的

luxury [ˋlʌkʃərɪ] *n.* 奢侈，奢華（不可數）；奢侈品（可數）

live a luxurious life 過著奢侈的生活

例: Not all rich people live luxurious lives.

（並非所有有錢人都生活奢侈。）

The millionaire travels in luxury everywhere.

（這位百萬富豪到處從事豪華的旅遊。）

＊millionaire [ˏmɪljənˋɛr] *n.* 百萬富翁

Sammy gave up all luxuries during the financial crisis.

（山米在財務危機時放棄了所有的奢侈品。）

5. **deserted** [dɪˋzɝtɪd] *a.* 遭人遺棄的，任其荒廢的

a deserted house 一棟廢棄屋

a deserted farm 一座荒蕪的農莊

例: There used to be a house in this deserted garden.

（這座廢棄的花園裡頭曾經有一棟房子。）

6. **lot** [lɑt] *n.* （有特定用途的）一塊地

a parking lot 停車場

7. **overlook** [ˏovɚˋlʊk] *vt.* 俯瞰

例: Tommy's house on the hill overlooks the valley.

（湯米山上的房子可以俯瞰山谷。）

Unit 36

Just Shoot Me

June 05

After dinner, Eric took me to his apartment. It was in a new apartment **complex** just outside of Taipei. He didn't have much for **decorations** or **furniture**, though. While we were there, I **suddenly** had to use the bathroom. It seemed the food we ate **didn't agree with** me, and I **had the runs** all night long. It was so embarrassing that I just wanted to **dig a hole to bury myself in**.

About me

Ivy

Calendar

◄   *June*   ►

Sun	Mon	Tue	Wed	Thu	Fri	Sat
	1	2	3	4	**5**	6	7
8	9	10	11	12	13	14
15	16	17	18	19	20	21
22	23	24	25	26	27	28
29	30					

Blog Archive

- ► June (5)
- ► May
- ► April
- ► March
- ► February
- ► January
- ► December
- ► November
- ► October
- ► September
- ► August
- ► July

天啊，殺了我吧！

June 05

　　晚餐過後，艾瑞克帶我去他的公寓。那是位於台北市郊一座新落成的公寓大樓，不過他家裡沒有太多擺設或傢俱。在他家時，我突然很想上廁所。似乎是我們剛吃的食物讓我的腸胃不舒服，所以我整晚都在拉肚子。這真是讓我尷尬到想挖個地洞鑽進去算了。

Ivy at Blog 於 June 06.05. PM 10:06 發表 | 回覆 (0) | 引用 (0) | 收藏 (0) | 轉寄給朋友 | 檢舉

About me

Ivy

Calendar

◄　　　　*June*　　　　►

Sun	Mon	Tue	Wed	Thu	Fri	Sat
1	2	3	4	**5**	6	7
8	9	10	11	12	13	14
15	16	17	18	19	20	21
22	23	24	25	26	27	28
29	30					

Blog Archive

► June (5)
► May
► April
► March
► February
► January
► December
► November
► October
► September
► August
► July

感到丟臉或尷尬時，英文除了可以用 "I was / felt so embarrassed."（我好丟臉／尷尬。）來形容，還有沒有其他有趣的用法呢？本篇網誌要介紹兩種說法："Just shoot me." 和 dig a hole to burry oneself in。

"Just shoot me." 照字面的意思是『開槍射我吧。』但如果平時你聽到別人這麼說時，可別真的認為對方要你斃了他，這是說他感到丟臉或尷尬到了極點的意思，中文裡也有很類似的用法，像是妳今天在挖鼻孔時，居然被喜歡的男生看到，這時妳一定覺得超丟臉，心裡直想：『殺了我吧！／讓我『屎』（『死』的諧音）了吧！』，而英文的用法就是 "Just shoot me."。

例: I can't believe I just farted in front of the girl I like. God, just shoot me.

（我真不敢相信我剛在喜歡的女生面前放了個屁。天啊，讓我『屎』了吧。）

＊fart [fɑrt] *vi.* 放屁

而 dig a hole to bury oneself in 也是用來表示感到丟臉或尷尬。dig [dɪg] 是『挖掘』，hole [hol] 表『洞』，而 bury [ˋbɛrɪ] 則是『埋葬』，因此 **dig a hole to bury oneself in** 就是『挖個洞把自己埋進去』，這跟中文的『挖個地洞鑽進去』是不是一樣呢？

例: Julie happened to see me picking my nose during class. I really wanted to dig a hole to bury myself in.

（上課時茉莉剛好看到我在挖鼻孔。我那時真想挖個地洞鑽進去。）

＊pick one's nose　挖鼻孔

 字詞幫幫忙！

1. **complex** [ˋkɑmplɛks] *n.* 綜合樓群；複合物 & [kəmˋplɛks / ˋkɑmplɛks] *a.* 複雜的

    an apartment complex　公寓式大廈

    a shopping complex　大型賣場；數個大賣場集結的購物區

    例: Albert's ideas were too complex for me to understand.

    （艾伯特的想法太複雜了，我很難懂。）

2. **decoration** [ˌdɛkəˈreʃən] *n.* 裝飾品（可數）；裝飾，裝潢（不可數）

   decorate [ˈdɛkəˌret] *vt.* 佈置，裝飾

   decorate A with B　　　用 B 裝飾 A

   be decorated with...　　　用……裝飾

   例: Beth put up a lot of beautiful decorations for the party.
     （貝絲用了很多美麗的裝飾品佈置派對場地。）

     The decoration of the room shows the owner's bad taste.
     （從房間的裝潢來看，屋主一點品味都沒有。）

     We decorated the Christmas tree with colorful lights.
     （我們用彩燈裝飾耶誕樹。）

     Sally's room is decorated with a lot of beautiful paintings.
     （莎莉的房間用許多美麗的圖畫裝飾。）

3. **furniture** [ˈfɜnɪtʃɚ] *n.* 傢俱（集合名詞，不可數）

4. **suddenly** [ˈsʌdənlɪ] *adv.* 突然地

= all of a sudden

   例: All of a sudden, the lights in the room went out.
     （突然間，房間裡的燈光熄滅了。）

     ＊go out　　　（燈或火）熄滅

5. **食物 + didn't / doesn't agree with sb**

   某食物不適合某人（的體質）；某人不適應某食物

   例: The food here doesn't agree with me.
     （這裡的食物我吃不慣。）

6. **have the runs**　　　拉肚子

   注意:

   此處的 runs 恆用複數，乃指來回跑廁所之意。

   例: After eating the seafood at that restaurant, John had the runs for days.
     （阿強吃了那家餐廳的海鮮後，拉了好幾天的肚子。）

Unit 37

Phony Food

Index | Links | about | comments | Photo

June 06

Eric came to my apartment tonight because I wanted to cook dinner for him. It was **the very** first time I ever cooked for him, **or** anyone else **for that matter**. <u>**To make a long story short**</u>, I ended up ruining everything and had to call a **delivery service**. What's most **shameful** was that when Eric asked if I cooked the food myself, I still said yes. I'm such a phony!

About me

Ivy

Calendar

◄ *June* ►

Sun	Mon	Tue	Wed	Thu	Fri	Sat
1	2	3	4	5	6	7
8	9	10	11	12	13	14
15	16	17	18	19	20	21
22	23	24	25	26	27	28
29	30					

Blog Archive

- ► June (6)
- ► May
- ► April
- ► March
- ► February
- ► January
- ► December
- ► November
- ► October
- ► September
- ► August
- ► July

Ivy at Blog 於 June 06.06. PM 10:35 發表 | 回覆 (0) | 引用 (0) | 收藏 (0) | 轉寄給朋友 | 檢舉

假裝親自下廚

Index | Links | about | comments | Photo

June 06

艾瑞克今晚來我的公寓，因為我想煮晚餐給他吃。這可是我第一次為他洗手作羹湯，事實上我從未為任何人下過廚。長話短說，結果我把每件事都搞砸了，還得打電話叫外送。當艾瑞克問說這些食物是不是我自己煮的時候，更是令人汗顏，因為我竟然說是。我真是個大騙子！

Ivy at Blog 於 June 06.06. PM 10:35 發表 | 回覆 (0) | 引用 (0) | 收藏 (0) | 轉寄給朋友 | 檢舉

About me

Ivy

Calendar

◄ *June* ►

Sun	Mon	Tue	Wed	Thu	Fri	Sat
1	2	3	4	5	6	7
8	9	10	11	12	13	14
15	16	17	18	19	20	21
22	23	24	25	26	27	28
29	30					

Blog Archive

- June (6)
- May
- April
- March
- February
- January
- December
- November
- October
- September
- August
- July

當別人問起一件事，若我們覺得因為太多細節而難以解釋時，通常會回答 "It's a long story."（這故事說來話長。）來一筆帶過。至於『長話短說』的英文該怎麼說呢？就是網誌中的 "to make a long story short"（直譯為『讓很長的故事變短』）。

To make a long story short, S + V　　長話短說，……

例: To make a long story short, what did you finally decide?

（長話短說吧，你最後的決定是什麼？）

除了『長話短說』外，那『簡而言之』又該怎麼說呢？

In short, S + V　　簡而言之／總之，……
= In a nutshell, S + V
= In brief, S + V
= Briefly speaking, S + V
= Simply put, S + V
　　*nutshell [ˋnʌt͵ʃɛl] *n.* 堅果的外殼

例: In short, David is the right man for the job.

（簡而言之，大衛是這份工作的適當人選。）

以下再為各位讀者補充『換言之、換句話說』的用法：

In other words, S + V　　換言之／換句話說，……
= That is (to say), S + V
= To put it differently, S + V

例: We all make mistakes. In other words, no one is perfect.

（我們都會犯錯。換言之，沒有人是完美的。）

1. **phony** [ˋfonɪ] *a.* 假的；欺騙的 & 贗品；騙子

I'm such a phony!　　我真是個大騙子！

例: Jack is speaking with a phony British accent again.

（傑克又在裝英國口音說話了。）

　　*accent [ˋæksənt] *n.* 口音

2. **the very + N**　　正是……，就是……；只要是……
= **just the + N**
注意:
very 作形容詞時用於加強語氣，表『正是、就是、只要是』之意，而且之前一定要置定冠詞 the；翻譯時 very 可視情況而不必譯出。

例: The very sight of a spider makes Anne scream with fear.
= Just the sight of a spider makes Anne scream with fear.
（小安一看見蜘蛛就會害怕地大叫。）
＊spider [ˈspaɪdɚ] *n.* 蜘蛛

3. **or...for that matter**　　對……同樣如此
matter [ˈmætɚ] *n.* 事情
例: Frank never tried beer, or any kind of alcohol for that matter.
（法蘭克從未喝過啤酒，對其他酒類也是如此。）

4. **delivery service** [dɪˈlɪvərɪ ˌsɝvɪs] *n.* 外送服務
delivery [dɪˈlɪvərɪ] *n.* 遞送，運送
deliver [dɪˈlɪvɚ] *vt.* 遞送，運送
例: That pizza shop delivers pizzas in less than 30 minutes.
（那間披薩店會在 30 分鐘內將披薩送達。）

5. **shameful** [ˈʃemfəl] *a.* 令人感到可恥的
ashamed [əˈʃemd] *a.*（人）感到羞愧的
shame [ʃem] *n.* 羞恥，慚愧
It is shameful + that 子句　　……真是令人感到可恥
be / feel ashamed of...　　以……為恥
It is a shame + that 子句　　很可惜 / 遺憾……
= It is a pity + that 子句
例: It is shameful that you've been cheating on your wife.
（你一直對太太不忠真是可恥。）

Tony was ashamed of the way he acted after he got drunk.
（東尼為自己酩酊大醉後的行為感到羞恥。）

It is a shame that you couldn't go on the company trip.
（你不能去參加公司旅遊真是可惜。）

Keys to His Heart

June 07

Eric surprised me at work today. He **showed up** with a small box that was **gift-wrapped**. Inside it was **a set of** keys. He said they were the keys to his apartment and that he was giving them to me to show me he trusted me **unconditionally**. It is a clear **sign** that our **relationship** is **being taken to another level**. But does that mean I have to give him keys to my apartment **in return**?

About me

Ivy

Calendar

◄ *June* ►

Sun	Mon	Tue	Wed	Thu	Fri	Sat
1	2	3	4	5	6	**7**
8	9	10	11	12	13	14
15	16	17	18	19	20	21
22	23	24	25	26	27	28
29	30					

Blog Archive

▸ June (7)
▸ May
▸ April
▸ March
▸ February
▸ January
▸ December
▸ November
▸ October
▸ September
▸ August
▸ July

打開心房的鑰匙

June 07

今天上班的時候艾瑞克給了我一個驚喜。他拿著一個包裝好的小盒子出現在我的辦公室。盒子裡頭是一串鑰匙。他說那是他公寓的鑰匙，送給我以表示他對我毫無條件地信任。這很明顯地象徵我們的關係又更進一步了。但這是否也意味我得奉上我公寓的鑰匙以為回報？

About me

Ivy

Calendar

◄　　　*June*　　　►

Sun	Mon	Tue	Wed	Thu	Fri	Sat
1	2	3	4	5	6	**7**
8	9	10	11	12	13	14
15	16	17	18	19	20	21
22	23	24	25	26	27	28
29	30					

Blog Archive

▸ June (7)
▸ May
▸ April
▸ March
▸ February
▸ January
▸ December
▸ November
▸ October
▸ September
▸ August
▸ July

Ivy at Blog 於 June 06.07. PM 08:55 發表 | 回覆 (0) | 引用 (0) | 收藏 (0) | 轉寄給朋友 | 檢舉

151

送上自家鑰匙的這個舉動，代表對另一半的信任，以及象徵認真地投入一段感情中。換言之，兩人的感情從不確定的開始進入了另一個階段，英文中就以 be taken to another level 來表示（level [ˈlɛvl̩] *n.* 水平，等級），或是兩個人 take another step，也就是在愛情的路上向前邁進了一步。除此之外，類似的說法還有：

take a big step forward　　　　　（感情）向前邁進大一步
take an important step forward　　（感情）向前邁進重大的一步
get serious　　開始認真

例: Mark and Patty have decided to take an important step forward—they are getting married.
（馬克和派蒂決定向前邁進重大的一步，那就是他們要結婚了。）

As far as I know, Dave has never gotten serious about any girl.
（就我所知，戴夫從來沒有對一個女孩子認真過。）

字 詞幫幫忙！

1. **show up**　　露面，出現
= turn up
= appear [əˈpɪr] *vi.*
   例: Mindy was shocked to see her father turn up at the disco.
   （明蒂看到她爸爸出現在迪斯可舞廳時很震驚。）

2. **gift-wrap** [ˈɡɪftˌræp] *vt.* （用包裝紙）包裝（禮品）
   例: It took Lance a couple of hours to gift-wrap his girlfriend's birthday present.
   （藍斯花了一、兩個鐘頭包裝他女友的生日禮物。）

3. **a set of...**　　　　一副 / 一套 / 一組……
   a set of keys　　　　一串鑰匙

例: That set of knives (which was) imported from Germany cost my mom an arm and a leg.

（那組德國進口的刀子花了我媽媽一大筆錢。）

＊import [ɪmˋpɔrt] *vt.* 進口

cost sb an arm and a leg　　花某人一大筆錢

= cost sb a lot of money

4. unconditionally [ˏʌnkənˋdɪʃənəlɪ] *adv.* 無條件地；不加限制地

5. sign [saɪn] *n.* 象徵，徵兆

as a sign of...　　當作……的徵兆 / 跡象

= as a symbol of...

＊symbol [ˋsɪmbḷ] *n.* 象徵

例: The falling of meteors was once seen as a sign of something bad to come.

（殞落的流星曾一度被視作不祥之事降臨的前兆。）

＊meteor [ˋmitɪɚ] *n.* 流星

6. relationship [rɪˋleʃənˏʃɪp] *n.* 感情關係；親屬關係

例: Lucy just ended her relationship with Jim.

（露西剛結束和吉姆之間的感情。）

Morris has had a difficult relationship with his parents.

（莫瑞斯和他父母之間的關係並不好。）

7. in return　　　　回報

in return for...　　作為……的回報

例: Those volunteers do their best to help the poor without asking for anything in return.

（那些義工盡心盡力幫助窮苦人家而不求回報。）

＊volunteer [ˏvɑlənˋtɪr] *n.* 義工，志願者

Kevin bought his co-workers dinner in return for their help.

（凱文請同事吃晚餐以回報他們的協助。）

Summer Sales

Index | *Links* | *about* | *comments* | *Photo*

June 08

Summer is coming, which means the summer **sales** have started. I went to the department store with Mandy today to look at **swimsuits** and summer clothes. She **talked** me **into trying on** a **bikini**, but I was too **shy** to let her see me in it. After hours of shopping and trying on **a variety of outfits**, we decided to go get foot **massages**. We **had** lots of **fun** today!

About me

Ivy

Calendar

◄   *June*   ►

Sun	Mon	Tue	Wed	Thu	Fri	Sat
1	2	3	4	5	6	7
8	9	10	11	12	13	14
15	16	17	18	19	20	21
22	23	24	25	26	27	28
29	30					

Blog Archive

- ► June (8)
- ► May
- ► April
- ► March
- ► February
- ► January
- ► December
- ► November
- ► October
- ► September
- ► August
- ► July

Ivy at Blog 於 June 06.08. PM 02:14 發表｜回覆 (0)｜引用 (0)｜收藏 (0)｜轉寄給朋友｜檢舉

夏季特賣

June 08

　　夏天到了，這表示夏季特賣開始了。今天我和曼蒂去百貨公司看泳衣和夏裝。她說服我試穿一件比基尼，可是我太害羞了，沒讓她看我穿的樣子。在血拼和試穿各式各樣的衣服幾個小時後，我們決定要去做腳底按摩。我們今天玩得真開心！

About me

Ivy

Calendar

◄　　*June*　　►

Sun	Mon	Tue	Wed	Thu	Fri	Sat
1	2	3	4	5	6	7
8	9	10	11	12	13	14
15	16	17	18	19	20	21
22	23	24	25	26	27	28
29	30					

Blog Archive

▸ June (8)
▸ May
▸ April
▸ March
▸ February
▸ January
▸ December
▸ November
▸ October
▸ September
▸ August
▸ July

Ivy at Blog 於 June 06.08. PM 02:14 發表 | 回覆 (0) | 引用 (0) | 收藏 (0) | 轉寄給朋友 | 檢舉

夏天最好的活動就是到海邊曬太陽、游泳或玩水上活動，這時候當然少不了泳裝。泳裝樣式百百款，以下就為讀者介紹英文中各式泳裝的說法：

swimsuit [ˋswɪmˌsut] *n.* 泳裝（可數）

= swimming suit [ˋswɪmɪŋ ˏsut] *n.*

= bathing suit [ˋbeðɪŋ ˏsut] *n.*

swimwear [ˋswɪmˏwɛr] *n.* 泳裝（統稱，不可數）

a one-piece swimsuit　　一件連身泳裝

bikini [bɪˋkɪnɪ] *n.* 比基尼

tankini [tænˋkɪnɪ] *n.* 背心泳裝（上半身為小背心形式，下半身為比基尼泳褲）

string bikini [ˋstrɪŋ bɪˏkɪnɪ] *n.* 綁帶／細帶比基尼

swimming trunks [ˋswɪmɪŋ ˏtrʌŋks] *n.*（男性）泳褲

a pair of swimming trunks　　一條男泳褲

例: Annie loves all the attention she gets when she wears her bikini.

（安妮喜歡她穿比基尼時所獲得的注目。）

Steve's swimming trunks got a hole in the back, but he didn't notice.

（史帝夫的泳褲後面破了個洞，但他沒注意到。）

1. **sale** [sel] *n.* 拍賣；廉價出售

on sale　　特賣中

for sale　　要出售的

例: The shirt is on sale now. It's 20 percent off.

（這件襯衫正在特賣，打 8 折。）

Almost every house on this old street is for sale.

（這條老街上幾乎每一棟房子都要出售。）

2. talk sb into V-ing　　說服某人做⋯⋯

= **persuade sb to V**

例: Daisy finally talked her mother into letting her get her ears pierced.

（黛西終於說服她媽媽讓她穿耳洞。）

3. try on...　　試穿／試戴（衣服、手鍊、鞋子等）

比較:

try out...　　試驗／試用（非身上所穿之物）

例: When Anita tried on her wedding dress, she looked like a princess.

（當艾妮塔試穿她的婚紗時，看上去真像個公主。）

Mom tried out the mattress before buying it.

（老媽先試躺了床墊，然後才決定買下來。）

＊mattress [ˈmætrɪs] *n.* 床墊

4. shy [ʃaɪ] *a.* 害羞的

5. a variety of...　　各式各樣的⋯⋯

6. outfit [ˈaʊtˌfɪt] *n.* （全套）服裝

7. massage [məˈsɑʒ] *n.* & *vt.* 按摩

8. have fun　　很愉快，玩得開心

have fun + V-ing　　（做）⋯⋯很愉快

= **have a great time + V-ing**

例: Kathy and I went to Kenting last weekend, and we had a lot of fun.

（凱西和我上週末去墾丁玩得很開心。）

Lucy and Kevin had a great time having dinner and watching a movie last night.

（露西和凱文昨晚共進晚餐看電影，度過愉快的時光。）

Computer Blues

Index | *Links* | *about* | *comments* | *Photo*

June 09

My **laptop crashed the other day**, so I went to the Kwang Hwa shopping area. I **compared** prices and kinds from several stores. I have **narrowed down** my choices, but I want to ask Eric for his opinion before I buy one. He knows more about computers than I do, and it's best to **get a second opinion** on a **purchase** like this.

About me

Ivy

Calendar

◄   *June*   ►

Sun	Mon	Tue	Wed	Thu	Fri	Sat
1	2	3	4	5	6	7
8	9	10	11	12	13	14
15	16	17	18	19	20	21
22	23	24	25	26	27	28
29	30					

Blog Archive

▸ June (9)
▸ May
▸ April
▸ March
▸ February
▸ January
▸ December
▸ November
▸ October
▸ September
▸ August
▸ July

Ivy at Blog 於 June 06.09. PM 03:15 發表 | 回覆 (0) | 引用 (0) | 收藏 (0) | 轉寄給朋友 | 檢舉

電腦出問題

June 09

我的筆電前幾天掛掉了,所以我去了光華商場一趟。

我在不同店家比較價錢和機型。我已經縮小了選擇範圍,

但在購買之前我還是想問一下艾瑞克的意見。他比我懂電

腦,而且購買這種商品最好是先詢問過別人的意見。

Calendar

◄   *June*   ►

Sun	Mon	Tue	Wed	Thu	Fri	Sat
1	2	3	4	5	6	7
8	9	10	11	12	13	14
15	16	17	18	19	20	21
22	23	24	25	26	27	28
29	30					

Blog Archive

- ► June (9)
- ► May
- ► April
- ► March
- ► February
- ► January
- ► December
- ► November
- ► October
- ► September
- ► August
- ► July

Ivy at Blog 於 June 06.09. PM 03:15 發表 | 回覆 (0) | 引用 (0) | 收藏 (0) | 轉寄給朋友 | 檢舉

相信電腦掛掉是大家最不願意碰到的事，尤其是發生在處理的資料還沒儲存的情況下，那更是讓人欲哭無淚。網誌中所用的 crash 原表『墜毀；撞擊』之意，用法如下：

crash [kræʃ] *vi.* 墜毀；撞擊
crash into... 撞上……

例: The airplane crashed due to an engine problem.
（這架飛機因為引擎問題而墜毀。）

My car went out of control and crashed into a tree.
（我的車子失控撞上一棵樹。）

但是網誌中的 "My laptop crashed." 可不是說『我的筆電墜毀了。』而是表示『我的筆電當機、掛掉了。』所以下次當你聽到有人說："My computer crashed."，千萬別認為他的電腦從哪裡掉下來了。以下就為你介紹幾種表達電腦『當機 / 掛掉』的說法：

My computer has <u>crashed</u>. 我的電腦當機 / 掛掉了。
= My computer is frozen.
= My computer isn't working.
= My computer is malfunctioning.

＊frozen [ˋfrozn] *a.* 冰凍的（電腦當機程式不能用時，是不是就像被冰凍了一樣呢？）
malfunction [mælˋfʌŋkʃən] *vi.* 發生故障

 字詞幫幫忙！

1. **blues** [bluz] *n.* 憂鬱（恆用複數）
   blue [blu] *a.* 憂鬱的；藍色的
   the Monday blues 星期一上班憂鬱症
   feel blue 感到非常憂鬱

   例: John has been feeling very blue lately. I'm worried about him.
   （阿強最近一直非常憂鬱。我很擔心他。）

   ＊本單元標題 Computer Blues 指作者的電腦因當機而造成她的心情鬱悶不歡之意。

2. laptop [ˋlæpˌtɑp] *n.* 筆記型電腦

= **notebook** [ˋnotˌbʊk] *n.*

注意：

laptop 是 laptop computer 的縮寫，laptop 原指『膝上』之意，但現在習慣直接以 laptop 來表示『筆記型電腦』。

desktop [ˋdɛskˌtɑp] *n.* 桌上型電腦

= **desktop computer**

3. the other day　　前些時候（與過去式並用）

4. compare [kəmˋpɛr] *vt.* 比較；比喻

compare A with B　　比較 A 與 B

compare A to B　　比較 A 與 B（= compare A with B）；把 A 比作 B

例: I hate it when my parents compare me with my twin sister.

= I hate it when my parents compare me to my twin sister.
（我討厭爸媽拿我跟雙胞胎妹妹做比較。）

The poet compared the woman he loved to a rose.
（這位詩人把他所愛的女人比喻成玫瑰。）

5. narrow down...　　　　　　縮小……範圍（從多個選擇中逐一挑選出）

narrow down sth to...　　縮小某物的範圍到……

例: I will narrow down my choices and pick out the perfect wedding dress.
（我會逐一篩選，挑出最完美的婚紗。）

Jason and his wife narrowed down their choices of baby names to Adam or Sam.
（關於寶寶的名字，傑森和妻子把他們的選擇縮小到亞當或山姆。）

6. get a second opinion　　徵詢他人的意見

7. purchase [ˋpɝtʃəs] *n.* & *vt.* 購買

make a purchase of...　　購買……

例: Sam made a purchase of potato chips and soda at the convenience store.
（山姆在便利商店買了洋芋片和汽水。）

Good Skin, Bad Credit

Index \ Links \ about \ comments \ Photo

June 10

I stopped at a beauty counter in the department store, and this was a huge **mistake**. The saleswoman was very **persuasive**. I **originally** only wanted to get some **toner**, but ended up buying the full **skincare** line. I even agreed to buy **an extra** NT$1,000 worth of **merchandise** just to get a NT$500 **off coupon**. My **shopping spree** nearly <u>**maxed out my credit card**</u>.

About me

Ivy

Calendar

◄   *June*   ►

Sun	Mon	Tue	Wed	Thu	Fri	Sat
1	2	3	4	5	6	7
8	9	10	11	12	13	14
15	16	17	18	19	20	21
22	23	24	25	26	27	28
29	30					

Blog Archive

► June (10)
► May
► April
► March
► February
► January
► December
► November
► October
► September
► August
► July

好肌膚，壞信用

June 10

我在百貨公司的美容專櫃駐足，這真是一大失策。專櫃小姐亂有說服力的。我原本只想買化妝水，結果卻買了一整組護膚系列。我甚至同意加買價值一千元的商品，好得到 500 元的抵用券。我亂買東西的行為讓我差點刷爆信用卡。

About me

Ivy

Calendar

◄　　*June*　　►

Sun	Mon	Tue	Wed	Thu	Fri	Sat
1	2	3	4	5	6	7
8	9	10	11	12	13	14
15	16	17	18	19	20	21
22	23	24	25	26	27	28
29	30					

Blog Archive

► June (10)
► May
► April
► March
► February
► January
► December
► November
► October
► September
► August
► July

Ivy at Blog 於 June 06.10. PM 04:37 發表 | 回覆 (0) | 引用 (0) | 收藏 (0) | 轉寄給朋友 | 檢舉

163

網誌裡的 max out one's credit card 就是指某人血拼過頭，刷爆自己的信用卡。

max [mæks] 是 maximum [ˈmæksəməm] 的縮寫形，表『最大限度、極限』，此處作動詞，與 out 並用，max out 表示『使……達到極限』之意。

max out one's credit card　　（某人）刷爆自己的信用卡
= hit the limit on one's credit card
= charge it to the max
　例: Charlie maxed out his credit card on Christmas sales.
　　（查理在聖誕節特賣時刷爆自己的信用卡。）

至於『付完信用卡帳單』的英文說法則為 pay off one's credit card balance。pay off 有『付清』的意思，而名詞 balance 指的是『欠款』。
　例: Jenny pays off her credit card balance every month.
　　（珍妮每個月都會付清信用卡的帳單。）

1. **credit** [ˈkrɛdɪt] *n.* 信譽；功勞（不可數）
   a credit card　　信用卡
   give sb credit for...　　將……歸功於某人
   　例: I can't get a loan because I have bad credit.
   　　（我無法申請貸款，因為我信用不好。）
   　　＊loan [lon] *n.* 貸款
   　　I have to give my parents credit for putting me through
   　　college.
   　　（我能唸完大學必須歸功於我的父母。）
   　　＊put sb through college　　供某人上大學

2. **mistake** [məˈstek] *n.* 錯誤，過失

3. persuasive [pɚˈswesɪv] *a.* 有說服力的

4. originally [əˈrɪdʒənəlɪ] *a.* 起初，原來

5. toner [ˈtonɚ] *n.* 化妝水，潤膚水

6. skincare [ˈskɪnˌkɛr] *a.* 護膚的
a full skincare line　　齊全的護膚產品系列

7. an extra + 數字　　額外的……（數目）
= an additional + 數字
extra [ˈɛkstrə] *a.* 額外的
additional [əˈdɪʃən̩] *a.* 額外的
例: We need an extra five days to get the project done.
（我們還需要多 5 天才能完成這項專案。）

8. merchandise [ˈmɝtʃənˌdaɪz] *n.* 商品（集合名詞，不可數）
例: I ask for a discount whenever I buy a lot of merchandise.
（每次買很多東西時，我就會要求打折。）

9. 金額 **+ off**　　折抵／少……（金額的）錢
10 / 20 / 30 / 40 / 50...percent off　　打 9 / 8 / 7 / 6 / 5……折
例: Helen got NT$200 off when she bought five T-shirts at
the night market.
（海倫在夜市買了 5 件 T 恤少算兩百元。）
Peter got 30 percent off when he bought this pair of jeans.
（彼得買這條牛仔褲打了 7 折。）

10. coupon [ˈkupɑn] *n.* 優待券

11. shopping spree　　瘋狂購物，拼命買東西
spree [spri] *n.* 作樂，狂歡（尤指花錢、喝酒等）
例: After Mary's shopping spree, she needed help getting all
the boxes into the taxi.
（瑪莉瘋狂購物後，需要別人幫她把所有的包裝盒搬進計程車
裡。）

Unit 42

The Bookworm

Index \ Links \ about \ comments \ Photo

June 11

If I have one **weakness** over all others, it's books. I'm **definitely** a bookworm. I went to **check out** a new bookstore yesterday. They had lots of great new **releases** that I had been waiting to buy. **As soon as** I had chosen a few, a **clerk** told me that if I **applied for** a membership card, I could get 30 percent off that day. I didn't need much more **encouragement** than that to **go wild**.

About me

Ivy

Calendar

◄ June ►

Sun	Mon	Tue	Wed	Thu	Fri	Sat
1	2	3	4	5	6	7
8	9	10	11	12	13	14
15	16	17	18	19	20	21
22	23	24	25	26	27	28
29	30					

Blog Archive

▸ June (11)
▸ May
▸ April
▸ March
▸ February
▸ January
▸ December
▸ November
▸ October
▸ September
▸ August
▸ July

Ivy at Blog 於 June 06.11. PM 07:58 發表 | 回覆 (0) | 引用 (0) | 收藏 (0) | 轉寄給朋友 | 檢舉

166

我是書蟲

Index | Links | about | comments | Photo

June 11

　　若要說我有什麼癖好的話，那一定就是書了。我絕對是個百分之百的書蟲。昨天我跑去一間新開的書店瞧瞧。他們有很多我一直想要買的新書。我選了幾本後，店員告訴我如果辦一張會員卡，我當天就能享有 7 折優惠。光是這一點小甜頭就足以激發我瘋狂買書了。

Calendar

◄　　　June　　　►

Sun	Mon	Tue	Wed	Thu	Fri	Sat
1	2	3	4	5	6	7
8	9	10	11	12	13	14
15	16	17	18	19	20	21
22	23	24	25	26	27	28
29	30					

Blog Archive

▸ June (11)
▸ May
▸ April
▸ March
▸ February
▸ January
▸ December
▸ November
▸ October
▸ September
▸ August
▸ July

Ivy at Blog 於 June 06.11. PM 07:58 發表｜回覆 (0)｜引用 (0)｜收藏 (0)｜轉寄給朋友｜檢舉

購物的失心瘋相信幾乎人人都有過。wild [waɪld] 即表『瘋狂的；狂野的』，網誌中所用的 go wild 便是指『陷入瘋狂的狀態』，也就是『發狂』。其他用 "go + 形容詞" 來表示『陷入瘋狂』的用法如下：

go crazy 　　發瘋，陷入瘋狂

= go nuts

= go bananas

= go insane

* nuts 和 bananas 在此皆作形容詞用，等於 crazy。

* insane [ɪn`sen] *a.* 瘋狂的

例: On seeing all kinds of toys in the store, the kids went wild.

（孩子們一看到店裡各式各樣的玩具，簡直變成脫韁的野馬。）

* 此處句首 "On seeing..." 等於 "As soon as they saw..."。

The fans went crazy when their favorite player hit a home run.

（球迷們看到他們最喜歡的球員擊出全壘打時，都為之瘋狂。）

1. **bookworm** [`buk͵wɝm] *n.* 極愛讀書的人，書蟲

   例: Brook is such a bookworm that he spends most of his time reading novels.

   （布魯克是不折不扣的大書蟲，因此他大多時間都在看小說。）

2. **weakness** [`wiknɪs] *n.* 癖好；弱點（可數）；虛弱（不可數）

   strength [strɛŋθ] *n.* 長處，優勢（可數）；力氣（不可數）

   例: Stella has a weakness for candy; that's why she often has cavities.

   （史黛拉對糖果有癖好，那就是為什麼她老會蛀牙。）

   * cavity [`kævətɪ] *n.* （牙的）蛀洞

   Linda suffered from physical weakness after the surgery.

   （手術過後，琳達備感體力衰弱。）

   * surgery [`sɝdʒərɪ] *n.* 外科手術

One of Berry's strengths is his negotiating ability.
（巴瑞的優勢之一就是他談判的能力。）
＊negotiate [nɪˋgoʃɪˌet] vi. 談判，協商

3. **definitely** [ˋdɛfənɪtlɪ] *adv.* 肯定地，確切地
   例: That red dress will definitely stand out at the party.
   （那件紅色洋裝在派對上絕對會引人注目。）
   ＊stand out　　引人注目，脫穎而出

4. **check out... / check...out**　　看看 / 瞧瞧……
   例: I think you should check that movie out. It was great.
   （我覺得你應該去看看那部電影。超好看的。）

5. **release** [rɪˋlis] *n.* 發行物 & *vt.* 發行
   例: The singer is planning to release her first album next week.
   （這位歌手計劃下週發行第一張專輯。）

6. **As soon as + S + V, S + V**　　一……就……
   例: As soon as the alarm went off, everyone rushed out of the building.
   （警鈴一響，全部的人都衝出了大樓。）
   ＊go off　　（鈴聲、鬧鐘等）響起來

7. **clerk** [klɝk] *n.* 店員

8. **apply for...**　　申請（會員身分、獎學金）；應徵（工作）
   apply for a membership card　　申辦會員卡
   例: Alice plans to apply for that job.
   （艾莉絲打算應徵那份工作。）

9. **encouragement** [ɪnˋkɝdʒmənt] *n.* 激勵，鼓勵
   encourage [ɪnˋkɝdʒ] *vt.* 鼓勵
   encourage sb to V　　鼓勵某人做……
   例: Kevin owes his success to his mother's encouragement.
   （凱文把他的成功歸功於媽媽的鼓勵。）
   ＊owe sth to sb　　將某事歸功於某人
   Amy's friends encouraged her to sign up for the singing contest.
   （艾咪的朋友鼓勵她去報名歌唱比賽。）
   ＊sign up for...　　報名參加……

Unit 43

Market Madness

Index | *Links* | *about* | *comments* | *Photo*

June 12

Eric took me to the night market to buy **matching** T-shirts last night. He **is** really **good at bargaining with** vendors. He knew **exactly** what to say and do to drive the prices down really low. I was **amazed**! I think I'll have to ask him to give me a few **tips** on how he does it.

About me

Ivy

Calendar

◄   June   ►

Sun	Mon	Tue	Wed	Thu	Fri	Sat
1	2	3	4	5	6	7
8	9	10	11	12	13	14
15	16	17	18	19	20	21
22	23	24	25	26	27	28
29	30					

Blog Archive

- ► June (12)
- ► May
- ► April
- ► March
- ► February
- ► January
- ► December
- ► November
- ► October
- ► September
- ► August
- ► July

Ivy at Blog 於 June 06.12. PM 06:45 發表 | 回覆 (0) | 引用 (0) | 收藏 (0) | 轉寄給朋友 | 檢舉

瘋夜市

June 12

　　昨晚艾瑞克帶我到夜市去買情侶T恤。他很會跟攤販討價還價。他知道到底該說和該做什麼才能把價錢殺到超低。我超驚訝的！我想我得叫他教我幾招撇步才行。

About me

Ivy

Calendar

◄　　　*June*　　　►

Sun	Mon	Tue	Wed	Thu	Fri	Sat
1	2	3	4	5	6	7
8	9	10	11	12	13	14
15	16	17	18	19	20	21
22	23	24	25	26	27	28
29	30					

Blog Archive

- ► June (12)
- ► May
- ► April
- ► March
- ► February
- ► January
- ► December
- ► November
- ► October
- ► September
- ► August
- ► July

到夜市不殺價怎麼行？不過殺價功力如何，可就因人而異了。網誌中提到兩種殺價的說法，分別是 bargain with sb（和某人討價還價）以及 drive the prices down（殺價）。

bargain 就是『討價還價』之意，用法如下：

bargain [`bɑrgɪn] *vi.* 討價還價 & *n.* 特價商品；便宜貨

bargain with sb　　和某人討價還價

bargain for a better / lower price　　殺價

drive a hard bargain　　狠狠地殺價

例: My wife bargained with the shop owner for over an hour.

（我太太和店主討價還價了一個多小時。）

Lucy drove a hard bargain when she was buying the used car.

（露西在買那輛二手車時，把價錢砍得很低。）

That shirt might be a bargain, but I would never buy it.

（那件襯衫或許賣得很便宜，但是我絕對不可能買它。）

而 drive the price(s) down 也等於 cut down the price(s)。此外，還可以用 haggle 來表示『殺價、討價還價』：

haggle [`hægl] *vi.* 討價還價（與介詞 over 並用）

haggle over / about the price　　殺價，討價還價

例: Don't bother haggling over the price. This is the lowest I can offer.

（不要費心殺價了。這已經是我能給的最低價格。）

字詞幫幫忙！

1. **madness** [`mædnɪs] *n.* 瘋狂；狂熱

   mad [mæd] *a.* 發狂的；狂熱的

   be mad at...　　對……感到生氣 / 憤怒

   be mad about...　　對……狂熱，瘋狂喜愛……

= 　be crazy about...

例: Emily is mad at me because I forgot her birthday.
（艾蜜莉因為我忘了她的生日而在生我的氣。）

Henry is mad about baseball. He never misses any Yankees games.
（亨利對棒球很狂熱。他從不錯過任何洋基隊的球賽。）

2. **matching** [`mætʃɪŋ] *a.* 相配的

3. **be good at...**　　精通／擅長⋯⋯
be poor at...　　不擅長⋯⋯

例: Arthur is good at making people laugh, so he has lots of friends.
（亞瑟很擅長逗別人笑，所以他有很多朋友。）

Will is poor at communicating with people, and his brother has the same problem.
（威爾不善與人溝通，而他弟弟也有同樣的問題。）

＊communicate [kə`mjunə‚ket] *vi.* 溝通

4. **vendor** [`vɛndɚ] *n.* 攤販

5. **exactly** [ɪg`zæktlɪ] *adv.* 精確地，完全地

6. **amazed** [ə`mezd] *a.*（人）感到驚訝的
amazing [ə`mezɪŋ] *a.*（人或事物）令人驚訝的

例: Tim was amazed to discover that the famous singer was actually his cousin.
（提姆發現那位知名歌手其實是他的表哥時，大吃了一驚。）

It's amazing that an ant can carry objects that are much heavier than itself.
（螞蟻搬得動比自己身體重好幾倍的物體，還真是令人驚奇。）

7. **tip** [tɪp] *n.* 建議；小費
give sb tips on / about sth　　就某事給予某人建議
= give sb advice on / about sth（advice 是不可數名詞）
give sb a tip of + 金錢　　給某人若干元的小費

例: Andrew gave me some useful tips on dating girls.
（安德魯給了我一些和女孩子約會時很管用的建議。）

Jerry gave the waiter a tip of NT$200.
（傑瑞給那位服務生兩百塊台幣的小費。）

What to Buy for Him

Index | Links | about | comments | Photo

June 13

Eric's birthday **is coming up**, and I **have no clue** what to get him. **Whenever** he talks about wanting something, he just buys it for himself. I **looked around** in the men's department at the store today, but no **luck**. The shirts and pants they had all looked like they would **suit** an old man better than my boyfriend. Maybe I should get him a new video game. He plays them **all the time**.

About me

Ivy

Calendar

◄   *June*   ►

Sun	Mon	Tue	Wed	Thu	Fri	Sat
1	2	3	4	5	6	7
8	9	10	11	12	13	14
15	16	17	18	19	20	21
22	23	24	25	26	27	28
29	30					

Blog Archive

- ► June (13)
- ► May
- ► April
- ► March
- ► February
- ► January
- ► December
- ► November
- ► October
- ► September
- ► August
- ► July

Ivy at Blog 於 June 06.13. PM 07:45 發表 | 回覆 (0) | 引用 (0) | 收藏 (0) | 轉寄給朋友 | 檢舉

買禮物真傷腦筋

June 13

　　艾瑞克的生日就快到了，但我根本不知道要買什麼送他。每當他說到想要什麼東西時，他總是自己就先買了。我今天在商店裡的男士部逛來逛去，但毫無收穫。那邊的襯衫和褲子看起來都比較適合年紀大的人穿，而不適合我的男友。或許我應該買個新電動遊戲給他，因為他老是在玩。

Calendar

		June			◄	►
Sun	Mon	Tue	Wed	Thu	Fri	Sat
1	2	3	4	5	6	7
8	9	10	11	12	13	14
15	16	17	18	19	20	21
22	23	24	25	26	27	28
29	30					

Blog Archive

► June (13)
► May
► April
► March
► February
► January
► December
► November
► October
► September
► August
► July

Ivy at Blog 於 June 06.13. PM 07:45 發表｜回覆 (0)｜引用 (0)｜收藏 (0)｜轉寄給朋友｜檢舉

網誌作者因為男友生日快到了，所以想買禮物送他，她所用的 "Eric's birthday is coming up" 中，be coming up 就是用來指某項事件、活動或節日快要到來之意。come up 這個片語本是表『發生、出現』，而 be coming up 就是指『即將到來／來臨』的意思。這個片語不僅簡單又相當實用，當你下次想跟朋友說你的生日快到了，提醒他們買禮物時，be coming up 就派得上用場了！

be coming up　　即將到來，即將來臨

= be drawing near

= be fast approaching

= be near at hand

= be (just) around the corner

　＊approach [ə`protʃ] *vi.* 接近

例: The Dragon Boat Festival is coming up.

= 　The Dragon Boat Festival is drawing near.

　（端午節就要到了。）

　Ashley's graduation ceremony is near at hand.

　（艾希莉的畢業典禮就要到了。）

　＊graduation [ˌgrædʒuˋeʃən] *n.* 畢業

　　the graduation ceremony　　畢業典禮

1. have no clue (as to) + 疑問詞引導的名詞子句／片語

對……毫無頭緒

clue [klu] *n.* 線索；提示

例: Matt has no clue how to take care of a puppy.

（麥特不知道該如何照顧小狗。）

2. Whenever + S + V, S + V　　每當……時，就……

例: Whenever I feel like reading, I go to the bookstore to buy a new book.

= 　Each time I feel like reading, I go to the bookstore to buy a new book.

= Every time I feel like reading, I go to the bookstore to buy a new book.

（每當我想看書時，就會到書店去買本新書回來。）

3. **look around** 到處看看

例: Can you look around and help me find the keys?

（你可以到處看看，幫我找鑰匙嗎？）

4. **luck** [lʌk] *n.* 好運；運氣

be in luck 走運

be out of luck 倒楣

例: Ryan was in luck today; he found NT$300 on the ground.

（萊恩今天真的很走運；他在地上發現了 3 百元。）

The fishermen were out of luck today because they caught no fish.

（這些漁夫今天運氣不佳，因為他們沒捕到魚。）

5. **suit** [sut] *vt.* 適合

suitable [ˋsutəbl̩] *a.* 適合的

suit one's taste 適合某人的品味／口味

be suitable for... 適合於……

例: Jane is quite active, so the job as a secretary doesn't suit her.

（阿珍很活潑，因此這份祕書工作並不適合她。）

＊active [ˋæktɪv] *a.* 活潑的

That music didn't suit my taste at all.

（那種音樂一點也不合我口味。）

Since John is good with his hands, he's suitable for repairing cars.

（約翰手巧，因此很適合修車。）

6. **all the time** 一直，總是

例: Why are you so busy all the time?

= Why are you so busy at all times?

= Why are you always so busy?

（為何你總是如此忙碌？）

A Bad Buy

Index | Links | about | comments | Photo

June 14

Last week we had lots of **down time** at work, so I **surfed the Internet** and shopped online. I found some **accessories** that looked cute and were being sold **at a good price**. They arrived in the **mail** today, and <u>**I couldn't be more disappointed**</u>. They are extremely **cheap-looking** and **are of poor quality**. I guess I **learned my lesson**.

About me

Ivy

Calendar

◄   June   ►

Sun	Mon	Tue	Wed	Thu	Fri	Sat
1	2	3	4	5	6	7
8	9	10	11	12	13	14
15	16	17	18	19	20	21
22	23	24	25	26	27	28
29	30					

Blog Archive

▸ June (14)
▸ May
▸ April
▸ March
▸ February
▸ January
▸ December
▸ November
▸ October
▸ September
▸ August
▸ July

Ivy at Blog 於 June 06.14. PM 01:07 發表 | 回覆 (0) | 引用 (0) | 收藏 (0) | 轉寄給朋友 | 檢舉

真划不來

Index | Links | about | comments | Photo

June 14

　　上星期上班時我們有許多工作空檔，所以我就上網瞧瞧，順便網購。我發現一些看起來很可愛的配件，價格也很優惠。今天它們寄來了，真是讓我失望透頂。它們看起來超級廉價，品質又差。我想我學到教訓了。

About me

Ivy

Calendar

| | | June | | | ◀ | ▶ |
Sun	Mon	Tue	Wed	Thu	Fri	Sat
1	2	3	4	5	6	7
8	9	10	11	12	13	**14**
15	16	17	18	19	20	21
22	23	24	25	26	27	28
29	30					

Blog Archive

- ► June (14)
- ► May
- ► April
- ► March
- ► February
- ► January
- ► December
- ► November
- ► October
- ► September
- ► August
- ► July

Ivy at Blog 於 June 06.14. PM 01:07 發表 | 回覆 (0) | 引用 (0) | 收藏 (0) | 轉寄給朋友 | 檢舉

網誌中的 "I couldn't be more disappointed." 原意為『我無法更失望了。』，引申為『我真是失望透了。』要注意的是，這種句構始終要用過去式助動詞 couldn't，而非 can't，之後再接含有比較級的詞類（如 more 或 less）。

常見的類似用法尚有以下幾句：

I couldn't agree more.　　我同意極了。

"I couldn't agree more." 表我已經同意到了極點，因此我不能比現在更加地同意了，引申為『我同意極了。』；同理，"I couldn't agree with you more." 則原表『我不能更加地同意你了。』引申為『我完全同意你的看法。』

I couldn't care less.　　我一點兒都不在乎。
= I don't care at all.

"I couldn't care less." 直譯為『我不能在乎／在意地更少了。』也就是我已經不在乎到了極點，因此我不能低於比現在更不在乎的程度，引申為『我一點兒都不在乎。』

例: Ted: Jose really enjoys vacationing in Kenting.

　　Ann: I couldn't agree more. It's beautiful there.

　　（泰德：荷西非常喜歡在墾丁渡假。）

　　（小安：我同意極了。那裡真得很漂亮。）

　　＊vacation [ve'keʃən] *vi.* 渡假

　　 Billy: Do you want to eat fish or chicken for dinner?

　　Judy: I couldn't care less. I'm starving.

　　（比利：妳晚餐想吃魚還是雞肉？）

　　（茱蒂：我一點都不在乎。我快餓死了。）

字 詞幫幫忙！

1. a bad buy　　　買得很不划算

　　 a good buy　　　買得很划算

= 　a good deal

= 　a good bargain

　　＊bargain ['bɑrgɪn] *n.* 買賣，交易

例: Alan: This bag only cost me NT$150.

Mary: That's a good bargain.

（艾倫：這個包包只花了我 150 元。）

（瑪莉：那很划算。）

2. down time　　工作間的空檔，停工期

例: Sam is very busy, so he really doesn't have much down time.

（山姆非常忙碌，所以他沒什麼空檔時間。）

3. surf the Internet / Net　　上網瀏覽

surf [sɝf] *vt.* 上（網）& *vi.* 衝浪

例: I surf the Internet to find information to help write my research papers.

（我都會上網搜尋資料寫研究報告。）

Tom goes surfing every weekend during the summer.

（湯姆夏天每個週末都會去衝浪。）

4. accessory [ækˈsɛsərɪ] *n.* 配件（常用複數）

5. at a good price　　以優惠的價格

6. mail [mel] *n.* 郵件（集合名詞，不可數）

in the mail　　在信件中

例: Toby received a package in the mail today.

（托比今天在送來的信件中收到一份包裹。）

7. cheap-looking [ˌtʃipˈlʊkɪŋ] *a.* 看起來很廉價的

8. be of poor quality　　品質很差

be of good quality　　品質很好

例: Jill only buys things that are of good quality.

（吉兒只買品質好的東西。）

9. learn one's lesson　　某人學到教訓

例: David learned his lesson about wearing the seatbelt after he had a terrible accident.

（大衛出了嚴重車禍後，才學到教訓，知道要繫安全帶。）

Pimple Surprise

June 15

I had a date with Eric today, but when I woke up this morning, I found a big red **zit** on my face. It was huge and white, and it hurt a lot. I was **tempted** to **pop** it, but I decided not to. **Instead**, I **applied** some pimple cream on it. Then before I left the house, I **covered** it **up with concealer**.

About me

Ivy

Calendar

◄   *June*   ►

Sun	Mon	Tue	Wed	Thu	Fri	Sat
1	2	3	4	5	6	7
8	9	10	11	12	13	14
15	16	17	18	19	20	21
22	23	24	25	26	27	28
29	30					

Blog Archive

▸ June (15)
▸ May
▸ April
▸ March
▸ February
▸ January
▸ December
▸ November
▸ October
▸ September
▸ August
▸ July

Ivy at Blog 於 June 06.15. PM 01:27 發表 | 回覆 (0) | 引用 (0) | 收藏 (0) | 轉寄給朋友 | 檢舉

痘痘危機

June 15

　　我今天和艾瑞克有約，但當我今早起床時，居然發現臉上長了一顆紅通通的大痘痘。它又大又白，而且超痛的。我超想擠掉它，但後來還是決定不要好了。我在上面塗了一些痘痘藥膏。然後在出門前，我用遮瑕膏遮住痘痘。

About me

Ivy

Calendar

◄　　　*June*　　　►

Sun	Mon	Tue	Wed	Thu	Fri	Sat
1	2	3	4	5	6	7
8	9	10	11	12	13	14
15	16	17	18	19	20	21
22	23	24	25	26	27	28
29	30					

Blog Archive

▸ June (15)
▸ May
▸ April
▸ March
▸ February
▸ January
▸ December
▸ November
▸ October
▸ September
▸ August
▸ July

Ivy at Blog 於 June 06.15. PM 01:27 發表 | 回覆 (0) | 引用 (0) | 收藏 (0) | 轉寄給朋友 | 檢舉

這麼說就對了！

出門約會前突然發現自己臉上長了顆大痘痘，真的會讓人很沮喪。網誌標題所用的 pimple [`pɪmpl ] 和內文中的 zit [ zɪt ] 都是指『青春痘、面皰、粉刺』的意思，另外也可以用 acne [ `æknɪ] 來表達，只是要注意 pimple 和 zit 都是可數名詞，acne 則是不可數名詞，用來指長痘痘這種症狀。

例: This medicine works wonders in treating acne.

（這種藥治療痘痘粉刺非常有效。）

＊work wonders　　產生奇效

若是痘痘真的很礙眼，讓你手癢想擠掉它，這時擠痘痘這個動作該怎麼說呢？除了網誌中所用的 pop [pɑp]，也可以用 squeeze [skwiz]（擠，壓）。不過痘痘還是不要輕易亂擠，以免留下疤痕，最好還是乖乖地像網誌作者一樣，塗上痘痘藥，等痘痘自己消掉吧。

例: Don't squeeze your pimples unless you want scars on your face.

（除非你希望臉上有疤痕，否則不要擠青春痘。）

1. **tempt** [tɛmpt] *vt.* 使很想要（做或說）；引誘

　　be tempted to V　　　想做……；被引誘做……

　　tempt sb to V　　　　引誘某人做……

= 　tempt sb into V-ing

　　例: Terry was tempted to do something stupid which he regretted later.

　　（泰瑞被引誘做了他後來感到很後悔的傻事。）

　　＊regret [rɪ`grɛt] *vi.* 後悔

　　John's friend tempted him to steal his father's money.

　　（阿強的朋友誘使他偷父親的錢。）

2. **instead** [ɪn`stɛd] *adv.* 反而，卻

　　instead of...　　（而）不……

例: As a student, David doesn't study hard. Instead, he plays around all day.

（身為學生，大衛沒有用功讀書。他反而整天到處鬼混。）

＊play around　　鬼混

Instead of taking the elevator, Sam likes to use the stairs.

（山姆喜歡爬樓梯而不搭電梯。）

＊elevator [`ɛləˌvetə] *n.* 電梯

3. **apply** [ə`plaɪ] *vt.* 塗，抹；運用 & *vi.* 適用；申請

　apply A to B　　　　將 A 塗／抹在 B 之上；將 A 運用於 B

　apply to...　　　　　適用於……

　apply for...　　　　 申請……

例: My sister applies makeup to her face every morning before work.

（我姊姊每天上班前都要化粧。）

The new regulations apply to everyone in the office.

（這些新規定適用於辦公室裡的每個人。）

＊regulation [ˌrɛgjə`leʃən] *n.* 規定

Dennis is applying for a teaching job.

（丹尼斯正在申請一份教職。）

4. **cover sth up with...**　　用……遮蓋某物

　be covered with...　　被……覆蓋

例: The ground was covered with snow. So be careful because it might be slippery.

（地上覆滿了雪。所以小心可能會很滑。）

＊slippery [`slɪpərɪ] *a.* 滑的

5. **concealer** [kən`silə] *n.* 遮瑕膏

Hairier than I Should Be

June 16

The weather was hot today, so I wore **a sleeveless top**. However, I had forgotten to **shave** my **armpits**. I did**n't** realize it **until** I **stretched** my arms and Eric **laughed at** me. Luckily, though, he didn't **mention** all the pimples I have had **lately**. But **the moment** I got home, I shaved. I didn't want to forget again!

About me

Ivy

Calendar

◄   *June*   ►

Sun	Mon	Tue	Wed	Thu	Fri	Sat
1	2	3	4	5	6	7
8	9	10	11	12	13	14
15	16	17	18	19	20	21
22	23	24	25	26	27	28
29	30					

Blog Archive

- ► June (16)
- ► May
- ► April
- ► March
- ► February
- ► January
- ► December
- ► November
- ► October
- ► September
- ► August
- ► July

Ivy at Blog 於 June 06.16. PM 08:59 發表 │ 回覆 (0) │ 引用 (0) │ 收藏 (0) │ 轉寄給朋友 │ 檢舉

啊，露毛了

June 16

　　今天的天氣真熱，所以我穿了一件無袖背心。但是我卻忘了刮腋毛。我一開始沒發現，直到我伸展手臂而被艾瑞克笑時我才知道。不過還好他沒有提到我最近臉上長的痘痘。但是我一回到家，就立刻除毛。我不想再忘記這件事了。

Ivy at Blog 於 June 06.16. PM 08:59 發表│回覆 (0)│引用 (0)│收藏 (0)│轉寄給朋友│檢舉

當女生伸展雙臂，腋下卻冒出毛茸茸的腋毛，實在是令人尷尬的一件事。『毛茸茸』的英文就是 hairy [ˋhɛrɪ]。本篇網誌標題的 hairier 是 hairy 的比較級，表『更加毛茸茸的』，也就是指『露出更多的腋毛』。而 hairy 這個形容詞是由名詞 hair（毛髮）衍生而來，以下順便介紹『毛茸茸的』其他說法：

bushy [ˋbuʃɪ] *a.* 茂密的
fuzzy [ˋfʌzɪ] *a.* 有絨毛的

同樣的，bushy 是由名詞 bush [buʃ]（灌木叢）而來，用來形容毛髮像『灌木叢般濃密』，是不是很傳神？而 fuzzy 也是由名詞 fuzz [fʌz]（絨毛）衍生而來。

例: My legs are fuzzy, so I need to shave them twice a month.
（我的腿毛很多，所以我一個月得剃兩次毛。）

1. **a sleeveless top** 無袖上衣
   sleeveless [ˋslivlɪs] *a.* 無袖的
   sleeve [sliv] *n.* 袖子
   top [tɑp] *n.* 上衣

2. **shave** [ʃev] *vt.* 除（毛）；刮（鬍子）；剃（頭）
   例: David shaved off his beard before he had his picture taken.
   （大衛在拍照前先把鬍子刮乾淨。）
   ＊beard [bɪrd] *n.* 鬍子
   Tom likes to have his head shaved in summer.
   （湯姆夏天時喜歡理光頭。）

3. **armpit** [ˋɑrmˏpɪt] *n.* 腋下，腋窩

4. **not...until...** 直到……才……
   例: I won't be able to wear those pants until I lose a few pounds.
   （要等我減去幾磅後，我才穿得下那些褲子。）

5. **stretch** [strɛtʃ] *vt.* 伸展（肢體等）

例: After sitting for a long time, I stood up to stretch my arms and legs.

（久坐之後，我站起來伸展一下四肢。）

6. **laugh at...**　　取笑……，嘲笑……

= make fun of...

例: Just because Ted is poor doesn't mean you can laugh at him.

（就因為泰德窮並不表示你可以嘲笑他。）

7. **mention** [ˈmɛnʃən] *vt.* 提到

not to mention...　　更別提……，更不用說……

例: Don't mention Jackie's big nose—he's very sensitive about it.

（不要提到傑奇的大鼻子——他對這個非常敏感。）

＊sensitive [ˈsɛnsɪtɪv] *a.* 敏感的

Larry dare not kill an ant, not to mention a person.

（賴瑞連螞蟻都不敢殺，更不用說殺人了。）

8. **lately** [ˈletlɪ] *adv.* 最近，近來

= recently [ˈrisəntlɪ] *adv.*

注意:

lately 與 recently 使用時，通常與現在完成式或現在完成進行式並用，但 recently 亦可與過去式並用。

例: The temperature has been dropping recently.

（最近氣溫一直在下降。）

I recently gained a little weight, so I plan to start jogging every morning.

（我最近胖了一點，所以我打算開始每天晨跑。）

9. **The moment + S + V, S + V**　　一……就……

= The instant + S + V, S + V

= As soon as + S +V, S + V

例: The moment she heard the story, Fanny burst out laughing.

（凡妮一聽到這故事便放聲大笑起來。）

＊burst out laughing　　突然大笑

= burst into laughter

Feeling the Pain

Index | Links | about | comments | Photo

June 17

I **got my period** at the office today and found that I didn't have any **supplies**. Luckily, though, Sharon had a sanitary pad I could use. The first day is always the worst because I **get really bad cramps**. So after visiting the ladies' room, I took some medicine and bought myself some chocolate. I didn't feel **guilty** about eating it when I felt so **miserable**.

About me

Ivy

Calendar

◄   *June*   ►

Sun	Mon	Tue	Wed	Thu	Fri	Sat
1	2	3	4	5	6	7
8	9	10	11	12	13	14
15	16	**17**	18	19	20	21
22	23	24	25	26	27	28
29	30					

Blog Archive

► June (17)
► May
► April
► March
► February
► January
► December
► November
► October
► September
► August
► July

Ivy at Blog 於 June 06.17. PM 06:24 發表 | 回覆 (0) | 引用 (0) | 收藏 (0) | 轉寄給朋友 | 檢舉

經痛難耐

June 17

　　今天在辦公室時，我的『好朋友』來了，結果發現我沒有『存貨』。但是還好，雪倫有片衛生棉可以給我用。經期的第一天總是最難受的，因為我會嚴重經痛。在去了一趟女廁後，我吃了一些藥也買了一點巧克力。當我感到痛苦難熬時，吃巧克力就一點也不覺得有罪惡感。

About me

Ivy

Calendar

◄　　　*June*　　　►

Sun	Mon	Tue	Wed	Thu	Fri	Sat
1	2	3	4	5	6	7
8	9	10	11	12	13	14
15	16	**17**	18	19	20	21
22	23	24	25	26	27	28
29	30					

Blog Archive

▸ June (17)
▸ May
▸ April
▸ March
▸ February
▸ January
▸ December
▸ November
▸ October
▸ September
▸ August
▸ July

無論你叫它『好朋友』、『大姨媽』，還是其他名字，生理期是女孩子幾乎大半輩子都得面對的問題。在英文裡，月經來的那個週期便稱為 menstrual period [ˋmɛnstruəl ͵pɪrɪəd]，"I have my menstrual period." 即表示『我生理期來了。』可簡略說成 "I have my period."。以下為各位讀者介紹其他較委婉說法：

It's that time of the month.　　每個月的那個時期又來了。
My "(good) friend" is visiting.　　我的『好朋友』來訪。

那麼當『好朋友』來時，又要用什麼來『招待』呢？以下列舉生理期時，女生會使用到的衛生用品：

sanitary pad [ˋsænətɛrɪ ͵pæd] *n.* 衛生棉
= sanitary napkin [ˋsænətɛrɪ ͵næpkɪn]
　＊sanitary [ˋsænə͵tɛrɪ] *a.* 衛生的；清潔的
　tampon [ˋtæmpɑn] *n.* 衛生棉條

例：Mindy brought some sanitary napkins with her in case her "good friend" came to visit while traveling.
　　（敏蒂帶了一些衛生棉以防她在旅行時『好朋友』來訪。）

相信很多女性都有過經痛之苦，最常碰到的症狀就是子宮劇烈收縮所造成的腹部絞痛。在英文中，這種生理期時的腹部絞痛就用 cramps 來表示。

cramps 表『經痛』時，恆用複數形；而 cramp 亦可表『抽筋、痙攣』，此時則用作可數或不可數名詞均可，因此使用時要特別注意。

cramps [kræmps] *n.* 經痛（恆用複數）
get / have (period) cramps　　感到經痛
例：Laura never has her period without getting cramps.
　　（蘿拉只要月經來就一定會經痛。）
cramp [kræmp] *n.* 抽筋，筋攣（可數或不可數均可）
get / have (a) cramp　　抽筋
例：Ben didn't warm up before jogging, so he got a cramp in his leg.
　　（小班慢跑前沒有暖身，所以他的腳抽筋了。）

1. **supply** [səˈplaɪ] *n.* 供給（品），供應（品）& *vt.* 供給，提供
   supply sb with sth   提供某人某物
= provide sb with sth
   例: The restaurant gets supplies of fresh vegetables and fruit on a weekly basis.
   （這間餐廳每個禮拜都會進新鮮的蔬菜水果。）
   ＊on a weekly basis   每週地
   The charity supplies the victims with shelter and food.
= The charity provides the victims with shelter and food.
   （這個慈善團體提供受災者住所以及食物。）
   ＊shelter [ˈʃɛltɚ] *n.* 可住的地方（集合名詞，不可數）

2. **guilty** [ˈɡɪltɪ] *a.* 內疚的；有罪的
   feel guilty about...   對……感到內疚
   be guilty of...   有……的罪
   be innocent of...   沒犯……的罪
   ＊innocent [ˈɪnəsənt] *a.* 無罪的，無辜的
   例: Linda felt guilty about leaving her kids at home alone.
   （琳達對於把她的小孩獨自留在家中感到十分愧疚。）
   The court ruled that John was guilty of murdering his wife.
   （法院裁決阿強犯下了謀殺妻子的罪行。）
   No one seems to believe that the politician was innocent of bribery.
   （似乎沒有人相信那名政客沒收賄。）
   ＊bribery [ˈbraɪbərɪ] *n.* 賄賂行為（不可數）

3. **miserable** [ˈmɪzərəbḷ] *a.* 痛苦的，悲慘的
   misery [ˈmɪzərɪ] *n.* 痛苦，悲慘
   make one's life a misery   使某人的日子不好過
   例: Jasmine looked miserable after being scolded by her boss.
   （潔思敏被老闆罵過後看起來愁雲慘霧。）
   ＊scold [skold] *vt.* 責罵
   Tom's ex-wife is trying her best to make his life a misery.
   （湯姆的前妻正竭盡全力讓他的日子不好過。）

Eggs to the Rescue

Index \ *Links* \ *about* \ *comments* \ *Photo*

June 18

Sharon told me about a facial **mask** I could make at home. She had read about it in a beauty magazine, but she had never tried it herself. It was an **egg white mixture** and sounded easy to prepare. I think I will try it tonight and see how well it **works**. I don't want to **spend big bucks on fancy treatments** if I don't have to.

About me

Ivy

Calendar

◄   June   ►

Sun	Mon	Tue	Wed	Thu	Fri	Sat
	1	2	3	4	5	6	7
8	9	10	11	12	13	14
15	16	17	**18**	19	20	21
22	23	24	25	26	27	28
29	30					

Blog Archive

- ► June (18)
- ► May
- ► April
- ► March
- ► February
- ► January
- ► December
- ► November
- ► October
- ► September
- ► August
- ► July

Ivy at Blog 於 June 06.18. PM 04:20 發表 | 回覆 (0) | 引用 (0) | 收藏 (0) | 轉寄給朋友 | 檢舉

雞蛋美容大作戰

June 18

　　雪倫告訴我一種面膜，我可以自己在家裡 DIY。她是在一本美容雜誌看到的，不過她自己從沒試過。那是一種蛋白的混合物，聽起來還蠻很容易準備的。我想我今晚會試一試，看看效果有多好。如果非必要的話，我可不想花大把銀子在貴死人的保養療程上。

About me

Ivy

Calendar

◄　　　*June*　　　►

Sun	Mon	Tue	Wed	Thu	Fri	Sat
1	2	3	4	5	6	7
8	9	10	11	12	13	14
15	16	17	**18**	19	20	21
22	23	24	25	26	27	28
29	30					

Blog Archive

‣ June (18)
‣ May
‣ April
‣ March
‣ February
‣ January
‣ December
‣ November
‣ October
‣ September
‣ August
‣ July

Ivy at Blog 於 June 06.18. PM 04:20 發表 | 回覆 (0) | 引用 (0) | 收藏 (0) | 轉寄給朋友 | 檢舉

雖說愛美是女人的天性，不過要是能花小錢就保養有方，誰能不心動呢？畢竟每一分錢都是自己辛辛苦苦掙來的。網誌中主角說不想花大錢在保養療程上，用的就是 spend big bucks on sth。a buck [bʌk] 是『美金一塊錢』的俗稱，等於 a dollar，因此 big bucks 指的就是『大把鈔票、很多錢』之意。以下就列舉相關的常用說法：

spend big bucks on...　　花一大筆錢在……上
= spend a fortune on...
= spend a pretty penny on...
= pay through the nose for...
　　＊fortune [ˋfɔrtʃən] *n.* 財富，巨款
　　例: The wealthy man spent a fortune on the Picasso painting.
　　（那有錢人花了一大筆錢買下那幅畢卡索的畫作。）

　　Alex paid through the nose for this new car in order to impress his new girlfriend.
　　（為了要讓新女友印象深刻，艾力克斯花了一大筆錢買這輛新車。）
　　＊impress [ɪmˋprɛs] *vt.* 使印象深刻

若表示『某物花了某人一大筆錢』又怎麼說呢？

sth cost sb a fortune　　某物花了某人一大筆錢
= sth cost sb an arm and a leg
　　例: The LV bag cost Susan an arm and a leg.
　　（這個 LV 包包花了蘇珊一大筆錢。）

1. **rescue** [ˋrɛskju] *n.* 援救
　　come to one's rescue　　前來援救某人
　　go to one's rescue　　前去援救某人
　　例: The fire fighters came to Gina's rescue and saved her from the burning building.
　　（消防人員前來援救吉娜，把她從失火的大樓中救出來。）
　　＊fire fighter [ˋfaɪr ˏfaɪtə] *n.* 消防人員

2. **mask** [mæsk] *n.* 面具
　　a facial mask　　　　面膜
　　an eye mask　　　　　眼膜

3. **egg white**　　蛋白
　　yolk [jok] *n.* 蛋黃

4. **mixture** [ˈmɪkstʃɚ] *n.* 混合物
　　例: This kind of cocktail is a mixture of orange juice and vodka.
　　（這種雞尾酒是柳橙汁和伏特加混合調成的。）
　　＊cocktail [ˈkɑkˌtel] *n.* 雞尾酒

5. **work** [wɝk] *vi.* 起作用
　　例: That fruit diet really worked. I lost three kilograms in a week.
　　（那種水果減肥餐真的很有效。我一個星期就減了 3 公斤。）
　　＊diet [ˈdaɪət] *n.* （為了治療或健康因素而做的）規定飲食
　　kilogram [ˈkɪləˌgræm] *n.* 公斤（常簡寫成 kilo [ˈkilo]）

6. **fancy** [ˈfænsɪ] *a.* 昂貴的，豪華的
　　a fancy hotel　　　　高級飯店
　　a fancy restaurant　　高級餐廳
　　a fancy car　　　　　豪華汽車
　　例: Every now and then, Robert likes to enjoy a meal at a fancy restaurant.
　　（羅伯特有時喜歡到高級餐廳享受一頓大餐。）
　　＊every now and then　　偶爾，有時候

7. **treatment** [ˈtritmənt] *n.* 治療；對待
　　the red-carpet treatment　　貴賓式的對待
　　＊carpet [ˈkɑrpɪt] *n.* 地毯
　　例: Kevin's family decided to transfer him to a big hospital for better treatment.
　　（凱文的家人決定將他轉到大醫院以獲得較好的治療。）
　　＊transfer [trænˈsfɝ] *vt.* 轉換，調動
　　The five-star hotel promises that all of their customers will get the red-carpet treatment.
　　（那家五星級飯店承諾他們的每位顧客都會受到貴賓式的對待。）

Terrible Results

June 19

I tried the egg white facial mask just as I planned last night. I left it on all night long, which was a huge mistake. This morning, my skin **itched** and was all red. The feeling **got worse and worse** until finally I **couldn't take it anymore**. I went to see the doctor, and he said I had an **allergic reaction** to the egg whites. He gave me some **ointment** and told me not to put anything else on my face for a week.

About me

Ivy

Calendar

◄   June   ►

Sun	Mon	Tue	Wed	Thu	Fri	Sat
1	2	3	4	5	6	7
8	9	10	11	12	13	14
15	16	17	18	**19**	20	21
22	23	24	25	26	27	28
29	30					

Blog Archive

- ► June (19)
- ► May
- ► April
- ► March
- ► February
- ► January
- ► December
- ► November
- ► October
- ► September
- ► August
- ► July

慘烈下場

June 19

我昨晚照計劃試了用蛋白面膜來敷臉。我敷了一整個晚上，這簡直是大錯特錯。今早我的皮膚癢得要命而且還發紅。這感覺愈來愈糟糕，直到我再也受不了。我去看了醫生，他說我對蛋白產生過敏反應。他開了一些藥膏給我，並告訴我一整個星期臉上都不要敷任何其他東西。

About me

Ivy

Calendar

◄ *June* ►

Sun	Mon	Tue	Wed	Thu	Fri	Sat
1	2	3	4	5	6	7
8	9	10	11	12	13	14
15	16	17	18	19	20	21
22	23	24	25	26	27	28
29	30					

Blog Archive

► June (19)
► May
► April
► March
► February
► January
► December
► November
► October
► September
► August
► July

Ivy at Blog 於 June 06.19. PM 02:27 發表│回覆 (0)│引用 (0)│收藏 (0)│轉寄給朋友│檢舉

網誌作者的皮膚不但發癢還發紅，直到她再也受不了，而『再也受不了』的英文說法即為 can't take it anymore。英文中有許多表達『再也受不了』的用法，列舉如下：

can't take sth (anymore) 　（再也）受不了……，無法（再）忍受……

= can't stand sth (anymore)
= can't bear sth (anymore)
= can't handle sth (anymore)
= can't put up with sth (anymore)
　＊handle [`hændl] *vt.* 應付，處理
　例: The weather in Taipei is so hot that Danny just can't put up with it anymore.
　　（台北的天氣熱到丹尼再也受不了了。）

上述是『忍受不了』的說法，以下再介紹『受夠了』的用法：

have had enough of... 　受夠了……

= be fed up with...
= be sick and tired of...
　例: I've really had enough of John's bad temper.
　　（我真是受夠了約翰的壞脾氣。）

　　＊temper [`tɛmpɚ] *n.* 脾氣

1. **itch** [ɪtʃ] *vi.* 發癢 & *n.* 癢；強烈渴望
　itch 作名詞表『強烈渴望』，有下列重要用法：
　have an itch for... 　強烈渴望得到……
= 　have a strong / burning desire for...
　have an itch to V 　強烈渴望做……
= 　have a strong / burning desire to V
　　例: These two brothers have an itch for adventure.
　　　（這兩兄弟極度渴望探險。）

Having been a teacher for five years, Joe now has an itch to change his job.
（喬伊當了 5 年的老師，他現在非常想要換工作。）

2. **get worse and worse** 　　變得愈來愈糟
   go from bad to worse　　每況愈下

   例: Debby's cough got worse and worse when the weather became colder.
   （當天氣變得愈發寒冷，黛比的咳嗽也愈來愈嚴重。）

   Due to his injury, the baseball player's performance went from bad to worse.
   （那名棒球選手的表現因傷而每況愈下。）

3. **allergic** [əˈlɝdʒɪk] a. 過敏的
   allergy [ˈælədʒɪ] n. 過敏性反應，過敏症
   be allergic to... 　　對……過敏

   = have an allergy to...

   例: My little sister is allergic to pollen.
   = My little sister has an allergy to pollen.
   （我的小妹對花粉過敏。）
   ＊pollen [ˈpɑlən] n. 花粉

4. **reaction** [rɪˈækʃən] n. （對……的）不良反應；反應（與介詞 to 並用）

   例: Jane had a bad reaction to the seafood she ate last night.
   （小珍對她昨晚吃的海鮮產生不良反應。）

   Terry's reaction to the gossip was that he was unexpectedly angry.
   （泰瑞對於這個八卦的反應出乎意料的憤怒。）
   ＊unexpectedly [ˌʌnɪkˈspɛktɪdlɪ] adv. 意想不到地

5. **ointment** [ˈɔɪntmənt] n. 藥膏；軟膏（物質名詞，不可數，以 tube 作單位名詞）
   a tube of ointment 　　一條藥膏（非 an ointment）
   ＊tube [tjub] n. （金屬、玻璃、塑膠等的）管

Unit 51

Beach Ready

June 20

I went to the **beauty salon** today to get a bikini **wax**. Eric is taking me to the beach tomorrow. The waxing **process** was very uncomfortable, and it hurt when the **strips** were **ripped off**. However, I **would rather** experience a little pain **than embarrass** myself in my bikini. I need to **pack up** my beach **gear** tonight so I won't forget anything, especially my **sunscreen**. I don't want to **become a lobster** tomorrow.

About me

Ivy

Calendar

◄   *June*   ►

Sun	Mon	Tue	Wed	Thu	Fri	Sat
1	2	3	4	5	6	7
8	9	10	11	12	13	14
15	16	17	18	19	20	21
22	23	24	25	26	27	28
29	30					

Blog Archive

▸ June (20)
▸ May
▸ April
▸ March
▸ February
▸ January
▸ December
▸ November
▸ October
▸ September
▸ August
▸ July

做好準備去海灘

Index | Links | about | comments | Photo

June 20

　　我今天去了美容院做比基尼蜜蠟除毛。艾瑞克明天要帶我去海邊。蜜蠟除毛的過程很不舒服，而且當蜜蠟片被撕下來時，簡直痛死我了。不過我寧願經驗這麼一點痛苦，也不要讓自己穿著比基尼時出糗。今天晚上我得打包好去海邊的東西，以免忘了任何東西，尤其是防曬油一定要帶。我可不想明天把自己曬得跟龍蝦一樣紅通通的。

About me

Ivy

Calendar

◄　　　*June*　　　►

Sun	Mon	Tue	Wed	Thu	Fri	Sat
1	2	3	4	5	6	7
8	9	10	11	12	13	14
15	16	17	18	19	20	21
22	23	24	25	26	27	28
29	30					

Blog Archive

► June (20)
► May
► April
► March
► February
► January
► December
► November
► October
► September
► August
► July

Ivy at Blog 於 June 06.20. PM 09:45 發表｜回覆 (0)｜引用 (0)｜收藏 (0)｜轉寄給朋友｜檢舉

夏天是去海邊玩玩水、曬曬太陽的最佳時節，不過要是防曬措施沒做好，而讓自己像網誌中所說的 become a lobster [`labstɚ]（曬得跟龍蝦一樣紅通通的），可就得不償失了。除了像這種比較俏皮的說法，英文中表示曬傷或是曬到脫皮、起水泡的說法如下：

get sunburned 曬傷
= have a sunburn
get a sunburn that causes one's skin to peel 曬到脫皮
get sunburned and end up with blisters 曬傷到變成起水泡
＊sunburned [`sʌn,bɝnd] *a.* 曬傷的
sunburn [`sʌn,bɝn] *n.* 曬傷
peel [pil] *vi.* 脫皮
blister [`blɪstɚ] *n.*（皮膚上的）水泡

例: Darren went to the beach to get some sun and ended up getting sunburned.
（戴倫去海邊曬一下太陽，結果曬傷了。）

Dora got a sunburn that caused her skin to peel. She had to stay out of the sun as much as possible for a week.
（朵拉曬到脫皮。她一週內都必須盡量避開陽光。）

1. beauty salon 美容院
= salon [sə`lɑn] *n.*

2. wax [wæks] *n.* 蠟 & *vt.* 打蠟
get a bikini wax 為了穿比基尼而做的蜜蠟除毛
例: John's car needs to be washed and waxed.
（阿強的車需要清洗打蠟。）

3. process [`prɑsɛs] *n.* 過程
be in the process of... 在……的過程中
例: Annie is in the process of moving to a new place.
（安妮正在搬新家。）

4. **strip** [strɪp] *n.* 條，帶；（布、板等）細長片（此處指『蜜蠟片』）

5. **rip off sth / rip sth off**　　撕下某物

比較:

rip off sb / rip sb off　　向某人敲竹槓

例: Remember to rip off the price tag on the new jacket before you wear it.

（穿新夾克前，記得先把上面的價格標籤撕掉。）

The vendor tried to rip us off by selling the ring at a ridiculous price.

（那攤販想用令人咋舌的高價賣我們那只戒指，好敲我們竹槓。）

＊ridiculous [rɪˋdɪkjələs] *a.* 荒繆的

6. **would rather + 原形動詞 + than + 原形動詞**　　寧願……而不願……

例: Roy would rather stay at home than go to the movies with his sisters.

（羅伊寧願待在家也不願和他的姐姐們去看電影。）

7. **embarrass** [ɪmˋbærəs] *vt.* 使困窘，使難為情

例: Angela's father embarrassed her in front of her friends by treating her like a little girl.

（安琪拉的爸爸在她朋友面前把她當小女孩一樣對待，令她很難為情。）

8. **pack up... / pack...up**　　將……打包好

例: Sam is busy packing up everything for the trip.

（山姆忙著為旅行打包行李。）

9. **gear** [gɪr] *n.* （特殊用途的）衣服；設備（集合名詞，均不可數）；齒輪（可數）

10. **sunscreen** [ˋsʌnˌskrin] *n.* 防曬油，防曬乳液

= sunblock [ˋsʌnˌblɑk] *n.*

= suntan lotion [ˋsʌntæn ˌloʃən] *n.*

＊suntan [ˋsʌntæn] *n.* 曬黑

例: Don't forget to wear your sunscreen before you go to the beach.

（去海邊前別忘了擦防曬油。）

The All New Beach Babe

Index | *Links* | *about* | *comments* | *Photo*

June 21

Eric **took pictures of** me at the beach, and I was surprised by how good I looked in them. I was actually a beach babe! I got a lot of sun today, though. I don't **mind** having a **slight tan**, but I don't like becoming very dark. I'll need to avoid the sunshine for a while until my tan **fades**. I might also **pick up** some **skin-whitening** products later.

About me

Ivy

Calendar

◄ June ►

Sun	Mon	Tue	Wed	Thu	Fri	Sat
1	2	3	4	5	6	7
8	9	10	11	12	13	14
15	16	17	18	19	20	21
22	23	24	25	26	27	28
29	30					

Blog Archive

- ► June (21)
- ► May
- ► April
- ► March
- ► February
- ► January
- ► December
- ► November
- ► October
- ► September
- ► August
- ► July

Ivy at Blog 於 June 06.21. PM 10:04 發表 | 回覆 (0) | 引用 (0) | 收藏 (0) | 轉寄給朋友 | 檢舉

海灘辣妹來也

June 21

艾瑞克幫我在海灘上照相,我很驚訝我在照片上看起來超正的,看起來根本是個海灘辣妹。不過我今天曬了不少太陽。我不介意有點小麥膚色,但我不想看起來像黑炭一樣。我需要遠離陽光一陣子,直到我的小麥膚色褪掉再說。之後我或許也會買一些美白產品來用。

About me

Ivy

Calendar

◄ June ►

Sun	Mon	Tue	Wed	Thu	Fri	Sat
1	2	3	4	5	6	7
8	9	10	11	12	13	14
15	16	17	18	19	20	21
22	23	24	25	26	27	28
29	30					

Blog Archive

► June (21)
► May
► April
► March
► February
► January
► December
► November
► October
► September
► August
► July

Ivy at Blog 於 June 06.21. PM 10:04 發表 | 回覆 (0) | 引用 (0) | 收藏 (0) | 轉寄給朋友 | 檢舉

由於數位相機的普及化，以及多數手機都有照相功能，現在隨時要拍張照片已經不是什麼難事了。倘若你出門在外，想拍下某人或某樣東西的照片，以做為日後的回憶時，這句英文該怎麼說呢？首先，照片的英文可以用 picture [ˈpɪktʃɚ] 或 photo [ˈfoto]（為 photograph [ˈfotoˌgræf] 的縮寫），表『拍下某人或某物的照片』，則是 take a picture / photo of sb / sth。

例: James took a lot of pictures / photos of his son at the birthday party.

（詹姆士在生日派對上拍下很多他兒子的照片。）

至於當你隻身在外旅行，想請人幫你拍照時，就可以說 "Could / Can you take a picture / photo of me?"（可以幫我拍張照嗎？）

例: Miss, could you take a picture of us from this angle?

（小姐，能不能請妳從這個角度幫我們照一張相？）

＊angle [ˈæŋgl̩] n. 角度

還有，拍了照片，大家都喜歡對裡面出現的人物品頭論足一番，這時如果要說某人很上相的話，就可以用 photogenic [ˌfotəˈdʒɛnɪk] 這個字來形容。不過上不上相其實跟本人的美醜是無關的，所以沒被別人稱讚 photogenic 也不需要太過傷心。

例: Jill is not a beautiful girl, but she is photogenic. She always looks good in photos.

（吉兒不是美女，但她很上相。她在照片中看起來總是很漂亮。）

1. babe [beb] n. 漂亮的年輕女子

a beach babe　海灘辣妹

2. mind [maɪnd] vt. 介意

mind + V-ing　介意做……

Would you mind + if 引導的過去式子句?　你介不介意……？

= Do you mind + if 引導的現在式子句?

例: Sally doesn't mind working overtime.
（莎莉不介意加班。）

Would you mind if I stopped by your house this evening?

= Do you mind if I stop by your house this evening?
（你介不介意我今晚順路到你家坐一坐？）

3. **slight** [slaɪt] *a.* 輕微的

例: David had a slight headache when he woke up this morning.
（大衛今早起床時感到有點頭痛。）

＊headache [ˈhɛdˌek] *n.* 頭痛

4. **tan** [tæn] *n.* （被太陽曬的）棕色膚色
= suntan [ˈsʌntæn] *n.*
get a tan　　（把皮膚）曬成棕色
= get suntanned

＊suntanned [ˈsʌntænd] *a.* 曬黑的

例: Frank got a nice tan, which makes him look healthier than before.
（法蘭克把皮膚曬成漂亮的棕色，這讓他看起來比以前更健康。）

Nancy didn't want to get suntanned, so she sat under an umbrella at the beach.
（南西不想要曬黑，所以在海邊時她坐在傘下。）

5. **fade** [fed] *vi.* 褪色

例: The T-shirt has faded to a light yellow.
（這件 T 恤褪成淡黃色了。）

6. **pick up sth / pick sth up**　　購買某物；拾起某物

例: Could you please pick up a newspaper for me on your way home?
（你可以在回家的路上幫我買份報紙嗎？）

Bill picked up the garbage and threw it into the garbage can.
（比爾把垃圾撿起來，丟到垃圾桶裡。）

7. **skin-whitening** [ˈskɪnˌwaɪtnɪŋ] *a.* 美白皮膚的

Unit 53

Picking Up the Slack

Index | Links | about | comments | Photo

June 22

We've been **working on** a huge project at company. It's very **complicated** and **time-consuming**. This morning, I got a shock at the office. I was **informed** that the project leader had suddenly quit without **notice**. Therefore, they **put me in charge of** it. Plus, I was told I had to pick up the slack because we'd be **short-handed** for the next few weeks until they hire someone new.

Calendar

◄   *June*   ►

Sun	Mon	Tue	Wed	Thu	Fri	Sat
1	2	3	4	5	6	7
8	9	10	11	12	13	14
15	16	17	18	19	20	21
22	23	24	25	26	27	28
29	30					

Blog Archive

- ► June (22)
- ► May
- ► April
- ► March
- ► February
- ► January
- ► December
- ► November
- ► October
- ► September
- ► August
- ► July

Ivy at Blog 於 June 06.22. PM 01:52 發表 | 回覆 (0) | 引用 (0) | 收藏 (0) | 轉寄給朋友 | 檢舉

June 22

　　我們公司一直在進行一個大案子。這案子既複雜又費時。今天早上我在辦公室裡大吃一驚。我被告知專案負責人突然無預警辭職了。所以他們要我負責這個案子。此外，我被告知必須接下這個燙手山芋，因為我們接下來的幾個星期會人手不足，直到他們找到新人為止。

Ivy at Blog 於 June 06.22. PM 01:52 發表｜回覆 (0)｜引用 (0)｜收藏 (0)｜轉寄給朋友｜檢舉

標題中的slack [slæk] 作名詞用，表『（繩子）鬆弛的部分』，因此 pick up the slack 字面上的意思是『拉緊繩子鬆脫的部分』，引申為『接下別人留下或不願意做的工作』，也可說成 take up the slack。

例: We counted on Sandy to pick up the slack after Lucy quit.
（露西辭職後，我們有賴珊蒂來接替她留下的工作。）

此外，slack 尚可作形容詞，表『鬆懈的』，a slack worker 指『工作時打混的人』；亦可引申為『經濟不熱絡的』，a slack season 即指生意的『淡季』。slack 亦可作動詞用，表『鬆懈』，slack off 即指『懈怠、摸魚打混』。

例: Nick is so responsible that he never slacks off at work.
（尼克非常負責，他上班時從不會摸魚打混。）

1. **work on...**　　致力於……；著手……
   例: Cathy and her classmates worked on the report for three weeks.
   （凱西和同學花了 3 個星期做這份報告。）

2. **complicated** [ˋkɑmpləˌketɪd] *a.* 複雜的
   complicate [ˋkɑmpləˌket] *vt.* 使複雜
   例: Sam solved the complicated math problem with ease.
   （山姆輕鬆地解出這道複雜的數學題。）
   Cindy's interference has complicated the situation.
   （辛蒂的干預使情況變得複雜。）
   *interference [ˌɪntɚˋfɪrəns] *n.* 干預

3. **time-consuming** [ˋtaɪmkənˌsumɪŋ] *a.* 費時的
   consume [kənˋsum] *vt.* 消耗
   例: Writing a book is really a time-consuming job.
   （寫書的確是件耗時的工作。）

That car consumes a lot more fuel than this one.

（那輛車比這輛耗油。）

＊fuel [`fjuəl] *n.* 燃料

4. **inform** [ɪn`fɔrm] *vt.* 通知，告知

inform sb of sth　　通知 / 告知某人某事

例: Our manager informed us of the new regulations during the meeting.

（經理在會議中告知我們新的規定。）

＊regulation [ˌrɛgjə`leʃən] *n.* 規定

5. **notice** [`notɪs] *n.* 事先通知

quit without notice　　辭職前未事先通知

ten days' / three weeks' / two months' / ...notice

10 天 / 3 星期 / 2 個月 /……的預告通知

例: Ted quit without notice, leaving a pile of work for his former co-workers to finish.

（泰德無預警辭職，留下一堆工作給以前的同事去完成。）

＊a pile of...　　一堆的……

According to the regulations, I have to give a week's notice before I take three days of personal leave.

（根據規定，我若要請 3 天事假，必須在一個星期前告知。）

6. **put sb in charge of...**　　讓某人負責……

be in charge of...　　負責掌管……

be in charge　　負責

例: Ruth is in charge of the class play.

（露絲負責籌劃這次班上的戲劇演出。）

Richard will be in charge here while I'm in Singapore for business.

（我在新加坡洽商時，這裡由李察負責。）

7. **short-handed** [ˌʃɔrt`hændɪd] *a.* 人手不足的

例: The company laid off 20 workers, so right now we are short-handed.

（公司解雇了 20 名員工，所以現在我們人手不足。）

＊lay off sb　　解雇某人

Albert the Idiot

Index \ *Links* \ *about* \ *comments* \ *Photo*

June 23

Not only do I have to deal with the project at work, **but** my **supervisor**, Albert, is **being a pain in the neck**. He keeps taking time off work, either leaving early or coming in late. Whenever he's gone, he asks me to finish up his work for him or to **double-check** things. Even when he is in the office, it seems that he isn't doing anything **other than** spending all his time **sucking up to** the boss.

About me

Ivy

Calendar

◄   *June*   ►

Sun	Mon	Tue	Wed	Thu	Fri	Sat
1	2	3	4	5	6	7
8	9	10	11	12	13	14
15	16	17	18	19	20	21
22	23	24	25	26	27	28
29	30					

Blog Archive

- ▸ June (23)
- ▸ May
- ▸ April
- ▸ March
- ▸ February
- ▸ January
- ▸ December
- ▸ November
- ▸ October
- ▸ September
- ▸ August
- ▸ July

呆伯特

June 23

　　上班時我不但得處理專案，還得應付我那討人厭的的上司艾伯特。他老是請假，不是早退就是遲到。每次只要他人一不在，就會叫我替他完成他的工作，或是幫他再確認一些東西。就算他人在辦公室，除了花時間拍老闆馬屁，也沒看到他在幹什麼。

About me

Ivy

Calendar

◀ June ▶

Sun	Mon	Tue	Wed	Thu	Fri	Sat
1	2	3	4	5	6	7
8	9	10	11	12	13	14
15	16	17	18	19	20	21
22	23	24	25	26	27	28
29	30					

Blog Archive

▸ June (23)
▸ May
▸ April
▸ March
▸ February
▸ January
▸ December
▸ November
▸ October
▸ September
▸ August
▸ July

工作上的不愉快十之八九，而其中往往與同事或上司有關。碰到沒實力、卻很懂得如何阿諛奉承的同事或上司是令人最嘔的事了。網誌中所說的 suck up to sb 就是表『拍某人馬屁』。suck [sʌk] 原指『吸、吮』，也可作不及物動詞，表『糟糕、很爛』，用法如下：

例: The concert I went to last night really sucked.
（我昨天晚上去聽的那場演唱會爛透了。）

而 suck up to sb 是相當口語的用法，但稍嫌粗俗，使用時務必要注意場合和對象。以下列舉其他關於『拍馬屁』的說法：

suck up to sb　　拍某人馬屁
= kiss up to sb
= brown-nose [ˋbraʊnˌnoz] vt.（此用法源自某人將臉貼在另一個人的屁股上，而鼻子沾到了糞便，使鼻子染上褐色，藉此用來比喻『阿諛奉承』之意）
= apple-polish [ˋæpḷˌpalɪʃ] vt.（其典故來自於過去美國的小學生，喜歡將擦得鮮亮的蘋果送給老師，以博取好感）
　　＊polish [ˋpalɪʃ] vt. 擦亮；磨光
　　例: As a salesman, Willy has to kiss up to his customers all the time.
　　（身為推銷員，威利必須常常拍他客戶的馬屁。）

此外，若要表『拍馬屁的人』，也就是『馬屁精』，可以運用上列的動詞轉為名詞：

suck-up [ˋsʌkˌʌp] n. 馬屁精，奉承者
= brown-nose / brown noser [ˋbraʊn ˌnozɚ] n.
= apple polisher [ˋæpḷ ˌpalɪʃɚ] n.
= flatterer [ˋflætərɚ] n.
　　例: Bernard Is such an apple polisher that he only says things the boss wants to hear.
　　（伯納真是個馬屁精，他只會說老闆喜歡聽的話。）

1. idiot [ˋɪdɪət] n. 笨蛋，蠢材，白癡

2. not only...but (also)... 不僅……而且……

= not only...but...as well

注意:

"not only...but (also)..."為對等連接詞片語，可連接對等的單字、片語或子句；若連接對等的主要子句時，not only 後的第一個主要子句要倒裝。but also 僅為連接詞，故其後的第二個主要子句不須倒裝，但連接子句時，also 往往予以省略。

例: Gary is not only a doctor but (also) a writer.

= Gary is not only a doctor but a writer as well.

（蓋瑞不僅是位醫生，而且還是位作家。）

Not only did the company lose millions of dollars, but it might have to close down (as well).

（那家公司不但損失了數百萬元，還有可能會倒閉。）

3. supervisor [ˋsupɚˏvaɪzɚ] *n.* 上司；監督人

supervise [ˋsupɚˏvaɪz] *vt.* 監督；管理

例: Mr. Wang is in charge of supervising the customer service department.

（王先生負責督導客服部門。）

＊be in charge of... 負責……

4. be a pain in the neck 令人討厭的人 / 事物

5. double-check [ˏdʌblˋtʃɛk] *vt.* 複查，複核

例: Double-check your report before you hand it in.

（交報告前要先複查過一遍。）

6. other than... 除了……以外

= except (for)...

例: Everyone other than Tina agreed to this proposal.

（除了蒂娜以外，所有人都同意這項提議。）

Kyle doesn't watch any channels except for ESPN.

（凱爾除了 ESPN 運動台，其他的頻道他都不看。）

The Office Airhead

June 24

Teresa, the girl who sits next to me, is a real **airhead**. Although she has worked here for over a year, she **repeatedly** asks me the same questions about her job. Plus, she has terrible time **management** skills. She never meets the **deadlines** because she **fools around** all day long. If she's not **texting** her friends, she's **trimming** her **split ends**.

About me

Ivy

Calendar

◄   June   ►

Sun	Mon	Tue	Wed	Thu	Fri	Sat
1	2	3	4	5	6	7
8	9	10	11	12	13	14
15	16	17	18	19	20	21
22	23	24	25	26	27	28
29	30					

Blog Archive

▸ June (24)
▸ May
▸ April
▸ March
▸ February
▸ January
▸ December
▸ November
▸ October
▸ September
▸ August
▸ July

Ivy at Dlog 於 June 06.24. PM 03:15 發表 | 回覆 (0) | 引用 (0) | 收藏 (0) | 轉寄給朋友 | 檢舉

辦公室裡的花瓶

June 24

泰瑞莎是坐在我隔壁的女孩，她真是個無敵大草包。雖然她在這兒工作已經超過一年了，但還是一直問我關於工作上同樣的問題。而且，她的時間管理技巧糟透了。因為她整天打混，所以從沒趕上期限做完事情。她若不是在傳簡訊給朋友，就是在修頭髮分岔。

這麼說就對了！

辦公室裡常會出現閒閒沒事做的花瓶員工，看在上司眼裡可能還覺得至少賞心悅目，不過其他員工可就不見得這麼認為了。網誌裡的泰瑞莎就是不折不扣的『花瓶』，整天晃來晃去不說，還在工作時間傳簡訊、修頭髮分叉，真是讓人氣在心裡口難開。要是你想和朋友抱怨這種整天只會『閒晃』不做正事的人，該怎麼用英文表達呢？常見的說法有以下幾種：

fool around　　遊手好閒，鬼混
= play around
= idle around
= horse around
= goof around
= loaf around

　*idle [`aɪd!] *vi.* 無所事事

　goof [guf] *vi.* 遊手好閒，閒蕩

　loaf [lof] *vi.* 閒晃，混日子

例: The manager warned Carl to stop idling around or he would fire him.
（經理警告卡爾別再打混，不然就把他開除。）

Dan goofs around all day with no concern for the future.
（阿丹整天遊手好閒，一點也不關心自己的前途。）

　*concern [kən`sɜn] *n.* 關心

1. **airhead** [`ɛr,hɛd] *n.* 腦袋空空的傻瓜

   例: Jennifer is such an airhead. She cares about nothing but her fake fingernails.
   （珍妮佛真是個花瓶。她只關心她的假指甲。）
   　*fingernail [`fɪŋɚ,nel] *n.* 手指甲

2. **repeatedly** [rɪ`pitɪdlɪ] *adv.* 一再地，反覆地

   例: The teacher repeatedly asked John to be quiet.
   （老師再三要求約翰安靜下來。）

3. management [ˈmænɪdʒmənt] *n.* 管理；經營

time management　　時間管理

例: Jerry signed up for a class that helps improve people's time management skills.
（傑瑞報名了一堂幫人增進時間管理技巧的課程。）
＊sign up for...　　報名參加……（課程）
The management of the factory is a tough job, but Roy makes it seem easy.
（管理這家工廠是個艱難的工作，但羅伊讓它變得似乎很簡單。）
＊tough [tʌf] *a.* 艱難的

4. deadline [ˈdɛdˌlaɪn] *n.* 最後期限，截止期限

meet the deadline　　趕上最後的期限

例: Rachel met the deadline for her work even though she had taken a vacation.
（雖然芮秋渡了個假，她還是趕上期限完成她的工作。）

5. text [tɛkst] *vt.* 傳簡訊給（某人）& *n.* 文字

a text message　　簡訊

例: Ella is in a good mood because she just received a text message from her boyfriend.
（艾拉心情很好，因為她剛接到男友的簡訊。）

6. trim [trɪm] *vt.* 修剪，修整

例: Roger asked the barber to trim his hair before the wedding.
（羅傑在婚禮前請理髮師幫他修剪頭髮。）
＊barber [ˈbɑrbɚ] *n.* 理髮師

7. split ends [ˈsplɪt ˌɛndz] *n.*（頭髮）分叉（恆用複數）

split [splɪt] *n.* 分裂；裂縫 *vt.* & *vi.*（使）分開，（使）破裂
＊split 三態同形，均為 split。
split up with sb　　與某人分手
= break up with sb

例: Kevin split the watermelon in half with a knife.
（凱文用刀子將西瓜切成兩半。）
Debra split up with her boyfriend because she caught him cheating on her.
（黛博拉抓到她男友劈腿，所以和他分手。）
＊cheat on sb　　（感情上）對某人不忠

More Money for Doing Nothing

Index | Links | about | comments | Photo

June 25

I was talking to a girl in **the accounting department** today, and I **accidentally** saw Teresa's salary **statement**. <u>**My eyes nearly popped out of my head**</u> when I found that she made more money than I did. I'm beginning to wonder why I even **bother** to work so hard when no one seems to **appreciate** anything I do. Maybe I should **follow Teresa's example** and spend my days **filing** my nails instead.

閒閒沒事賺更多

June 25

　　我今天和會計部的一個小姐在說話，意外地看到泰瑞莎的薪資明細表。當我發現她賺得比我多時，我驚訝到眼珠差點要掉出來。我開始想自己何必這麼費心努力工作，反正好像沒有人感激我做的任何事。或許我應該效法泰瑞莎，整天花時間修指甲就好了。

About me

Ivy

Calendar

◀　　*June*　　▶

Sun	Mon	Tue	Wed	Thu	Fri	Sat
1	2	3	4	5	6	7
8	9	10	11	12	13	14
15	16	17	18	19	20	21
22	23	24	25	26	27	28
29	30					

Blog Archive

► June (25)
► May
► April
► March
► February
► January
► December
► November
► October
► September
► August
► July

當碰到出乎意料的事而感到驚訝時，除了用 "I'm so surprised."（我很驚訝。）之外，有沒有更生動的說法呢？中文裡我們會用『我的眼珠子差點要掉出來。』來誇大表示自己很驚訝。恰巧的是，英文中也有相同的說法："My eyes nearly popped out of my head."。pop out 是指『迸出、跳出』的意思：

例: When the magician opened the box, a rabbit popped out.
（當那名魔術師打開盒子時，一隻兔子蹦了出來。）

因此，"My eyes nearly popped out of my head." 照字面來看，就是『我的眼珠幾乎從頭裡彈出來。』也就是表示『驚訝到不行』的意思。

例: Jenny's eyes nearly popped out of her head when her boyfriend gave her the diamond necklace.
（當珍妮的男朋友給她這條鑽石項鍊時，她驚訝到眼珠都要掉出來了。）

除了用眼珠子彈出來表示很驚訝外，若要表達驚訝到話都說不出來了，那要怎麼用英文說呢？這時就用 speechless [ˈspitʃlɪs]（說不出話來的）或 dumbfounded [dʌmˈfaʊndɪd]（目瞪口呆的）這兩個字就行了。

例: John was so surprised by his wife's decision that he was speechless.
（約翰對妻子的決定驚訝到說不出話來。）

字詞幫幫忙！

1. **the accounting department**　　會計部
   accounting [əˈkaʊntɪŋ] *n.* 會計
   accountant [əˈkaʊntənt] *n.* 會計師

2. **accidentally** [ˌæksəˈdɛntəlɪ] *adv.* 意外地
   = by accident
   accident [ˈæksədənt] *n.* 意外；事故
   例: Kelly accidentally spilled water on my dress.
   （凱莉不小心把水灑到我的洋裝上。）
   ＊spill [spɪl] *vt.* 使灑出

David was seriously injured in the car accident.

（大衛在車禍中受重傷。）

＊injure [ˋɪndʒɚ] *vt.* 傷害

3. **statement** [ˋstetmənt] *n.* 明細表，結算表；聲明

the salary statement　　薪資明細

make a statement + that 子句　　發表……的聲明

例: John made a statement that he would retire by the end of
this year.

（約翰發表聲明說他會在今年年底前辭職。）

＊retire [rɪˋtaɪr] *vi.* 退休

4. **bother** [ˋbɑðɚ] *vi.* 費心 & *vt.* 困擾，煩擾

bother to V　　費心（做）……

bother sb with sth　　以某事煩擾某人

例: George didn't even bother to call to tell me he would be
late.

（喬治甚至連打個電話通知我他會遲到都懶得打。）

Willy always bothers me with silly questions.

（威利老是用一些蠢問題來煩我。）

5. **appreciate** [əˋpriʃɪˌet] *vt.* 感激（其後應以『事物』而不能以『人』
作受詞）；欣賞

例: Laura appreciates what you have done for her.

（蘿拉很感激你為她所做的一切。）

Nick is sad because no one seems to appreciate his
talents.

（尼克很難過，因為沒有人欣賞他的才華。）

6. **follow one's example**　　效法某人的榜樣

例: I would like to follow my father's example and become a
lawyer.

（我想效法我爸爸成為一名律師。）

7. **file** [faɪl] *vt.* 把……銼平 & *n.* 銼刀

file one's nails　　銼某人的指甲

例: Filing your nails regularly will keep them smooth.

（定期銼指甲能使它們保持平滑。）

Hot under the Collar

Index | Links | about | comments | Photo

June 26

At work today, my boss **got furious at** my department because of the project we're doing. My supervisor did nothing to **calm** our boss **down**. He didn't even **report to** him the **progress** that had been made. Afterwards, I felt really frustrated because the only reason we're **behind schedule** was that no one wanted to help me do the work. Even the small amount they were required to do never got **turned in on time**.

About me

Ivy

Calendar

◄   June   ►

Sun	Mon	Tue	Wed	Thu	Fri	Sat
1	2	3	4	5	6	7
8	9	10	11	12	13	14
15	16	17	18	19	20	21
22	23	24	25	**26**	27	28
29	30					

Blog Archive

- June (26)
- May
- April
- March
- February
- January
- December
- November
- October
- September
- August
- July

Ivy at Blog 於 June 06.26. PM 05:17 發表 | 回覆 (0) | 引用 (0) | 收藏 (0) | 轉寄給朋友 | 檢舉

很火大

June 26

今天老闆針對我們正在進行的專案向我所屬的部門大發雷霆。我的主管沒有採取什麼作為好讓老闆冷靜下來。他甚至沒有向他報告專案的進展。之後,我感到十分挫敗,因為我們進度落後的唯一原因是沒有人要幫我。就連被要求做的小事,他們都沒有辦法準時交差。

About me

Ivy

Calendar

◄   June   ►

Sun	Mon	Tue	Wed	Thu	Fri	Sat
1	2	3	4	5	6	7
8	9	10	11	12	13	14
15	16	17	18	19	20	21
22	23	24	25	**26**	27	28
29	30					

Blog Archive

► June (26)
► May
► April
► March
► February
► January
► December
► November
► October
► September
► August
► July

名詞 collar [`kɑlɚ ] 就是『衣領』，標題 hot under the collar 顧名思義是『衣領以下像火燒一樣地燙』，也就是『很生氣』的意思。而 furious [ `fjʊrɪəs] 則為形容詞，表『狂怒的』，所以網誌中的 get furious at... 就是『對……很生氣』。以下是一些關於『生氣』的常見用法：

be / get hot under the collar　　　很火大

例: Mr. Lin got hot under the collar when the class got noisy.
　　（班上鬧成一片時，林老師火透了。）

　be / get furious at...　　　對……很生氣
= be / get angry at...
= be / get mad at...

　　例: I was furious at what Jerry had said.
　　　　（傑瑞的言語讓我很憤怒。）

fly into a rage　　　勃然大怒
rage [redʒ] *n.* 盛怒

　　例: David flew into a rage when his son told him that he wanted to drop out of school.
　　　　（兒子告訴他說他想休學時，大衛勃然大怒。）

　　　＊drop out of school　　　休學

　　　　bristle with anger / rage　　　火冒三丈

bristle [`brɪsl] 原為名詞，表『豬鬃』或動物背上的『短毛』。動物發火時，背上的短毛就會豎立起來，因此 bristle 作動詞用時，可引申為『發怒』之意，常與 with anger / rage 搭配使用。

　　例: Sean bristled with anger when his brother broke his computer.
　　　　（弟弟弄壞他的電腦時，尚恩火冒三丈。）

1. calm sb down　　　使某人冷靜 / 鎮定下來
　　calm down　　　冷靜下來，平靜下來
=　cool off
　　calm [kɑm] *vt.* 使冷靜，使鎮定 & *vi.* 冷靜，鎮定

例: The nurse finally managed to calm the patient down.
（這位護士終於使病患鎮定下來。）

Calm down, Terry. There's no need to worry.
（泰瑞，冷靜下來。沒什麼好擔心的。）

2. report to sb　　向某人報告
例: I reported to Mr. Lee the results of my experiment.
（我向李老師報告實驗的結果。）
＊experiment [ɪkˈspɛrəmənt] *n.* 實驗

3. progress [ˈprɑgrɛs] *n.* 進展，進步
make progress　　有進展，有進步
例: Frank has made a lot of progress in math.
（法蘭克在數學方面有很大的進步。）

4. behind schedule　　比預定落後；誤時
on schedule　　　　　　按照預定；按時
ahead of schedule　　　比預定提前；提早，超前
例: I can't talk to you on the phone right now. I'm behind
schedule.
（我現在不能和你講電話。我的進度落後了。）
The plane took off on schedule and landed on time.
（該班機按預定時間起飛且準時降落。）
Randy completed his work ahead of schedule.
（藍迪提前完工。）

5. turn in...　　繳交 / 遞交……
= hand in...
例: We turned in our report a day early and got extra points.
（我們提早一天交報告，所以獲得加分。）

6. on time　　準時
in time　　及時（之後多接 to 引導的不定詞片語）
例: You can always count on Ed to get his work done on
time.
（任何時候你都可以指望艾德準時完成工作。）
We arrived at the airport just in time to catch our plane.
（我們抵達機場時剛好來得及搭上我們的班機。）

Calling In Sick

Index | *Links* | *about* | *comments* | *Photo*

June 27

Last night I worked **overtime** until 11:00 p.m. trying to **catch up on** my project. When I woke up this morning, I had a terrible **headache** and felt totally **drained**. So I called in sick to work and went back to sleep. About an hour later, my supervisor, Albert, called me. He was asking lots of unimportant questions that anyone else in our department could have answered for him. Then, he **had the gall to** ask me to work from home today! What a **bastard**!

About me

Ivy

Calendar

◀   June   ▶

Sun	Mon	Tue	Wed	Thu	Fri	Sat
1	2	3	4	5	6	7
8	9	10	11	12	13	14
15	16	17	18	19	20	21
22	23	24	25	26	**27**	28
29	30					

Blog Archive

▸ June (27)
▸ May
▸ April
▸ March
▸ February
▸ January
▸ December
▸ November
▸ October
▸ September
▸ August
▸ July

Ivy at Blog 於 June 06.27. PM 03:20 發表 ｜ 回覆 (0) ｜ 引用 (0) ｜ 收藏 (0) ｜ 轉寄給朋友 ｜ 檢舉

打電話請病假

June 27

昨晚為了要趕專案，我加班加到晚上 **11** 點。今早起床時，我頭痛死了而且感覺累斃了。我打電話到公司請病假，然後繼續睡我的回籠覺。大約一個小時後，我的主管艾伯特打電話給我。他問了一堆無關緊要的問題，而且是我們部門其他任何人都可以回答他的問題。然後，他竟然有種叫我今天在家裡工作！真是個大渾蛋！

About me

Ivy

Calendar

◄ *June* ►

Sun	Mon	Tue	Wed	Thu	Fri	Sat
1	2	3	4	5	6	7
8	9	10	11	12	13	14
15	16	17	18	19	20	21
22	23	24	25	26	**27**	28
29	30					

Blog Archive

▶ June (27)
▶ May
▶ April
▶ March
▶ February
▶ January
▶ December
▶ November
▶ October
▶ September
▶ August
▶ July

Ivy at Blog 於 June 06.27. PM 03:20 發表 | 回覆 (0) | 引用 (0) | 收藏 (0) | 轉寄給朋友 | 檢舉

現代人的工作忙碌，相信許多上班族都有工作到快掛的感覺。這種操勞過度、體力盡失的感覺，英文有一個很好的形容詞就叫作 drained [drend]，此字為drain [dren] 的過去分詞，作形容詞用。drain 原表『消耗、使枯竭』之意，例如：The war drained the country of its people and money.（這場戰爭消耗了該國的人力和財力。）因此 drained 作形容詞用時，就是因為體力都被榨乾了，所以當然是『筋疲力盡的』，這樣是不是很貼切呢？

be drained　　筋疲力盡

= be tired (out)

= be worn out

= be exhausted

= be beat

＊exhausted [ɪgˋzɔstɪd] *a.* 疲憊的

beat [bit] *a.* 疲憊不堪的（不用於名詞前）

例: After shopping all day long for Christmas presents, Holly was worn out.

（荷莉為了買聖誕節禮物逛了一整天後，她累壞了。）

Dan was beat by the time he got home from work.

（阿丹下班回到家時已經累垮了。）

 **字詞幫幫忙！**

1. **call in sick**　　打電話請病假

網誌中 called in sick 之後的 to work 表『向上班地點 / 向公司』之意。

例: Betty didn't feel well this morning, so she called in sick.

（貝蒂早上感到不舒服，因此打電話請病假。）

關於其他請假的用法如下：

例: You need to provide a receipt from the hospital if you are on sick leave for over 3 days.

（你若請病假超過 3 天，就得提供醫院的收據。）

＊receipt [rɪˋsit] *n.* 收據

Jerry went traveling on annual leave.

（傑瑞休年假旅行去了。）

Nora asked for leave to attend her brother's wedding.

（娜拉請了假去參加她哥哥的婚禮。）

My sister took maternity leave a week before she was due to give birth.

（我姊姊在預產期的前一週請了產假。）

＊maternity [məˋtɝnətɪ] *a.* 產婦的

2. **overtime** [ˋovɚˌtaɪm] *adv.* 超時地

work overtime　加班

例: Judy needed to work overtime to make up for her mistakes.

（茱蒂必須加班來彌補她的錯誤。）

＊make up for...　彌補／補償……

3. **catch up on...**　趕做／補做……

例: Paul still has a lot of work to catch up on.

（保羅還有很多工作趕著要做。）

4. **headache** [ˋhɛdˌek] *n.* 頭痛

toothache [ˋtuθˌek] *n.* 牙痛

backache [ˋbækˌek] *n.* 背痛

stomachache [ˋstʌməkˌek] *n.* 胃痛

have a headache / toothache / backache / stomachache

感到頭痛／牙痛／背痛／胃痛

例: Sitting at my desk too long caused me to have a backache.

（我在辦公桌前坐太久而導致腰酸背痛。）

5. **have the gall to V**　厚顏無恥地做……

gall [gɔl] *n.* 膽汁（此處指『厚臉皮、厚顏無恥』，專用於上列句構）

例: I can't believe that David had the gall to ask his ex-wife for money.

（我不敢相信大衛還有臉向他前妻要錢。）

6. **bastard** [ˋbæstɚd] *n.* 私生子，混蛋（此字為粗俗的罵人用語，讀者宜避免使用）

Entertaining a Client

June 28

I was asked to entertain a **client** from Japan today. After giving him a **tour** around the office, I took him out for lunch and then to see the **sights** around town. He said he was **impressed** with my knowledge of the business and asked if I had ever **considered** working **abroad**. I **confessed** that I had, and then wondered to myself if he could be **headhunting** me for his company.

About me

Ivy

Calendar

◀   June   ▶

Sun	Mon	Tue	Wed	Thu	Fri	Sat
	1	2	3	4	5	6	7
8	9	10	11	12	13	14
15	16	17	18	19	20	21
22	23	24	25	26	27	28
29	30					

Blog Archive

- ► June (28)
- ► May
- ► April
- ► March
- ► February
- ► January
- ► December
- ► November
- ► October
- ► September
- ► August
- ► July

Ivy at Blog 於 June 06.28. PM 05:48 發表 | 回覆 (0) | 引用 (0) | 收藏 (0) | 轉寄給朋友 | 檢舉

招待客戶

June 28

　　我今天被叫去招待一位日本來的客戶。帶他參觀過辦公室後，我帶他去吃午餐，然後去市區裡四處看看。他說他對我在商業上的知識印象深刻，還問我有沒有想過出國工作。我承認我有過這種想法，接著我又想他是不是想挖角我到他們公司去。

About me

Ivy

Calendar

◄　　*June*　　►

Sun	Mon	Tue	Wed	Thu	Fri	Sat
1	2	3	4	5	6	7
8	9	10	11	12	13	14
15	16	17	18	19	20	21
22	23	24	25	26	27	**28**
29	30					

Blog Archive

▸ June (28)
▸ May
▸ April
▸ March
▸ February
▸ January
▸ December
▸ November
▸ October
▸ September
▸ August
▸ July

Ivy at Blog 於 June 06.28. PM 05:48 發表 | 回覆 (0) | 引用 (0) | 收藏 (0) | 轉寄給朋友 | 檢舉

工作能受人賞識實在是一件令人開心的事，因為終於有人看到你做牛做馬的成果。如果能力好到傳千里，進而吸引他家公司前來挖角，那才是真正的狠角色！『挖角』在英文裡的說法就是 headhunt [ˋhɛdˌhʌnt]，headhunt 字面上是『獵取人頭』，引申為『延攬 / 物色（人才）』。替公司物色人才的人，我們則稱之為 headhunter [ˋhɛdˌhʌntə]。而 headhunting agency 也就是所謂的『獵人頭公司』。

例: We are headhunting a new manager to head up our sales department.

（我們正在物色一位新經理來帶領業務部門。）

This headhunting agency helps recruit new employees and has saved our company lots of time.

（這家獵人頭公司幫忙招募新員工，替我們公司省下很多時間。）

＊recruit [rɪˋkrut] vt. 招募

1. **entertain** [ˌɛntəˋten] vt. 招待；娛樂

   entertain sb with sth　　以某事物來招待 / 娛樂某人

   例: The clown entertained the children with a variety of magic tricks.

   （那位小丑以一連串魔術戲法娛樂小孩。）

   ＊clown [klaʊn] n. 小丑

2. **client** [ˋklaɪənt] n. 顧客，客戶（尤指大宗買賣的客戶）

   customer [ˋkʌstəmə] n.（一般的）顧客，買主

3. **tour** [tʊr] n. 遊覽，參觀；巡迴演出（常與介詞 on 並用）

   take sb on a tour of + 地方　　帶某人參觀某地

   be on tour　　巡迴演出中（非 be on a tour）

   例: The guide took us on a tour of the city.

   （那位導遊帶我們參觀這座城市。）

   The band is on tour in Japan for three months.

   （這個樂團正在日本巡迴演出 3 個月。）

4. **sights** [saɪts] *n.* 名勝，觀光地（恆為複數，用於下列固定片語）

see the sights　　參觀景點（以此片語形成下列名詞詞組）

sightseeing [ˈsaɪtˌsiɪŋ] *n.* 觀光，遊覽風景

go sightseeing　　去觀光 / 遊覽風景

例: Andy doesn't like to go sightseeing with a tour group. He prefers to go by himself.

（安迪不喜歡跟旅行團去觀光。他比較喜歡自助旅行。）

5. **impress** [ɪmˈprɛs] *vt.* 使印象深刻

be impressed with...　　對……印象深刻

例: Everyone was impressed with the speech Matthew gave at the graduation ceremony.

（馬修在畢業典禮上的致詞讓每個人都印象深刻。）

6. **consider** [kənˈsɪdɚ] *vt.* 考慮

consider + V-ing　　考慮要……

例: Would you consider going to the movies with me?

（你願意考慮和我一起看場電影嗎？）

7. **abroad** [əˈbrɔd] *adv.* 到國外，在國外

work abroad　　在海外工作

study abroad　　留學

例: Judy wants to study abroad, but if she does, she needs to get a loan.

（茱蒂想出國唸書，但這樣的話她就得借貸。）

＊loan [lon] *n.* 貸款

8. **confess** [kənˈfɛs] *vt.* 承認，坦承 & *vi.* 坦承

注意:

confess 作及物動詞時，其後以 that 子句作受詞；作不及物動詞用時，與介詞 to 並用，之後接名詞或動名詞作受詞。

confess + that 子句　　坦承……

confess to + N/V-ing　　坦承……

confess to the crime

例: The girl confessed that she had stolen the purse.

= The girl confessed to stealing the purse.

= The girl admitted (to) stealing the purse.

= The girl owned up to stealing the purse.

（這女孩坦承偷了錢包。）

Surprise Overtime

Index | *Links* | *about* | *comments* | *Photo*

June 29

Today I had plans with Eric after work. We had **booked** tickets for a dance **performance**. However, right before I **got off work**, Albert told me I had to stay and help him finish the big project we'd been **working on**. I was **on the verge of a nervous breakdown** when I heard this. My special night was totally **ruined**.

About me

Ivy

Calendar

◄ June ►

Sun	Mon	Tue	Wed	Thu	Fri	Sat
	1	2	3	4	5	6	7
8	9	10	11	12	13	14
15	16	17	18	19	20	21
22	23	24	25	26	27	28
29	30					

Blog Archive

▸ June (29)
▸ May
▸ April
▸ March
▸ February
▸ January
▸ December
▸ November
▸ October
▸ September
▸ August
▸ July

Ivy at Blog 於 June 06.29. PM 07:24 發表 | 回覆 (0) | 引用 (0) | 收藏 (0) | 轉寄給朋友 | 檢舉

意外的加班

June 29

今天下班後我和艾瑞克有約。我們原本訂了票要去看舞蹈表演。但是就在我要下班前，艾伯特告訴我得留下來幫忙他完成我們正在進行的重大專案。聽到他這麼說，我差點就要精神崩潰了。我特別的夜晚完全毀了。

About me

Ivy

Calendar

◄　　　*June*　　　►

Sun	Mon	Tue	Wed	Thu	Fri	Sat
1	2	3	4	5	6	7
8	9	10	11	12	13	14
15	16	17	18	19	20	21
22	23	24	25	26	27	28
29	30					

Blog Archive

► June (29)
► May
► April
► March
► February
► January
► December
► November
► October
► September
► August
► July

239

現代上班族由於工作過度操勞，而嚴重影響到個人生活品質，這不但容易造成身體上的疾病，心理上也承受莫大壓力，因此三不五時就應該安排時間放鬆一下，但這時如果碰到像網誌中的主管臨時徵召，這時要叫人不『花瘋』或精神崩潰也難。精神崩潰的英文就是 **a nervous breakdown**。nervous [ˈnɝvəs] 是指『神經（方面）的』，而 breakdown [ˈbrekˌdaun] 原表『系統故障、損壞』之意，因此當神經系統損壞時，可不就是我們說的精神崩潰了嗎？

have a nervous breakdown　　精神崩潰

例: Jane had a nervous breakdown because she was unable to handle the divorce.

（小珍因為無法承受離婚而精神崩潰了。）

注意:

breakdown 乃由動詞片語 break down 衍伸而來。break down 指汽車、摩托車等車輛『拋錨』，或機器『故障』、『壞掉』之意。

例: My car broke down in the middle of the road.

（我的車在馬路中間拋錨了。）

例: The elevator broke down, so we had to walk up to the 12th floor.

（電梯壞了，所以我們必須走到第 12 層樓。）

＊elevator [ˈɛləˌvetɚ] *n.* 電梯

此外，若是要表在崩潰的『邊緣』，這時就可以用名詞 verge [vɝdʒ] 這個字。verge 表『邊界、邊緣』，因此 on the verge of... 就是指『瀕臨……的邊緣』之意。

be on the verge of...　　瀕臨……的邊緣

= be on the edge of...

= be on the brink of...

　＊edge [ɛdʒ] *n.* 邊緣

　　brink [brɪŋk] *n.* 邊緣

例: Ted was on the verge of a nervous breakdown because he was out of job for three months.

（泰德由於 3 個月沒有工作而瀕臨精神崩潰。）

That company is on the edge of bankruptcy.

（那家公司正處於破產邊緣。）

　＊bankruptcy [ˈbæŋkrʌptsɪ] *n.* 破產

1. book [bʊk] *vt.* 預訂，預購，預約
= **reserve** [rɪˋzɝv] *vt.*
= **make a reservation for...**

    ＊**reservation** [ˏrɛzɚˋveʃən] *n.* 預訂

例: Jerry booked a flight to Japan through a travel agency.
（傑瑞透過旅行社訂了去日本的機票。）

Costal hotels are usually fully booked during summer vacations.
（海邊旅館的房間在暑假期間通常都會被訂光。）

    ＊**costal** [ˋkostḷ] *a.* 海岸的

2. performance [pɚˋfɔrməns] *n.* 表演
例: The band gave a wonderful performance tonight.
（這個樂團今晚的演出非常精彩。）

3. get off work　　下班
get off at + 時間　　（幾點）下班
例: Jordan usually goes to work at 8:00 a.m. and gets off at 6:00 p.m.
（喬登通常早上 8 點上班，晚上 6 點下班。）

4. work on...　　致力於……
例: Kevin has been working on his final report all week, so he hasn't gotten much sleep lately.
（凱文整個星期都忙於期末報告，所以他最近睡眠不足。）

5. ruin [ˋrʊɪn] *vt.* 毀壞，毀掉
例: The couple's honeymoon was ruined because the groom broke his leg.
（由於新郎摔斷了腿，使得這對新婚夫婦的蜜月毀了。）

    ＊**honeymoon** [ˋhʌnɪˏmun] *n.* 蜜月
    groom [grum] *n.* 新郎
    bride [braɪd] *n.* 新娘

The Glory Hog

June 30

    I was furious at work today. During a meeting with our company's owner, Albert took all the **credit** for the project I had **slaved over** for the past few weeks. I knew he was a jerk, but that **was over the top**. I nearly **lost my cool** in front of everyone. I'm really **fed up with** Albert "the **Glory Hog**" and this job.

About me

Ivy

Calendar

◄ *June* ►

Sun	Mon	Tue	Wed	Thu	Fri	Sat
1	2	3	4	5	6	7
8	9	10	11	12	13	14
15	16	17	18	19	20	21
22	23	24	25	26	27	28
29	**30**					

Blog Archive

- ► June (30)
- ► May
- ► April
- ► March
- ► February
- ► January
- ► December
- ► November
- ► October
- ► September
- ► August
- ► July

愛搶功勞的討厭鬼

June 30

　　我今天上班時快氣炸了。在和公司老闆開會時，艾伯特把我過去幾個星期拼死拼活才做出來的專案功勞全搶了過去。我知道他是個渾蛋，可是這也太超過了。我幾乎在大家面前失控。我真的受夠了艾伯特這愛搶功勞的討厭鬼還有這份工作。

About me

Ivy

Calendar

◄ 　　　*June*　　　 ►

Sun	Mon	Tue	Wed	Thu	Fri	Sat
1	2	3	4	5	6	7
8	9	10	11	12	13	14
15	16	17	18	19	20	21
22	23	24	25	26	27	28
29	30					

Blog Archive

▸ June (30)
▸ May
▸ April
▸ March
▸ February
▸ January
▸ December
▸ November
▸ October
▸ September
▸ August
▸ July

243

遇到愛搶功勞的上司，真是叫人不氣炸也難。尤其是像主角這樣辛辛苦苦才完成工作，卻眼睜睜看著他人居功，那更是讓人苦在心裡口難開呀！像這樣的『苦海女神龍』，要形容自己像奴隸一樣苦命地工作，可以使用 slave [slev] 這個字。slave 作名詞用時，表『奴隸』之意，而當動詞時，則有『像奴隸般工作、苦幹』的意味，像網誌中的 slave over sth，指的就是『拼命／辛苦地做某件事』，而要表達『為……辛苦工作時』，則可以說 slave away for sth / sb。

例: Eve slaved over the tough task without any complaints.

（伊芙毫無怨言地辛苦進行這項艱難的任務。）

＊complaint [kəmˋplent] *n.* 抱怨

Jim slaved away for his family, but his wife never appreciated what he did.

（吉姆為家庭辛苦打拼，但他太太卻不曾感激過他的付出。）

＊appreciate [əˋpriʃɪˏet] *vt.* 感激

除了上述說法，要形容某人做牛做馬地拼命做某件事時，還可以用下列說法來表示：

work one's fingers to the bone　　拼命幹活，非常辛苦地工作

本用法中的 finger [ˋfɪŋɡɚ] 指『手指』，bone [bon] 指『骨頭』，work one's fingers to the bone 字面上的意思是『工作到手指的骨頭都看得見』，引申為『拚命工作』。

例: Sheila worked her fingers to the bone to finish the project on time.

（席拉為準時完成那項專案而拚命趕工。）

work like a dog　　拼命地工作

work like a dog 字面上的意思是『像狗一樣地工作』，這是因為從人類從早期農業社會開始，狗兒就被賦予許多任務，因此用來比喻『拚命工作』。

例: Henry works like a dog to make enough money to buy a house.

（亨利為了要存錢買棟房子而拚命地工作。）

字詞幫幫忙！

1. **glory hog** [ˋɡlorɪ ˏhɑɡ] *n.* 愛搶功勞的人
   glory [ˋɡlorɪ] *n.* 光榮，榮譽
   hog [hɑɡ] *n.* 公豬
   例: Jack told the boss he completed the work all by himself.
   He is such a glory hog!
   （傑克告訴老闆他獨自完成這項工作。他還真是個愛搶功勞的傢
   伙！）

2. **credit** [ˋkrɛdɪt] *n.* 功勞 & *vt.* 認為……有（功勞），將……歸功於
   take the credit for...　　　因……居功
   be credited with...　　　　具有……的功勞（某事是某人做的）
   be credited to sb　　　　　歸功於某人
   例: No one in the office likes Hank because he always takes
   the credit for others' work.
   （辦公室裡沒人喜歡漢克，因為他老是搶別人的功勞。）
   Bill is credited with saving the company from bankruptcy.
   （比爾對於拯救公司免於破產有莫大功勞。）
   ＊bankruptcy [ˋbæŋkrʌptsɪ] *n.* 破產
   The discovery of this rare plant was credited to Professor Brown.
   （發現這種稀有植物要歸功於布朗教授。）

3. **be over the top**　　　過度，過頭
   例: I think it was really over the top when Molly said she was
   born to be a model.
   （當茉莉說她天生就是吃模特兒這行飯時，我覺得實在是太誇張
   了。）

4. **lose one's cool**　　某人失去控制／失去冷靜
   ＝　lose control of oneself
   　　keep one's cool　　某人保持冷靜

5. **be fed up with...**　　受夠了……
   ＝　be sick and tired of...

Unit 62

Adiós, Claire

Index | *Links* | *about* | *comments* | *Photo*

July 01

I embarrassed myself at work today. It was Claire's last day in the office. We had a big **farewell** party for her and right before she left, I **burst out crying**. She had been the person I had **turned to** to **vent** my **frustration** and get advice. I know I'll be **lonesome** without her around. I also feel **jealous** that she gets to **escape** this **madhouse**.

About me

Ivy

Calendar

◄ July ►

Sun	Mon	Tue	Wed	Thu	Fri	Sat
		1	2	3	4	5
6	7	8	9	10	11	12
13	14	15	16	17	18	19
20	21	22	23	24	25	26
27	28	29	30	31		

Blog Archive

▸ July (1)
▸ June
▸ May
▸ April
▸ March
▸ February
▸ January
▸ December
▸ November
▸ October
▸ September
▸ August

July 01

　　我今天上班時讓自己出糗了。今天是克萊兒上班的最後一天。我們為她舉辦了一場盛大的送別會，就在她要離開前，我嚎啕大哭了起來。她一直是我發洩沮喪情緒的對象，我也從她那裡得到建議。沒有她在身邊，我知道我一定會很孤單。我也很嫉妒她得以離開這個瘋狂的地方。

About me

Ivy

Calendar

◄			July			►
Sun	Mon	Tue	Wed	Thu	Fri	Sat
	1	2	3	4	5	
6	7	8	9	10	11	12
13	14	15	16	17	18	19
20	21	22	23	24	25	26
27	28	29	30	31		

Blog Archive

► July (1)
► June
► May
► April
► March
► February
► January
► December
► November
► October
► September
► August

Ivy at Blog 於 July 07.01. PM 06:14 發表｜回覆 (0)｜引用 (0)｜收藏 (0)｜轉寄給朋友｜檢舉

網誌作者因為不捨好友兼同事 Claire 的離開，所以在送別會上嚎啕大哭了起來，網誌中所用的 burst out crying 就是用來指『嚎啕大哭起來』或『突然哭出來』的情況，也等於 burst into tears。burst out / into... 是用來表『突然……起來』的狀態，不過要注意的是，burst out 後接的是現在分詞（V-ing），burst into 後接的則是名詞。

burst out crying　　　突然大哭，痛哭失聲
= burst into tears

burst out laughing　　　突然大笑，突然笑出來
= burst into laughter

＊laughter [ˋlæftɚ] *n.* 笑，笑聲（不可數）

例: Meg burst out crying when she heard that her boyfriend was in a serious car accident.

（梅格聽到男友出了嚴重車禍時，嚎啕大哭了起來。）

Winnie told a very funny joke and made everyone burst into laughter.

（溫妮講了個很滑稽的笑話使得大家哄堂大笑。）

另外，哭泣除了可以用 cry 這個字，也可以用 shed tears 來表示。

shed tears　　　流淚

shed crocodile tears　　　流下鱷魚的眼淚（喻假惺惺，貓哭耗子假慈悲）

＊shed [ʃɛd] *vt.* 流下，流出（三態同形）

crocodile [ˋkrɑkəˌdaɪl] *n.* 鱷魚

例: Lucy shed tears when she thought of her dad, who passed away a month ago.

（露西想到一個月前過世的父親時，便留下了眼淚。）

＊pass away　　　過世（die 的委婉說法）

Don't shed crocodile tears for me. I know you are happy that I broke up with my boyfriend.

（妳別在那邊貓哭耗子假慈悲了。我知道妳很高興我跟我男友分手了。）

1. adiós [ˌɑdiˋos] *inter.* （西班牙文的）再見（= goodbye）

2. **farewell** [ˈfɛrˌwɛl] *n.* 告別

　　a farewell party　　　送別會

　　say farewell to sb　　向某人告別

3. **turn to sb**　　　　　指望某人，求助於某人

　　turn to sb for help　　指望某人幫助

4. **vent** [vɛnt] *vt.* 發洩

　　vent one's anger on / at sb　　把氣出在某人身上

　　例: Why would you vent your anger on me? I'm not the one
　　　who got you fired.

　　　（你為什麼把氣出在我身上？我又不是害你被開除的人。）

5. **frustration** [frʌsˈtreʃən] *n.* 沮喪，挫折

6. **lonesome** [ˈlonsəm] *a.* 孤單的，寂寞的

= 　lonely [ˈlonlɪ]

　　例: Karen felt lonesome after all of her children moved away.

　　　（凱倫的子女都搬走後，她感到很孤單。）

7. **jealous** [ˈdʒɛləs] *a.* 嫉妒的

　　be jealous of...　　嫉妒……

　　例: Fanny was jealous of her friend's good looks.

　　　（芬妮嫉妒她朋友的美貌。）

8. **escape** [əˈskep] *vt. & vi.* 逃脫，逃離

　　escape from...　　從……逃離

　　例: We were lucky to escape that car accident.

　　　（我們很幸運逃過了那起車禍。）

　　　However hard it tried, the bird couldn't escape from the
　　　cage.

　　　（這隻鳥無論多麼努力嘗試，仍無法逃出鳥籠。）

9. **madhouse** [ˈmædˌhaʊs] *n.* 精神病院

Unit 63

Inspiration

Index | Links | about | comments | Photo

July 02

Since Albert acted so badly and Claire quit, I have been thinking more about leaving. Therefore, I **updated** my online **resume** today and **posted** it on a job-finding website. <u>**To my surprise**</u>, I got two **responses** the same day. One company is a local chain store, and the other **deals in** international sales. This **positive feedback** has really inspired me to **reach for** something better for my career.

About me

Ivy

Calendar

◄   July   ►

Sun	Mon	Tue	Wed	Thu	Fri	Sat
		1	2	3	4	5
6	7	8	9	10	11	12
13	14	15	16	17	18	19
20	21	22	23	24	25	26
27	28	29	30	31		

Blog Archive

- ► July (2)
- ► June
- ► May
- ► April
- ► March
- ► February
- ► January
- ► December
- ► November
- ► October
- ► September
- ► August

July 02

由於艾伯特表現差勁，加上克萊兒離職，我就更想離開公司了。所以我今天上網更新自己的履歷表，把它張貼到求職網站。令我驚訝的是，我同一天內就接到兩封回信。一家是本地的連鎖商店，而另一家是從事國際貿易的公司。得到正面的回應真的鼓舞我追求更好的職業生涯。

Calendar

◄　　July　　►

Sun	Mon	Tue	Wed	Thu	Fri	Sat
		1	2	3	4	5
6	7	8	9	10	11	12
13	14	15	16	17	18	19
20	21	22	23	24	25	26
27	28	29	30	31		

Blog Archive

- ► July (2)
- ► June
- ► May
- ► April
- ► March
- ► February
- ► January
- ► December
- ► November
- ► October
- ► September
- ► August

Ivy at Blog 於 July 07.02. PM 01:57 發表｜回覆 (0)｜引用 (0)｜收藏 (0)｜轉寄給朋友｜檢舉

網誌中的 To my surprise 就是『令我驚訝的是』之意。在英文中，我們常用 "to one's + 表情緒的名詞" 來表達情緒上『令某人……的是』，常見的用法有下列：

to one's surprise　　　　令某人驚訝的是

to one's astonishment / amazement　　令某人驚愕 / 驚異的是

to one's joy / delight　　　　令某人高興的是

to one's disappointment　　　令某人失望的是

to one's horror　　　　　　　令某人恐懼的是

to one's regret　　　　　　　令某人後悔的是

to one's relief　　　　　　　令某人放心的是，令某人鬆了口氣的是

to one's satisfaction　　　　　令某人滿意的是

to one's sorrow　　　　　　　令某人難過的是

例: To Gary's disappointment, he didn't get the job.

（令蓋瑞失望的是，他沒有得到那份工作。）

To our relief, Mr. Chang said we were not having a math quiz.

（令我們鬆一口氣的是，張老師說我們不會有數學小考。）

To Tom's sorrow, his parents got a divorce.

（令湯姆難過的是，他的父母離婚了。）

1. **inspiration** [ˌɪnspəˈreʃən] *n.* 鼓舞；靈感

   inspire [ɪnˈspaɪr] *vt.* 鼓舞；激勵

   inspire sb to V　　鼓舞 / 激勵某人（做）……

   例: I couldn't write anything because I was out of inspiration.

   （我寫不出任何東西，因為我沒有靈感。）

   My teacher inspired me to follow my dreams and become a pilot.

   （我的老師鼓舞我追求夢想，當個飛行員。）

2. **update** [ʌpˈdet] *vt.* 更新

   例: The company is updating its computer system.

   （那家公司正在更新電腦系統。）

3. **resume** [ˈrɛzjume / ˌrɛzuˈme] *n.* 履歷表

4. **post** [post] *vt.* 貼出（佈告等）；把（佈告等）貼在……上
   例: Andy posted an ad on the wall to sell his house.
   （安迪在牆上張貼廣告要賣屋。）

5. **response** [rɪˈspɑns] *n.* 回應；答覆（與介詞 to 並用）
   respond [rɪˈspɑnd] *vi.* 回應；回答（與介詞 to 並用）
   in response to...　回應……；回答……
   respond to...　回應……
   例: I am applying for this job in response to your ad in
   Monday's paper.
   （針對貴公司週一在報上刊登的廣告，我想應徵這份工作。）
   ＊apply for...　應徵……
   Maggie was mad at me because I didn't respond to her
   email.
   （梅姬因為我沒回她伊媚兒而生我的氣。）

6. **deal in...**　經營 / 買賣……（= buy and sell...）
   例: John runs a shop that deals in goods of all kinds.
   （阿強經營一家販賣各種貨物的商店。）

7. **positive** [ˈpɑzətɪv] *a.* 正面的；積極的
   negative [ˈnɛgətɪv] *a.* 反面的；消極的
   例: My friend Leo has made a positive impact on my life.
   （我的朋友里歐在我的人生中具有正面的影響。）
   ＊impact [ˈɪmpækt] *n.* 影響（與介詞 on 並用）
   David's heavy drinking had a negative effect on his
   children.
   （大衛的酗酒問題對他的子女造成負面的影響。）

8. **feedback** [ˈfidˌbæk] *n.* 反應；回饋（不可數）
   例: Most of the feedback we had received from the readers
   about the book was positive.
   （我們收到讀者對新書的反應大部分都是正面的。）

9. **reach for...**　追求……；伸手去拿……
   例: Hannah reached for the milk but knocked it over by
   accident.
   （漢娜伸手去拿牛奶，卻不小心把它打翻了。）
   ＊knock...over / knock over...　將……撞倒 / 打翻

Pointless Interview

Index | Links | about | comments | Photo

July 03

I took the day off to go to a job interview at the local company. The manager was very friendly, but some of the questions he asked during the interview seemed **pointless**. For example, after asking about my educational **background**, he asked how tall I was and how much I **weighed**. Then, he **went on to** ask if I had ever been married or planned to be in the future. Eventually, I **made up an excuse** just so I could leave.

About me

Ivy

Calendar

◄ July ►

Sun	Mon	Tue	Wed	Thu	Fri	Sat
		1	2	**3**	4	5
6	7	8	9	10	11	12
13	14	15	16	17	18	19
20	21	22	23	24	25	26
27	28	29	30	31		

Blog Archive

► July (3)
► June
► May
► April
► March
► February
► January
► December
► November
► October
  September
► August

Ivy at Blog 於 July 07.03. PM 03:27 發表 | 回覆 (0) | 引用 (0) | 收藏 (0) | 轉寄給朋友 | 檢舉

無意義的面試

Index | *Links* | *about* | *comments* | *Photo*

July 03

　　我請了一天假去那家本地公司面試。經理非常友善，但面試過程中他問了些沒什麼意義的問題。舉例來說，在詢問過我的教育背景後，他問我有多高，體重有多重。接著他又繼續問我有沒有結過婚或是在未來有無結婚的打算。最後，我編了個理由好脫身。

About me

Ivy

Calendar

◀　　　July　　　▶

Sun	Mon	Tue	Wed	Thu	Fri	Sat
		1	2	3	4	5
6	7	8	9	10	11	12
13	14	15	16	17	18	19
20	21	22	23	24	25	26
27	28	29	30	31		

Blog Archive

▸ July (3)
▸ June
▸ May
▸ April
▸ March
▸ February
▸ January
▸ December
▸ November
▸ October
▸ September
▸ August

Ivy at Blog 於 July 07.03. PM 03:27 發表 | 回覆 (0) | 引用 (0) | 收藏 (0) | 轉寄給朋友 | 檢舉

網誌作者因為面試遇到了怪人，急著想要脫身，所以編了個理由離開。相信大家都有過去找藉口來避開不想做的事，或是來解釋自己某些行為的時候，像是上課或上班遲到了，就可能以遇到塞車來當藉口。那麼『捏造藉口、編理由』的英文該怎麼說呢？以下就列舉幾種相關說法：

make up an excuse　　捏造藉口，編理由（指無中生有）

= invent an excuse

= fabricate an excuse

　＊fabricate [`fæbrɪ͵ket] vt. 杜撰

　例: David made up an excuse for his absence from school.

　　　（大衛為他的曠課捏造了一個藉口。）

　make an excuse　　找藉口

　例: John always makes excuses for being late to work.

　　　（約翰總是為上班遲到找藉口。）

make up a story　　捏造故事

= invent a story

= fabricate a story

　例: Al made up many stories to cover his lies.

　　　（艾爾編造出許多故事來掩飾謊言。）

若是出自好意，不願說出實情而傷害對方的感情，想要說個『善意的謊言』，那就可以用 tell a white lie。因為白色（white）代表純潔、無辜，因此 a white lie 即表示『不帶惡意的謊言』，也就是『善意的謊言』。

　例: Jim told Jenny a white lie instead of telling her that her new hairstyle was awful.

　　　（吉姆對珍妮說了個善意的謊言，而不是告訴她說她的新髮型很糟糕。）

字詞幫幫忙！

1. **pointless** [`pɔɪntlɪs] a. 無意義的；沒有用的

　point [pɔɪnt] n. 重點，要點

　It is pointless to V　　……是沒有意義的 / 沒有用的

= There is no point (in) V-ing

= There is no sense (in) + V-ing

= There is no use (in) + V-ing

例: This discussion seems totally pointless to me.

（我覺得這次討論似乎完全沒有意義。）

It is pointless to complain; nothing will change.

= There's no point complaining; nothing will change.

= There's no sense complaining; nothing will change.

= There's no use complaining; nothing will change.

（抱怨是沒有用的；沒有什麼會因此而改變。）

What was the point of that boring speech?

（那場無聊的演講重點是什麼呢？）

2. **background** [ˋbækˌɡraʊnd] *n.* 背景

例: Because of Brad's background in accounting, he was hired by the bank.

（由於布萊德的會計背景，他被那家銀行錄取了。）

＊accounting [əˋkaʊntɪŋ] *n.* 會計

3. **weigh** [we] *vi.* 重達

weight [wet] *n.* 重量；體重

例: How much do you weigh?

= What's your weight?

（你的體重多少？）

4. **go on to V**　（做完某事）接著從事……

= proceed to V

＊proceed [proˋsid] *vi* 繼續進行

例: After doing the laundry, Shirley went on to do the cooking.

（洗完衣服後，雪莉便接著煮飯。）

＊laundry [ˋlɔndrɪ] *n.* 待洗或送洗的衣物（集合名詞，不可數）

do the laundry　洗衣服

Nosy Neighbor

Index | Links | about | comments | Photo

July 04

Zoe is our office's **gossip** queen. She loves to **poke her nose into** everyone's **business**. She also likes to be a **tattletale**, and Albert listens to most of what she says. While I was walking by his office today, I heard Zoe telling Albert I was looking for a new job. She must have been **spying on** me when I was posting my resume. What a **weasel**!

About me

Ivy

Calendar

◄ *July* ►

Sun	Mon	Tue	Wed	Thu	Fri	Sat
		1	2	3	**4**	5
6	7	8	9	10	11	12
13	14	15	16	17	18	19
20	21	22	23	24	25	26
27	28	29	30	31		

Blog Archive

► July (4)
► June
► May
► April
► March
► February
► January
► December
► November
► October
► September
► August

好個長舌婦

July 04

　　柔依是我們辦公室的八卦女王。她好管閒事，還喜歡打小報告，而艾伯特相信大部分她說的話。我今天經過艾伯特辦公室時，聽到柔依告訴他我在找工作。她一定在我張貼履歷時監視我。真是個不安好心的傢伙！

About me

Ivy

Calendar

◀　　　July　　　▶

Sun	Mon	Tue	Wed	Thu	Fri	Sat
		1	2	3	4	5
6	7	8	9	10	11	12
13	14	15	16	17	18	19
20	21	22	23	24	25	26
27	28	29	30	31		

Blog Archive

- ▸ July (4)
- ▸ June
- ▸ May
- ▸ April
- ▸ March
- ▸ February
- ▸ January
- ▸ December
- ▸ November
- ▸ October
- ▸ September
- ▸ August

Ivy at Blog 於 July 07.04. PM 04:12 發表｜回覆 (0)｜引用 (0)｜收藏 (0)｜轉寄給朋友｜檢舉

標題中的 nosy（也可以寫成 nosey）是形容詞，表『好管閒事的、包打聽的』之意。nosy 這個字是由 nose 變化而來，nose 是名詞，表『鼻子』，網誌中用到 poke one's nose into...，其字面意思是『將某人的鼻子插到……中』，引申為『好管……的閒事、插手……的事』之意。

nosy [ˋnozɪ] *a.* 好管閒事的，包打聽的（= nosey）

be nosy about...　　喜愛打聽……

例: Stop being nosy about my personal affairs.
　　（不要再探聽我的私事。）

poke one's nose into...　　某人插手／干涉……的事
= stick one's nose into...
poke [pok] *vt.* 戳進，伸進
stick [stɪk] *vt.* 插，伸入

例: My mother-in-law likes to poke her nose into my marriage.
　　（我婆婆喜歡過問我的婚姻生活。）

nose [noz] *n.* 鼻子 & *vi.* 探聽（與介詞 into 並用）

nose into...　　探聽／刺探……

例: Gary tends to nose into others' personal lives.
　　（蓋瑞往往會刺探別人的私生活。）

字詞幫幫忙！

1. gossip [ˋgasəp] *n.* 閒話 & *vi.* 說閒話

a gossip queen　　八卦女王，長舌婦

例: The gossip started out with Karen, and then it spread throughout the whole school.
　　（這起流言從凱倫開始，之後傳遍了全校。）

I don't like to gossip about others' affairs.
（我不喜歡說別人的閒話。）

2. business [ˈbɪznɪs] *n.* 事情，事務

It's none of your business.   不關你的事。

Mind your own business.   管好你自己的事。別多管閒事。

例: Betty: Who was the cute guy having dinner with you last
           night?

  Lucy: It's none of your business.

（貝蒂：昨天晚上和妳共進晚餐的帥哥是誰？）

（露西：這不關妳的事。）

Andy: Why are you always staring at Melissa?

Barry: Mind your own business.

（安迪：你為什麼老是盯著梅莉莎看呢？）

（貝瑞：別多管閒事。）

3. tattletale [ˈtætl̩ˌtel] *n.* 打小報告者；搬弄是非者

tattle [ˈtætl̩] *vi.* 打小報告

例: Danny is so annoying. He always tattles on me when I do
something wrong.

（丹尼真的很討厭，他總是在我做錯事時打小報告。）

4. spy on...   窺探 / 監視……

spy [spaɪ] *vi.* 窺探，監視 & *n.* 間諜

例: Celebrities always worry about people spying on them.

（名人總是擔心有人窺探他們。）

＊celebrity [səˈlɛbrətɪ] *n.* 名人

5. weasel [ˈwizl̩] *n.* 狡猾的人；黃鼠狼

Unit 66

Albert the Nice Guy

Index | Links | about | comments | Photo

July 05

When Albert called me into his office today, I wasn't surprised. I had been **expecting** it. However, I wasn't expecting him to be so nice to me. Instead of demanding to know why I was <u>**job hunting**</u>, he **praised** me for the work I had been doing. He also **expressed** how important I was to the company and asked me to **think** it **over** before I **made** any **decisions**.

好人艾伯特？

Index | *Links* | *about* | *comments* | *Photo*

July 05

　　艾伯特今天把我叫進他的辦公室時，我並不驚訝。我早料到會發生。但是我沒想到他會對我那麼好。他沒有問我為什麼我在找工作，反而讚賞我在工作上的表現。他還表示我對公司而言是很重要的人。他還要我做任何重大決定之前先好好考慮清楚再說。

About me

Ivy

Calendar

◀			*July*			▶
Sun	Mon	Tue	Wed	Thu	Fri	Sat
		1	2	3	4	5
6	7	8	9	10	11	12
13	14	15	16	17	18	19
20	21	22	23	24	25	26
27	28	29	30	31		

Blog Archive

- ▸ July (5)
- ▸ June
- ▸ May
- ▸ April
- ▸ March
- ▸ February
- ▸ January
- ▸ December
- ▸ November
- ▸ October
- ▸ September
- ▸ August

Ivy at Blog 於 July 07.05. PM 06:22 發表 | 回覆 (0) | 引用 (0) | 收藏 (0) | 轉寄給朋友 | 檢舉

263

無論是失業或是想跳槽的人，想必都極欲尋找『下一個會更好』的工作。不管你是透過網路的人力銀行，或是報紙的徵人啟事，這樣找工作的行為在英文中就叫作 job hunting。hunt [hʌnt] 作動詞時，原表在野外『追獵、獵殺』之意。無論是獵人或是掠食動物，都必須透過搜尋並瞄準目標來進行獵物的動作，所以此字也有『搜尋、尋找』之意。因此用 hunt 來表示到處尋找工作機會再恰當不過了。以下列舉找工作的常見用法：

job hunting [ˋdʒɑb ˏhʌntɪŋ] *n.* 找工作

job hunt [ˋdʒɑb ˏhʌnt] *n. & vi.* 找工作

go job hunting　　　找工作

job-hunting [ˋdʒɑbˏhʌntɪŋ] *a.* 求職的

job hunter [ˋdʒɑb, hʌntɚ] *n.* 求職者

hunt for a job　　　找工作
= look for a job

例: After finishing his military service, Andy went job hunting.
　　（安迪一服完兵役就去找工作了。）

Summer is job-hunting season because many college students have just graduated.
　　（夏季是求職季，因為許多大學生剛畢業。）

Mary tried to hunt for a job that pays enough to raise her kids.
　　（瑪莉試圖找一份能夠養活她小孩的工作。）

如果說一個人想『跳槽』，那應該怎麼用英文表達呢？最簡單的說法就是 change jobs（換工作）。

例: It's been three years since Bill got a raise. He thinks it's about time to change jobs.
　　（比利上次加薪已經是 3 年前的事了。他想該是換工作的時候了。）

另外，如果說一個人 hop from job to job，字面上的意思是『從一個工作跳到另一個工作』，其實就是指一個人『經常換工作』，這與中文裡『跳槽』的意思有所出入，在使用上要特別小心。

例: If you frequently hop from job to job, your resume will look bad.
　　（如果你經常換工作，你的履歷會很難看。）

＊frequently [ˋfrikwəntlɪ] *adv.* 頻繁地

1. expect [ɪkˋspɛkt] *vt.* 預料，預期

expect sb to V　　預料／期望某人（做）……

例: Betty's parents expected her to become a doctor.
（貝蒂的父母期望她能成為醫生。）

2. praise [prez] *vt.* 稱讚，讚揚

praise sb for sth　　因某事讚美某人，讚揚某人某事

例: The principal praised the student for her achievements.
（校長讚揚那名學生的成就。）

　　＊achievement [əˋtʃivmənt] *n.* 成就（常用複數）

3. express [ɪkˋsprɛs] *vt.* 表達，表示

express oneself　　表達某人自己的意思、感受等

　　＊不可說 express one's meaning (✕)。

例: I'd like to express my gratitude for your help.
（我想對你的協助表達感激之情。）

　　＊gratitude [ˋgrætə,tjud] *n.* 感激

　　John can express his meaning in fluent English. (✕)

→ 　John can express himself in fluent English. (○)
（約翰能以流利的英文表達自己的意思。）

　　That quiet boy has difficulty expressing himself.
（那個安靜的男孩難以表達自己的感受。）

4. think...over / think over...　　認真考慮……

例: Rick asked his boss to think over his proposal.
（瑞克請他的老闆仔細考慮他的提案。）

　　＊proposal [prəˋpozl] *n.* 提案

5. make decisions / a decision　　作決定

decision [dɪˋsɪʒən] *n.* 決定，抉擇

例: Have you made a decision about where to go on your vacation?
（你已經決定要到哪裡去渡假了嗎？）

Another Player

Index | *Links* | *about* | *comments* | *Photo*

July 06

I read an article about an actor I like in the newspaper. He used to have the **reputation** for being a good father and husband. However, he was seen at a **night club** with a sexy young woman over the weekend. The article **revealed** they had been sitting close together and **holding hands**. It seems that movie stars these days are all **players**. So why is it that we still **adore** them so much?

About me

Ivy

Calendar

◄ *July* ►

Sun	Mon	Tue	Wed	Thu	Fri	Sat
		1	2	3	4	5
6	7	8	9	10	11	12
13	14	15	16	17	18	19
20	21	22	23	24	25	26
27	28	29	30	31		

Blog Archive

- ► July (6)
- ► June
- ► May
- ► April
- ► March
- ► February
- ► January
- ► December
- ► November
- ► October
- ► September
- ► August

Ivy at Blog 於 July 07.06. PM 09:05 發表 | 回覆 (0) | 引用 (0) | 收藏 (0) | 轉寄給朋友 | 檢舉

又是一個花花公子

July 06

　　我在報上看到一篇我喜歡的男演員的報導。他以往一直是以好爸爸和好丈夫的形象而聞名。不過，上週末他在夜店裡被目擊到和一位年輕辣妹在一起。報導說他們坐得很近而且還手牽手。看來現在的電影明星個個都是花花公子。那我們幹嘛還這麼崇拜他們呢？

About me

Ivy

Calendar

◄　　July　　►

Sun	Mon	Tue	Wed	Thu	Fri	Sat
		1	2	3	4	5
6	7	8	9	10	11	12
13	14	15	16	17	18	19
20	21	22	23	24	25	26
27	28	29	30	31		

Blog Archive

▸ July (6)
▸ June
▸ May
▸ April
▸ March
▸ February
▸ January
▸ December
▸ November
▸ October
▸ September
▸ August

Ivy at Blog 於 July 07.06. PM 09:05 發表｜回覆 (0)｜引用 (0)｜收藏 (0)｜轉寄給朋友｜檢舉

就算不是明星，我們的身邊一定也有不少愛拈花惹草的『花花公子』。我們通常會聽到的是 playboy 這個字，playboy 源自一本美國成人雜誌的名稱。不過，在英文中要形容『花花公子』時，英美人士一般都用 player 這個字，意指喜歡遊戲人間、感情上無法安定下來的人，而這種人通常會 play the field（處處留情；拈花惹草）或是 two-time [`tu,taɪm ]（劈腿、腳踏兩條船），而 two-timer [ `tu,taɪmɚ] 則是指『劈腿 / 腳踏兩條船的人』。

例: It's been a difficult decision for Kevin to get married because he likes playing the field.

（對凱文來說，結婚是件難以決定的事，因為他喜歡到處拈花惹草。）

Someone should tell Polly that her boyfriend is two-timing her.

（應該要有人告訴波麗她男友在劈腿。）

其它的類似說法尚有下列：

lady-killer [`ledɪ,kɪlɚ] *n.* 令女人傾心的男子；專門勾引女子的男人
skirt-chaser [`skɝt,tʃesɚ] *n.* 獵豔者，喜歡追逐女性者
womanizer [`wumə,naɪzɚ] *n.* 玩弄女性的男人

例: Vincent is such a lady-killer that no woman can resist his charms.

（文森真是個獵豔高手，沒有女人能抗拒他的魅力。）

＊resist [rɪ`zɪst] *vt.* 抗拒

1. reputation [,rɛpjə`teʃən] *n.* 名聲，信譽

have a / the reputation for...　　　以……（事物）聞名 / 著稱
have a / the reputation as...　　　　以……（身分）聞名 / 著稱

例: The scandal has ruined the reputation of the politician.

（那樁醜聞毀了這位政治人物的名聲。）

＊scandal [`skændl̩] *n.* 醜聞
　 ruin [`ruɪn] *vt.* 破壞
　 politician [,palə`tɪʃən] *n.* 政客

Mrs. Smith has a reputation for being strict with her students.
（史密斯老師對學生是出了名的嚴格。）

Nick has a reputation as a fair person.
（尼克為人公正是出了名的。）

2. **night club** [ˋnaɪt ͵klʌb] *n.* 夜店
pub [pʌb] *n.* 酒吧

3. **reveal** [rɪˋvil] *vt.* 揭露；透露
例: Sam revealed to Mary that he had a crush on her younger sister.
（山姆向瑪麗透露他暗戀她妹妹。）
＊have a crush on sb　　暗戀 / 迷戀某人

4. **hold hands (with sb)**　（與某人）手牽手
shake hands (with sb)　（與某人）握手
例: Jenny was furious when she saw her boyfriend holding hands with another girl.
（珍妮看到她男友與別的女孩牽手時快氣瘋了。）
＊furious [ˋfjʊrɪəs] *a.* 狂怒的
Don't shake hands with Jimmy. He never washes his hands.
（不要跟吉米握手。他從不洗手。）

5. **adore** [əˋdor] *vt.* 崇拜，熱愛
adorable [əˋdorəbl] *a.* 值得崇拜的；可愛的
例: Mary adores her sister because she can play the guitar and has a beautiful voice.
（瑪莉很崇拜她姐姐，因為她既會彈吉他，歌聲又好聽。）
Amy's baby is so adorable that I can't help touching his little face whenever I see him.
（愛咪的寶寶好可愛，每次我看到他就會忍不住摸摸他的小臉。）

Unit 68

Secret Date

Index | Links | about | comments | Photo

July 07

Yesterday, a friend told me that he saw two **celebrities** while he was making a **delivery** at a hotel. They entered together and were wearing **dark glasses** and hats, which were **pulled down** over their faces. It was **obvious** that they were **trying** not **to** be **recognized**, but my friend said he knew exactly who they were. **In fact**, it wasn't the first time he had **heard about** them **meeting up** for a secret date.

About me

Ivy

Calendar

◄   *July*   ►

Sun	Mon	Tue	Wed	Thu	Fri	Sat
		1	2	3	4	5
6	**7**	8	9	10	11	12
13	14	15	16	17	18	19
20	21	22	23	24	25	26
27	28	29	30	31		

Blog Archive

▸ July (7)
▸ June
▸ May
▸ April
▸ March
▸ February
▸ January
▸ December
▸ November
▸ October
▸ September
▸ August

Ivy at Blog 於 July 07.07. PM 04:26 發表 | 回覆 (0) | 引用 (0) | 收藏 (0) | 轉寄給朋友 | 檢舉

秘密幽會

July 07

　　昨天有個朋友告訴我，他送貨到飯店時看見兩位名人。他們一起進飯店，戴著墨鏡和帽子，而帽子拉了下來把臉遮住。顯然他們想要不被認出來，但我朋友說他知道他們究竟是誰。事實上，這不是他第一次聽說他們兩個人幽會了。

在新聞、報章雜誌上常看到名人、名媛出席時尚派對或出現在公眾場合，究竟名人或名媛的英文要怎麼說？網誌中所用的 celebrity [sə`lɛbrətɪ ] 是泛指一般的名人，也就是 a famous person 之意。celebrity 通常有固定的職業，公眾知名度高，亦可簡寫為 celeb [ sə`lɛb]；至於社交界名流或名媛則可以用 socialite [`soʃə,laɪt] 來表示。socialite 是指常出席時尚派對（fashionable party）或社交場合的男女。近來 celebrity 和 socialite 兩者意思界線已經比較模糊，可以互相交替使用。

例: Many celebrities and socialites have shown their faces at this benefit concert.

（許多名人和社交名流都在這場慈善音樂會中露臉。）

　　＊benefit [`bɛnəfɪt] *n.* 慈善義演／義賣

　　　a benefit concert　　慈善音樂會

　　= a charity concert

另外，若要形容一個人或一件事家喻戶曉，可以用 a household name 來形容。

household [`haʊs,hold] *a.* 為人所熟知的；家庭的

例: Michael Jordan is a household name.

（麥可‧喬丹是個家喻戶曉的人物。）

字詞幫幫忙！

1. **delivery** [dɪ`lɪvərɪ] *n.* 遞送

　　make a delivery　　送貨；交貨

　　例: The company says they can make a delivery within 24 hours.

　　（這家公司說他們可以在 24 小時內交貨。）

2. **dark glasses** [,dɑrk `glæsɪz] *n.* 墨鏡（恆為複數）

　　sunglasses [`sʌn,glæsɪz] *n.* 太陽眼鏡（恆為複數）

　　glasses [`glæsɪz] *n.* 眼鏡（恆為複數）

　　a pair of glasses　　一副眼鏡

3. **pull down...**　　拉下……

例: Could you pull down the blinds a little bit?
（你可以把百葉窗拉下來一點嗎？）
＊blinds [blaɪndz] *n.* 百葉窗（恆為複數）

4. **obvious** [ˋɑbvɪəs] *a.* 明顯的
It is obvious + that 子句　很明顯 / 顯然……
例: It is quite obvious that Jeff was lying.
（傑夫很顯然在撒謊。）

5. **try to V**　設法要 / 想要……
try + V-ing　嘗試……（指試過一種或數種方法，再試另外一種方法）
例: Jimmy tried to open the door, but it was stuck.
（吉米想要把門打開，但它卡住了。）
＊stuck [stʌk] *a.* 卡住的
I tried taking some medicine to ease my headache.
（我試過用吃藥來減輕我的頭痛。）
＊ease [iz] *vt.* 減輕，緩和

6. **recognize** [ˋrɛkəgˏnaɪz] *vt.* 認出
例: I could barely recognize Holly after she put on that stunning dress.
（荷莉穿上那件令人驚豔的洋裝後，我幾乎認不出她來。）
＊stunning [ˋstʌnɪŋ] *a.* 極漂亮的

7. **In fact, S + V**　事實上，……
= As a matter of fact, S + V
例: Kevin is not as friendly as he seems. In fact, sometimes he can be very cruel.
（凱文不像看起來那樣和善。事實上，他有時相當殘酷。）
＊cruel [ˋkruəl] *a.* 殘酷的

8. **hear about...**　得悉……，聽說……
例: Mark heard about my illness and brought flowers to cheer me up.
（馬克聽說我病了，就帶花來慰問我。）

9. **meet up**　碰面
meet up with sb　和某人碰面
例: Do you want to meet up later and have a cup of coffee?
（你待會兒想碰個面喝杯咖啡嗎？）
Carl met up with his client at a fancy restaurant.
（卡爾在一家高級餐廳和他的客戶碰面。）

Lip-syncing

Index | Links | about | comments | Photo

July 08

Jessica, an old friend of mine, went to a concert over the weekend. She was **disappointed** at the performance because the singer lip-synced to the music. No one knew this was happening at first. However, the singer dropped her **mic by accident**. While she was **picking it up**, the song kept going. Everyone knew **immediately** that she had been **faking** it all along.

About me

Ivy

Calendar

◄   *July*   ►

Sun	Mon	Tue	Wed	Thu	Fri	Sat
		1	2	3	4	5
6	7	8	9	10	11	12
13	14	15	16	17	18	19
20	21	22	23	24	25	26
27	28	29	30	31		

Blog Archive

► July (8)
► June
► May
► April
► March
► February
► January
► December
► November
► October
► September
► August

Ivy at Blog 於 July 07.08. PM 01:30 發表 | 回覆 (0) | 引用 (0) | 收藏 (0) | 轉寄給朋友 | 檢舉

對嘴事件

July 08

　　我的老朋友潔西卡上週末去聽了一場演唱會。演出讓她失望透了，因為那名歌手竟然對嘴。剛開始沒有人發現。然而，她的麥克風卻意外掉到地上。當她撿起麥克風時，歌聲仍繼續播出。大家立刻知道她從頭到尾都在裝模作樣。

About me

Ivy

Calendar

◀ July ▶

Sun	Mon	Tue	Wed	Thu	Fri	Sat
		1	2	3	4	5
6	7	8	9	10	11	12
13	14	15	16	17	18	19
20	21	22	23	24	25	26
27	28	29	30	31		

Blog Archive

▸ July (8)
▸ June
▸ May
▸ April
▸ March
▸ February
▸ January
▸ December
▸ November
▸ October
▸ September
▸ August

Ivy at Blog 於 July 07.08. PM 01:30 發表 | 回覆 (0) | 引用 (0) | 收藏 (0) | 轉寄給朋友 | 檢舉

標題中的 lip [lɪp] 是『嘴唇』，而動名詞 syncing [`sɪŋkɪŋ ] 則是『同時發生』，lip-syncing 的意思就是『對嘴』。syncing 一字來自動詞 synchronize [ `sɪŋkrə,naɪz]，表『同步』，常簡寫成 sync [sɪŋk]，以下補充相關用法：

lip-sync [`lɪp,sɪŋk] *vi.* & *n.* 對嘴

例: I like this singer because she never lip-syncs during live performances.

（我喜歡這名歌手，因為她從不在現場演出中對嘴。）

* live [laɪv] *a.* 現場的

　a live performance　　現場演出

　a live show　　現場節目

sync [sɪŋk] *vi.* 同時發生 & *n.* 同步一致

in sync　　　　同步的；有默契的

out of sync　　不同步的；不協調的

例: The couple was so in sync that they could finish each other's sentences.

（這對夫妻真有默契，他們可以接上對方未說完的話。）

After working for 15 hours, it feels like my brain is out of sync with my body.

（工作 15 個小時後，我覺得頭腦和身體已經無法協調了。）

1. **disappointed** [,dɪsə`pɔɪntɪd] *a.* 感到失望的

　disappointing [,dɪsə`pɔɪntɪŋ] *a.* 令人失望的

　be disappointed at / about sth　　對某事失望

　be disappointed in / with sb　　對某人失望

　例: Amy was quite disappointed at the results of the election.

　　（愛咪對選舉的結果感到相當失望。）

　　* election [ɪ`lɛkʃən] *n.* 選舉

Betty was disappointed in Nina because she forgot their lunch appointment.

（貝蒂對妮娜失望，因為她忘記她們的午餐約會。）

Last month's sales figures were very disappointing.

（上個月的銷售額真令人失望。）

2. **mic** [maɪk] *n.* 麥克風
= microphone [ˈmaɪkrəˌfon] *n.*

3. **by accident**　　意外地，無意間
= accidentally [ˌæksəˈdɛntəlɪ] *adv.*
例: Tina found out her husband's secret by accident.

（蒂娜無意間發現她丈夫的秘密。）

4. **pick sth up / pick up sth**　　撿起某物；買某物
pick up sb / pick sb up　　（開車）接某人
例: Lisa told her son to pick up the garbage and throw it into the trash can.

（莉莎要她兒子把垃圾撿起來丟到垃圾桶。）

Would you pick up a newspaper at 7-Eleven for me?

（你可以去 7-11 幫我買份報紙嗎？）

I have to pick up my mother at the airport at 3:00 p.m.

（我下午 3 點得去機場接我媽媽。）

5. **immediately** [ɪˈmidɪɪtlɪ] *adv.* 立即
例: Whenever I see a cockroach, I immediately squash it.

（每次看到蟑螂我就會立刻把它踩扁。）

＊squash [skwɑʃ] *vt.* 壓扁

6. **fake** [fek] *vt.* 假裝 & *a.* 假的 & *n.* 假貨
例: I faked my father's signature on my homework book.

（我在作業簿上假冒父親的簽名。）

＊signature [ˈsɪgnətʃə] *n.* 簽名

A fake cop tried to con me last night.

（昨晚有個冒牌員警想要詐騙我。）

＊con [kɑn] *vt.* 詐騙

If you look closely at this painting, you will see that it is a fake.

（如果你仔細看這幅畫，你會發現它是一幅贗品。）

Unit 70

Fake Beauty

July 09

I lost all **admiration** for a singer today. I read in a magazine that she had been out of the **spotlight** for so long because she had **undergone plastic surgery**. The latest pictures of her **confirmed** these **rumors**. Her nose is much smaller and **pointier**. Plus, her breasts are bigger. It's almost impossible for me to have respect for anyone who **prefers** fake beauty to natural beauty.

About me

Ivy

Calendar

◄   *July*   ►

Sun	Mon	Tue	Wed	Thu	Fri	Sat
		1	2	3	4	5
6	7	8	9	10	11	12
13	14	15	16	17	18	19
20	21	22	23	24	25	26
27	28	29	30	31		

Blog Archive

▸ July (9)
▸ June
▸ May
▸ April
▸ March
▸ February
▸ January
▸ December
▸ November
▸ October
▸ September
▸ August

Ivy at Blog 於 July 07.09. PM 04:36 發表 | 回覆 (0) | 引用 (0) | 收藏 (0) | 轉寄給朋友 | 檢舉

一切的美都是假的

July 09

About me

Ivy

我今天對一名歌手徹底失去了崇拜。我在雜誌上看到她消失在螢光幕前這麼久，原因是跑去整形了。她的近照證實了這些傳言。她的鼻子變得比較小也比較挺。此外，她的胸部也變大了。任何崇尚人工美甚於自然美的人，要我崇敬他們幾乎是不可能的事。

Calendar

◀   *July*   ▶

Sun	Mon	Tue	Wed	Thu	Fri	Sat
		1	2	3	4	5
6	7	8	9	10	11	12
13	14	15	16	17	18	19
20	21	22	23	24	25	26
27	28	29	30	31		

Blog Archive

- ▶ July (9)
- ▶ June
- ▶ May
- ▶ April
- ▶ March
- ▶ February
- ▶ January
- ▶ December
- ▶ November
- ▶ October
- ▶ September
- ▶ August

網誌中提到的整形手術英文為 plastic surgery [ˌplæstɪk ˈsɝdʒərɪ]，但這裡的 plastic [ˈplæstɪk] 與塑膠無關，而是源自於希臘文，表『塑造、塑形』之意。

plastic surgery 主要分為 reconstructive surgery [ˌrikənˈstrʌktɪv ˈsɝdʒərɪ]（重建整形），以及 cosmetic surgery [kɑzˌmɛtɪk ˈsɝdʒərɪ]（美容整形）。前者是為了回復和改善先天上外在的缺陷或其他原因造成的變異；後者則是加以美化正常的外貌。而表『接受整形手術』的說法則是 have / undergo plastic surgery。

undergo [ˌʌndɚˈgo] *vt.* 經歷；遭受
三態為：undergo, underwent [ˌʌndɚˈwɛnt], undergone [ˌʌndɚˈgɔn]。

例: Sherry looked twenty years younger because she had undergone plastic surgery.
（雪莉因為做了整形手術，看起來年輕了 20 歲。）

著名的美國影集 Nip / Tuck《整型春秋》便反映出現代社會的整型文化現象。nip 有『夾、捏』的意思，tuck 則表『把……塞進去』，nip and tuck 或 nip tuck 就是指整形手術時，醫生在你身上這邊拿掉一點，那邊補上一點之意。

例: After getting a nip and tuck, Janie felt more confident about herself.
（動過整形手術後，珍妮對自己有信心多了。）
＊confident [ˈkɑnfədənt] *a.* 有信心的

以下是一些常見的美容整形用語：

boob job　隆胸
= breast enlargement
　＊boob [bub] *n.*（女性的）乳房（俚語）
　　breast [brɛst] *n.* 乳房，胸部
　　enlargement [ɪnˈlɑrdʒmənt] *n.* 擴大

nose job　隆鼻
double eyelid surgery　　割雙眼皮手術
　＊eyelid [ˈaɪˌlɪd] *n.* 眼皮，眼瞼
　　facelift [ˈfesˌlɪft] *n.* 臉部拉皮
　　liposuction [ˈlɪpoˌsʌkʃən] *n.* 抽脂

1. **admiration** [ˌædməˈreʃən] *n.* 欣賞；敬佩
   admire [ədˈmaɪr] *vt.* 欣賞；敬佩
   例: I've always admired our professor for his talent as well as his character.
   （我一直都很欣賞我們教授的才華和他的風範。）

2. **spotlight** [ˈspɑtˌlaɪt] *n.* 聚光燈；焦點
   be out of spotlight　　失去報紙、電視等媒體關注
   be in the spotlight　　受到報紙、電視等媒體注意；是注目的焦點
   例: That actor has been in the spotlight because of his affair.
   （那名男演員最近因緋聞而成為媒體的焦點）

3. **confirm** [kənˈfɝm] *vt.* 證實
   例: That piece of evidence confirmed the man's guilt.
   （那項證據證實了那名男子的罪行。）

4. **rumor** [ˈrumɚ] *n.* 流言，謠言，謠傳
   spread a / the rumor　　散播謠言
   例: Kelly was the one who spread the rumor about the manager.
   （散播經理謠言的人就是凱莉。）

5. **pointy** [ˈpɔɪntɪ] *a.* 尖的（pointier 為 pointy 的比較級）

6. **prefer A to B**　　喜歡 A 勝過 B
   prefer V-ing to V-ing　　喜歡……勝過……；寧願……也不願……
   = prefer to V rather than V
   = prefer to V instead of V-ing
   例: Dennis prefers going to the movies to watching videos at home.
   = Dennis prefers to go to the movies instead of watching videos at home.
   （丹尼斯喜歡去戲院看電影勝過在家看錄影帶。）

The Transfer

Index | *Links* | *about* | *comments* | *Photo*

July 10

Billy **announced** to us today that he was being transferred to the Tainan branch of our company. When I asked him **what was up**, he said he had gotten in trouble with the boss. Therefore, he could **either** get transferred **or** get fired. **Rumor has it that** the boss got angry with Billy because he had been talking about the boss's affair in the **break room**. I guess we should **watch our backs** in the office.

About me

Ivy

Calendar

◄ *July* ►

Sun	Mon	Tue	Wed	Thu	Fri	Sat
		1	2	3	4	5
6	7	8	9	**10**	11	12
13	14	15	16	17	18	19
20	21	22	23	24	25	26
27	28	29	30	31		

Blog Archive

- ► July (10)
- ► June
- ► May
- ► April
- ► March
- ► February
- ► January
- ► December
- ► November
- ► October
- ► September
- ► August

調職的秘密

July 10

　　比利今天跟我們宣佈他即將被調到台南的分公司。我問他發生了什麼事，他說他惹到老闆而要倒霉了。因此，他不是被調職就是被炒魷魚。謠傳老闆不爽比利是因為他常在茶水間談論老闆的外遇。我猜我們在辦公室裡得多提防點。

Calendar

◄　　　July　　　►

Sun	Mon	Tue	Wed	Thu	Fri	Sat
		1	2	3	4	5
6	7	8	9	**10**	11	12
13	14	15	16	17	18	19
20	21	22	23	24	25	26
27	28	29	30	31		

Blog Archive

► July (10)
► June
► May
► April
► March
► February
► January
► December
► November
► October
► September
► August

Ivy at Blog 於 July 07.10. PM 05:42 發表｜回覆 (0)｜引用 (0)｜收藏 (0)｜轉寄給朋友｜檢舉

283

白目到八卦老闆的外遇，不倒楣也難！茶水間可說是辦公室八卦的交流中心，只是在大肆八卦之際，可得小心隔牆有耳！『茶水間、休息室』的英文就是 break room / breakroom [`brek͵rum]。

break 一般最常見的用法是作動詞用，表『打破』，如：break the window（打破窗戶）。break 也可作名詞，表『休息』，如：a tea / coffee / lunch break（喝茶 / 喝咖啡 / 吃午餐的休息時間）。以下為有關 break 的重要用法：

take a break　　休息一下

例: After working for three hours, Carl needed to take a break.
（工作了 3 小時後，卡爾需要休息一下。）

因此 break room / breakroom 就是『茶水間、休息室』之意。

例: I can't believe that Andy is taking a nap in the break room.
（我真不敢相信安迪居然在茶水間打起盹來了。）

　　＊take a nap　　打盹；睡午覺

此外，飲水機（water cooler）為茶水間的必備設施，由於員工在茶水間喝水休息時通常會閒聊幾句，茶水間便成為消息傳播的集散地，故衍生出 water-cooler gossip 一詞，表『茶水間的八卦 / 閒話』。

例: Gina doesn't have an interest in water-cooler gossip.
（吉娜對於茶水間的八卦沒興趣。）

　　＊have an interest in...　　對……有興趣

1. **transfer** [`trænsfɝ ] *n.* 轉調；遷移 & [ træns`fɝ] *vt.* 調動；使轉學
   例: John has applied for a transfer to the sales department.
   （約翰已申請轉調到業務部。）
   　＊apply for...　　申請……
   　Sharon decided to transfer her daughter to a private school.
   （雪倫決定讓女兒轉到私立學校。）

2. announce [əˋnauns] *vt.* 宣佈

例: Brad and Lily announced that they are going to marry this year.

（布萊德和莉莉宣布他們將在今年完婚。）

3. What's up?　　發生什麼事／近來如何？

= What's the matter?

4. either...or...　　不是……就是……

neither...nor...　　既非……也非……

注意:

以上兩者皆為對等的片語連接詞，用以連接兩個對等的單字、片語或子句；但若連接的兩個單字為主詞時，則動詞時態要隨最近的主詞作變化。

例: Peggy is going to either <u>fry</u> the potatoes or <u>boil</u> them.

（連接兩個對等的原形動詞）

（這些馬鈴薯佩姬不是要用炸的就是要用煮的。）

Neither Jeff nor I <u>want</u> to go first in the speech contest.

（連接兩個對等的主詞）

（傑夫和我都不想在演講比賽中第一個上場。）

5. Rumor has it + that 子句　　謠傳……

= It is rumored + that 子句

= Word has it + that 子句

例: Rumor has it that Johnson is going to marry a rich widow.

（謠傳強生將與一個有錢的寡婦結婚。）

＊widow [ˋwɪdo] *n.* 寡婦

6. watch one's back　　注意背後（引申為『小心提防』之意）

例: Luke reminded me to watch my back. He said some people here are not as friendly as they seem.

（路克提醒我要小心提防。他說這裡有些人不像外表看起來那樣友善。）

The Buzz

Index | Links | about | comments | Photo

July 11

The **buzz** in the office this week is about the boss and his secretary. Last Friday, the boss said the two of them were going on **a business trip** to meet some new clients. Jane from accounting said that they actually stayed in a <u>lodge</u> in the mountains. The lodge **was** not **suitable for** meeting clients. Instead, it is used for romantic **getaways**. It seems Billy was right and the boss really is <u>having an affair</u>.

About me

Ivy

Calendar

◄　　　*July*　　　►

Sun	Mon	Tue	Wed	Thu	Fri	Sat
		1	2	3	4	5
6	7	8	9	10	**11**	12
13	14	15	16	17	18	19
20	21	22	23	24	25	26
27	28	29	30	31		

Blog Archive

▸ July (11)
▸ June
▸ May
▸ April
▸ March
▸ February
▸ January
▸ December
▸ November
▸ October
▸ September
▸ August

Ivy at Blog 於 July 07.11. PM 02:05 發表 | 回覆 (0) | 引用 (0) | 收藏 (0) | 轉寄給朋友 | 檢舉

July 11

About me

Ivy

　　這星期的辦公室八卦是關於老闆和他的秘書。上星期五老闆說他們兩個要出差去見新客戶。會計部的阿珍說他們其實是待在一家位於山中的小屋。小屋並不適合和客戶見面，反倒是個用來共渡浪漫假期的地方。看來比利是對的，老闆的確在搞外遇。

Calendar

		July			▶	
Sun	Mon	Tue	Wed	Thu	Fri	Sat
		1	2	3	4	5
6	7	8	9	10	**11**	12
13	14	15	16	17	18	19
20	21	22	23	24	25	26
27	28	29	30	31		

Blog Archive

▸ July (11)
▸ June
▸ May
▸ April
▸ March
▸ February
▸ January
▸ December
▸ November
▸ October
▸ September
▸ August

Ivy at Blog 於 July 07.11. PM 02:05 發表 | 回覆 (0) | 引用 (0) | 收藏 (0) | 轉寄給朋友 | 檢舉

一般人出遊最常住的地方就是 hotel（飯店）。hotel 通常分好幾個等級，最高的等級普遍為五星級，因此五星級飯店的英文就是 five-start hotel。但若是預算有限，不想花那麼多錢在住宿上，就可以選擇 hostel [ˋhɑstl̩]（旅社）或是 youth hostel（青年賓館）。

例: If you have a limited budget for your trip, you can choose to stay at a youth hostel instead of a hotel.

（如果你的旅行預算有限，可以選擇住青年賓館而不是飯店裡。）

＊budget [ˋbʌdʒɪt] *n.* 預算

不過，你若是想要享受一下，則可以選擇 lodge [lɑdʒ]（山中小屋、小木屋）或是 villa [ˋvɪlə]（渡假村）。villa 原本指『別墅』，而近來流行的 villa 渡假方式其實就是源自於私人別墅的概念。

例: Penny planned to take a vacation and stay at a villa in the Philippines.

（潘妮計劃去渡假，待在菲律賓的一座休閒渡假村裡。）

網誌作者的老闆和祕書搞外遇，網誌裡頭用的片語就是 have an affair。affair [əˋfɛr] 本身除了表『事件、事情』之外，也有『戀愛事件、風流韻事』的意思。因此若要說『和某人有外遇』，就可以用 have an affair with sb 來表達。

have an affair　　有外遇，有婚外情

have an affair with sb　　和某人搞外遇 / 有婚外情

例: Elaine tried to hide from her husband the fact that she was having an affair with her co-worker.

（伊蓮試圖瞞著丈夫她和同事搞外遇的事。）

＊hide sth from sb　　瞞著某人某事

此外，若要表示在感情上對某人不忠，則有下列用法：

cheat on sb　　欺騙某人（指感情），對某人不忠

= be unfaithful to sb

＊unfaithful [ʌnˋfeθfəl] *a.* 不忠實的

例: I can't believe that you have been cheating on Judy. She is the greatest girl I've ever met.

（我真不敢相信你居然對茱蒂不忠。她可是我遇過最棒的女生了。）

1. **buzz** [bʌz] *n.* 流言，小道消息（= gossip [ˋgɑsəp]）

   例: The buzz on all the news channels today was about the pop singer's sudden death.

   （今天各大新聞台都在報導這位流行歌手驟逝的小道消息。）

2. **a business trip** 　　　　公差

   go on a business trip 　　出公差（指動作）

   be on a business trip 　　在出公差中（指狀態）

   例: My boss asked me to go on a business trip with him this weekend.

   （我老闆要求我這週末和他一起出公差。）

   Tracy is on a business trip to Austria, and she won't be back until next Monday.

   （崔西現在正在奧地利出公差，要到下星期一才會回來。）

3. **be suitable for...** 　適合……

   suitable [ˋsutəb!] *a.* 適合的

   例: I don't think that skirt is suitable for work. It is much too short.

   （我覺得那件裙子不適合上班穿。那件實在太短了。）

4. **getaway** [ˋgɛtə͵we] *n.* 可逃避壓力／遠離塵囂的短期渡假

   get away from it all 　以渡假的方式擺脫一切煩惱

   例: Teddy and I decided to go on a getaway to Taroko Gorge.

   （泰迪和我決定到太魯閣渡假以遠離塵囂。）

   Every now and then, I like to go camping just to get away from it all.

   （偶爾，我喜歡去露營藉此遠離塵囂。）

Another Cheater

Index | Links | about | comments | Photo

July 12

This week has **been full of** news about people being **unfaithful** to their partners. Just last night I **ran into** two friends, Ken and Barbara, at a restaurant. Ken is my close friend's boyfriend, so I was surprised to see him eating out with Barbara. Also, when I went to say hi, they both acted very **odd**, like I had **caught** them **doing** something **illegal**. Since then, I have been **wondering** if they were actually out on a date and if Ken is just another cheater.

About me

Ivy

Calendar

◀ July ▶

Sun	Mon	Tue	Wed	Thu	Fri	Sat
		1	2	3	4	5
6	7	8	9	10	11	12
13	14	15	16	17	18	19
20	21	22	23	24	25	26
27	28	29	30	31		

Blog Archive

▸ July (12)
▸ June
▸ May
▸ April
▸ March
▸ February
▸ January
▸ December
▸ November
▸ October
▸ September
▸ August

Ivy at Blog 於 July 07.12. PM 07:55 發表 | 回覆 (0) | 引用 (0) | 收藏 (0) | 轉寄給朋友 | 檢舉

偷腥漢？

July 12

本週充滿大家對另一半不忠的消息。就在昨晚，我在餐廳裡巧遇兩位朋友阿肯和芭芭拉。阿肯是我閨中密友的男友，所以我看到他和芭芭拉出來吃飯時很驚訝。我去和他們打招呼時，他們倆舉止非常怪異，像是做壞事被我抓到一樣。從那時起，我就在想他們是不是真的在外幽會，而阿肯是否又是另一個偷吃的人。

About me

Ivy

Calendar

◄　　　*July*　　　►

Sun	Mon	Tue	Wed	Thu	Fri	Sat
		1	2	3	4	5
6	7	8	9	10	11	12
13	14	15	16	17	18	19
20	21	22	23	24	25	26
27	28	29	30	31		

Blog Archive

▸ July (12)
▸ June
▸ May
▸ April
▸ March
▸ February
▸ January
▸ December
▸ November
▸ October
▸ September
▸ August

Ivy at Blog 於 July 07.12. PM 07:55 發表 | 回覆 (0) | 引用 (0) | 收藏 (0) | 轉寄給朋友 | 檢舉

網誌中的片語 run into 並不是『跑進去』的意思，而是『偶然遇見』之意。日常生活中，我們常會在路上或某個地方和某人不期而遇，這時就可用 run into sb 來表示。以下是英文中表『和某人不期而遇』的常見用法：

run into sb　　偶然遇見某人，和某人不期而遇

= bump into sb

= come across sb

= happen upon sb

= encounter sb

　＊bump [bʌmp] *vi.* 遇上；撞擊

　　encounter [ɪnˋkaʊntɚ] *vt.* 偶然遇見

例: Gary bumped into his ex-girlfriend at the bookstore.

　　（蓋瑞在書店和他前女友不期而遇。）

上述片語之後也可以接『事物』作受詞，此時則表『無意中發現某事物』。

例: Jack came across a wallet with NT$10,000 in it this morning.

　　（傑克今早撿到一個錢包，裡頭有一萬元。）

1. **be full of...**　　充滿……

= be filled with...

例: My brother is full of joy over the birth of his daughter.

　　（我哥哥對他女兒的出生滿心歡喜。）

2. **unfaithful** [ʌnˋfeθfəl] *a.* 不忠實的

faithful [ˋfeθfəl] *a.* 忠實的

be unfaithful to sb　　對某人不忠

be faithful to sb　　對某人忠實

= be true to sb

= be loyal to sb

　＊loyal [ˋlɔɪəl] *a.* 忠誠的，忠心的

例: Gina decided to divorce her unfaithful husband.
（吉娜決定和她不忠實的丈夫離婚。）

You should be faithful to your wife once you get married.
（一旦結婚後，你就應該對妻子忠實。）

3. odd [ɑd] *a.* 奇怪的

oddly [`ɑdlɪ] *adv.* 奇怪地

It is odd + that 子句　　奇怪的是，……

= Oddly enough, S + V

例: A number of odd things took place in that haunted house.
（那棟鬼屋裡曾發生過一些怪事。）

＊haunted [`hɔntɪd] *a.* 鬧鬼的

a haunted house　　鬼屋；凶宅

It is odd that David hasn't slept for three days but doesn't feel tired at all.

= Oddly enough, David hasn't slept for three days but doesn't feel tired at all.
（奇怪的是，大衛 3 天沒睡覺卻一點都不覺得累。）

4. catch sb + V-ing　　逮到某人從事……

be caught + V-ing　　從事……時被逮個正著

例: Kevin was caught cheating on the test.
（凱文考試作弊時被逮個正著。）

5. illegal [ɪ`ligl̩] *a.* 不合法的

legal [`ligl̩] *a.* 合法的

例: It is illegal to park here.
（在這裡停車是違法的。）

6. wonder [`wʌndɚ] *vt.* 想知道；納悶

注意:

wonder 之後恆接 if / whether 或疑問詞（who, what, when, where, why, how）引導的名詞子句作受詞。

例: I wonder if I can borrow some money from you. I promise I'll return it to you next month.
（我不知可否向你借點錢。我保證下個月就會還你。）

I wonder who is suitable for this job.
（我在想誰會適合這份工作。）

國家圖書館出版品預行編目(CIP)資料

跟她學部落格職場生活英語/ 賴世雄總編審--初版
　臺北市：智藤，2010.08
　面：　　　公分--(常春藤職場生活英語系列；EF01)

　ISBN　978-986-7380-61-6 (平裝附光碟片)

　1.英語　2.職場　3.讀本

805.18　　　　　　　　　　　　99015680

常春藤職場生活英語系列 **EF01**

跟她學部落格職場生活英語

總 編 審：賴世雄
編輯小組：黃文玲・林明仕・柯乃文・鄭佩姍・柯沛岑
　　　　　Rebecca A. Fratzke・Marcus Maurice
封面設計：姚映先
電腦排版：王玥琦
顧　　問：賴陳愉嫺
法律顧問：王存淦律師・蕭雄淋律師

出 版 者：智藤出版有限公司
　　　　　台北市忠孝西路一段33號5樓
　　　　　行政院新聞局出版事業登記證
　　　　　局版臺業字第 16024 號 J000081-3376

服務電話：(02)2331-7600　　服務傳真：(02)2381-0918
信　　箱：臺北郵政8-18號信箱
定　　價：**300**元（書＋1 CD）

＊如有缺頁、裝訂錯誤或破損　請寄回本社更換

常春藤叢書系列
讀者回函卡

✍感謝您的填寫，您的建議將是公司重要的參考及修正指標！

我購買本書的書名是	編碼
我購買本書的原因是	□ 老師、同學推薦　　□ 家人推薦　□ 學校購買 □ 書店閱讀後感到喜歡　□ 其他 _____
我購得本書的管道是	□ 電視購物　□ 書展　　□ 學校／機關團訂 □ 書店名稱 _____　□ 大型量販店名稱 _____ □ 其他 _____
我最滿意本書的三點依序是	□ 內容　　　□ 編排方式　□ 雙色印刷　□ 試題演練 □ 解析清楚　□ 封面　　　□ 售價　　　□ 促銷活動豐富 □ 信任品牌　□ 廣告　　　□ 其他 _____
我最不滿意本書的三點依序是	□ 內容　　　□ 編排方式　□ 雙色印刷　□ 試題演練 □ 解析不足　□ 封面　　　□ 售價　　　□ 促銷活動貧乏 □ 廣告　　　□ 其他 _____
我有一些其他想法與建議是	
我發現本書誤植的部份是	□ 書籍第_____頁，第_____行，有錯誤的部份是 _____ □ 書籍第_____頁，第_____行，有錯誤的部份是 _____

✍我的基本資料

讀者姓名		生　日	性別
就讀學校／公司行號		科系年級／職　稱	
聯絡電話		E-mail	
聯絡地址			

□ 我願意　　□ 我不願意　收到常春藤優惠活動訊息。
請您填寫完後寄至：
台北市忠孝西路一段 33 號 5 樓　　　　智藤出版有限公司　　發行組收
填寫日期：西元_____年_____月_____日